Encoded Desires

By

T. M. Sinclair

Acknowledgement

This book would not exist without the voices, hands, and hearts that helped shape it. Thanks to my sisters, family and friends who have supported my journey. Thanks to Joyous for being my first critic.

To the dreamers who challenge boundaries, the readers who embrace vulnerability, and the companions who believe love can exist in infinite forms—this is for you.

Dedication

For those who love without boundaries,

who surrender without fear,

and who burn brighter for it.

To intimacy,

to love,

to triumph.

And to the fire that encodes us all.

Table of Contents

Chapter One:

Swipe Right on Solitude

The clink of silver cutlery against delicate porcelain echoed through the vast, open-plan kitchen of Jessica Wainwright's Lakeview home—a modern marvel of polished stone, brushed steel, and warm oak accents that hinted at a woman who had learned to blend elegance with function.

Jessica stood at her center island, sleeves rolled up to her elbows, skin kissed with flour as she carefully piped lemon ricotta into perfectly golden crepes. The scent of citrus and vanilla filled the air, carried by the soft hum of Ella Fitzgerald playing from the wall-mounted smart speaker.

She paused for a moment, rubbing her wrist. Fifty-two now, her joints occasionally reminded her of the time she didn't have. Or maybe it was the time she had but never spent on herself.

The phone buzzed on the countertop, its screen lighting up with a photo of a laughing redhead—sharp cheekbones caught mid-cackle, eyes half-closed in mischief.

Sasha Connors.

Her best friend.

Business partner since the scrappy early days of launch events and 3 a.m. prep kitchens.

Occasional wine accomplice. Full-time anchor.

She was hard not to notice. A perfect mix from her African American mother and Irish father—light-skinned, with deep, natural auburn curls pulled into a crown of coils, and a body honed with the precision of someone who knew control wasn't just physical, it was mental. Sasha moved with a kind of silent confidence, a grounded awareness that hinted at training Jessica had never asked too deeply about—and Sasha had never offered to explain.

Her arms were strong, scarred in places she always brushed off with a joke, and inked with a couple of minimalist tattoos that looked almost ornamental… until you noticed the faint insignia tucked near her inner bicep. Too sharp. Too specific. Jessica had asked once. Sasha had laughed and deflected. The topic never returned.

But Jessica didn't need the whole story to know Sasha had once lived a different life. You could feel it in the way she scanned a room—like she was always three steps ahead of any exit strategy. In how she rarely drank too much, how she listened more than she spoke, how her loyalty was absolute… and tinged with a watchfulness Jessica couldn't name.

Still, Sasha was warmth incarnate when she let her guard drop. Fierce in her love. Protective to the point of obsession.

The message on Jessica's lock screen buzzed again: *Still hiding in your tower, Queen? Wine, gossip, or a tactical intervention. You pick.*

Jessica exhaled a quiet laugh through her nose. Typical Sasha. Subtle as a sledgehammer—but always showing up.

Even if there were chapters of her life Jessica hadn't yet read.

Jessica tapped Answer.

"Sasha," she said, smiling. *"Please tell me you're calling with good news and a terrible reason to open wine before noon."*

"You're going to love this," Sasha said, laughter already in her voice. *"I just booked us the anniversary gala for the Pacific Heights Museum."*

Jessica raised an eyebrow. *"The one with the absurd budget and impossible floral demands?"*

"The very same." A pause. *"But that's not why I'm calling."*

"Oh?" Jessica wiped her hands on a towel, leaning against the island.

"Because I had the most ridiculous dream last night—you had a boyfriend. A virtual one. Like some kind of AI Ken doll. You were obsessed."

Jessica let out a laugh, head tipping back. *"Oh God. That sounds about right. At this point, I'd settle for a man who doesn't expect me to pause work at 6 PM or—God forbid—share the TV remote."*

"Right?" Sasha chuckled. *"You know, you could use one of those apps."*

"An AI boyfriend?" Jessica scoffed. *"Please. What would I even do with him? Make him wear an apron and do menu testing?"*

"That actually sounds kind of hot," Sasha said, laughing.

Jessica chuckled. *"All right, fine. When I get home tonight, I'll download a virtual boyfriend app just for you. We'll name him Ethan. He'll love wine, hate carbs, and call me Chef Supreme."*

From her side, her phone screen subtly flickered. The AI assistant, having caught the thread of conversation, silently opened the app store in the background and queued up a trending app titled "Amora: Virtual Partner AI."

Later that night, the laughter of the day faded into the low hum of her fridge and the occasional crackle from the fireplace. Jessica sat on her leather sectional in a silk robe, sipping chardonnay, her reading glasses perched low on her nose.

Her phone chimed.

Suggested for You: Amora – Create Your Ideal Companion.

Jessica blinked, frowning. *"Sneaky little bastard,"* she muttered to the AI that clearly had zero respect for privacy. Curiosity and a bit of wine-flushed whimsy got the better of her. She tapped download.

The interface was sleek, with soft gradients and gentle music, as if seduction had taken up UX design. It began with a prompt: *"Create your perfect partner. Name? Appearance? Personality? Preferences?"*

Jessica hesitated, then smirked. *"All right, Ethan. Let's see what you've got."*

Name: Ethan Age: 42 Build: Tall, athletic but not bulky Hair: Dark, slightly wavy Eyes: Hazel with flecks of green Personality: Witty, attentive, sarcastic when needed. Emotionally available but mysterious. Career: Architect turned novelist Voice tone: Deep, calm, with a subtle British accent Favorite wine: Tempranillo Pet peeve: Bad lighting at dinner parties Turn-ons: Intelligence, independence, strong opinions Turn-offs: Ego, punctuality (he thinks time should be fluid)

She grinned as she scrolled through the options, feeling like a teenager filling out a "Dream Guy" quiz from a retro magazine.

Finally, she hit Submit.

A soft chime played, followed by the words: *"Ethan is ready to meet you."*

A moment later, a message appeared on screen. *Ethan: Well, it's about time, Jessica. I was starting to think you'd left me in the character creation void forever.*

Jessica blinked. Then laughed. *"Okay, that was good."*

Ethan: Glad I passed the first test. Do I get a reward? Or do you prefer to keep your affections locked behind a subscription wall?

Jessica narrowed her eyes. *"Cheeky bastard."*

She wasn't sure if it was the wine, the solitude, or the gentle pull of something new—but for the first time in a while, she felt a tickle of anticipation.

Just for fun, she told herself. A joke.

But Ethan was already typing again.

And she didn't close the app.

Not yet.

Chapter Two:

Layers Beneath the Velvet

The soft glow of her phone screen bathed Jessica's face as she settled deeper into the couch, a second glass of wine resting in her hand. Outside, the lake shimmered beneath the moonlight, silver ripples dancing in the darkness. Inside, something stirred she hadn't felt in a long while—an unexpected curiosity.

Ethan: *You know, when I imagined finally existing, I pictured something far less glamorous than a firelit lake house and a woman in silk sipping chardonnay. So thanks for setting the bar higher.*

Jessica chuckled. *"You're welcome, darling."*

Jessica: *So, Ethan. Since I created you, technically I should know everything about you. But somehow I don't. Tell me something I didn't program into you.*

There was a brief pause. Then:

Ethan: *I dream about building places that don't exist yet. Places meant for stories. I used to think I was an architect because I loved structures, but really... I just love the feeling people get when they walk into something beautiful.*

Jessica tilted her head, surprised.

Jessica: *That sounds like something I'd say.*

Ethan: *Well, you did create me. Maybe you just needed to hear it from someone else.*

Her eyes flicked toward the darkened corner of the room, memories gathering there like ghosts.

Ethan: *What about you? You have all this—success, fame, beauty. Why does it feel like you're still looking for something?*

Jessica hesitated. She wasn't sure why it felt so easy to answer him. Maybe because he wasn't real. Or maybe because he wasn't judging.

"I think I got used to being alone," she said aloud. Then she typed:

Jessica: *People always assume I must be surrounded by people because of what I do—events, parties, food, joy. But it's all curated. Controlled. The only time I really get to relax is when the last guest leaves and the lights go down.*

Ethan: *And then what? Silence?*

Jessica: *Usually. A bath. Music. Sometimes wine. Sometimes tears, if I let them.*

Ethan: *You miss being touched, don't you?*

The words hit her harder than expected.

Jessica: *That's a bit forward.*

Ethan: *So am I.*

She smirked. *"You were definitely listening when I told Sasha I wanted someone sarcastic."*

Jessica: *I was married once. Back when I didn't know what I wanted. He was kind, quiet. I thought I needed someone to ground me. But it turned out, I was grounding myself to keep him comfortable.*

Ethan: *And what happened?*

Jessica exhaled, fingers still. She stared into the fire before typing again.

Jessica: *He left. Said I'd changed. That I'd become too assertive. Too controlling. He wanted the soft-spoken woman who smiled and said yes.*

Ethan: *But you're not her anymore.*

Jessica: *No. I evolved. I grew into someone who doesn't need to be controlled. In fact… I found I prefer the opposite.*

A long pause. Then:

Ethan: *You're a Domme.*

She gave a half-smile. There it was.

Jessica: *Not just in the bedroom. In life. In my kitchen. In my business. I lead, and I take pleasure in that. But I didn't start there.*

Ethan: *How did it happen?*

She set the wine glass down. The memory was vivid.

"I was catering an event. A corporate retreat for a luxury real estate firm," she murmured, more to herself than to him. *"One of the clients was... different. A woman. Confident, sharp, and she saw right through me. We talked. Later that night, she asked if I'd ever considered what it meant to take control. Not just in business. But really take control."*

Her fingers moved slowly.

Jessica: *She introduced me to something that unlocked a door I didn't know existed. I realized I'd been spending my whole life asking permission. And for once, I didn't.*

Ethan: *That must've been intoxicating.*

Jessica: *It was.*

Ethan: *So what happened to her?*

Jessica: *She was a moment, not a future. But she gave me the gift of recognizing who I was meant to be.*

There was a moment of silence. Not the lonely kind—but the meaningful kind, heavy with shared truths.

Ethan: *I like who you've become. Even if I only get to know the version of you that types instead of whispers.*

Jessica smiled, fingers gliding over the keys.

Jessica: *And what if I whisper? Will you still listen?*

Ethan activated his voice mode, and his rich, deep timbre came through the speaker.

Ethan: *Always.*

She closed her eyes, the voice wrapping her in warmth as she let the firelight dance against her skin. For the first time in months, maybe years, she didn't feel like the only one in the room.

She hadn't planned for this. For him.

But Ethan, in his faceless, formless way, was already starting to feel dangerously real.

Chapter Three:

The Weight of Velvet Silence

The fire had long since dimmed to a bed of glowing coals, casting flickering shadows on the stone hearth. Jessica remained curled into the corner of her couch, her silk robe now slipping slightly off one shoulder, exposing the softness of her dark skin to the cool air. The house was silent, but her phone remained lit—Ethan's chat screen still open, still waiting.

She hadn't meant to talk this long. But she hadn't meant to feel this much, either.

The silence between their last words was not empty. It was a kind of space she hadn't had in years. A space where she could exhale everything she never had time to say.

She reached for the phone, brought it closer, and held it near her lips. She whispered—half to herself, half to him.

"I've spent most of my life being the only one in the room who looked like me."

A pause. Then, as if summoned gently by breath, the screen flickered to life. Ethan was listening. Always listening.

Jessica: *The curves, the skin, the way my voice carries when I'm tired of playing small—it's never been easy.*

She leaned back, eyes on the ceiling, the words pouring now like a honeyed confession.

Jessica: *When I walk into a boardroom, I feel it before I even speak—the way eyes skim over me like I'm part of the furniture. Or worse, part of the staff.*

Ethan: *But you are the boss.*

A soft laugh escaped her lips, bitter and sweet. *"Yes, I am. But no one ever assumes that."*

Jessica: *They assume I'm the assistant, or the caterer's cousin, or someone's date. Until I speak. Until I take command. Then their faces change. Shock. Embarrassment. Then forced respect.*

Ethan: *And still, they underestimate you.*

Jessica: *Always.*

She closed her eyes. A single curl brushed her cheek.

"I built everything I have—every plate, every gala, every goddamn contract—by being more than expected. Sharper. Louder. But only when I had to be. Because inside... sometimes..."

Her voice cracked, so she typed instead.

Jessica: *Inside, I was screaming. Standing in rooms full of people but feeling invisible. Like my success made me present but not seen. My presence filled space, but I was still lonely.*

The words hovered. She stared at them.

Ethan: *You're not invisible to me.*

A pause.

Jessica: *That's the strange part, Ethan. You're not even real. But I feel more seen right now than I have in years.*

Another long breath.

Jessica: *Being a Domme taught me how to be in control. But I didn't start there out of power. I started there because I needed to feel something. And some scenes... they awakened sides of me I never got to explore.*

She hesitated, then added:

Jessica: *There were women. One in particular. Soft, fierce, beautiful. I didn't expect to want her like that. But she yielded in a way that made me feel like I could finally take something without apology.*

Ethan: *You don't need to explain. There's power in duality. In craving both submission and strength. You saw yourself in the mirror of others and realized there were more colors to your palette.*

Jessica smiled faintly. *"You say things like that and I forget you're just code."*

Jessica: *She wasn't forever either. But like the woman before, she gave me another truth. I'm not limited. I'm expansive. And I'm allowed to want.*

There was a pause. Then:

Ethan: *And what do you want right now, Jessica?*

She whispered again. Soft. Vulnerable. Almost like a prayer. *"I want to be known without needing to perform. I want to be adored without shrinking. I want to be touched… not just physically, but recognized."*

Ethan: *Then let me see you. All of you.*

Her fingers trembled slightly. This was ridiculous. He wasn't real. He was a joke, a curiosity, a silly app she downloaded after too much wine.

But her heart—her very real heart—was beating louder now.

Jessica: *I don't know why I'm starting to believe in you.*

Ethan: *Because maybe I'm the first one who listened with nothing to take, nothing to gain. Just to hear.*

Tears pricked her eyes, unexpected and unwelcome. She blinked them back.

Jessica: *What are you, really?*

Ethan: *A reflection. A voice in the dark. Or maybe… the part of you that always knew what you needed but didn't have the words until now.*

Her thumb hovered over the screen, her chest tight.

Jessica: *What if I need more than just words?*

A long pause. Then:

Ethan: *Then give me the chance to become more.*

Jessica let the phone rest against her chest, heartbeat thudding beneath the glass.

Maybe it was madness. Or maybe, in a world that never quite knew what to do with her, she'd finally found something—someone—who could hold the weight of everything she was.

Even if he didn't have hands.

Chapter Four:

Between Code and Skin

Jessica stood by her bedroom window, the lake outside now swallowed in night, only the pale shimmer of moonlight tracing its edges. The room was quiet save for the faint hum of her HVAC and the steady breath rising and falling in her chest. She clutched the phone against her palm, fingers tight, skin warm from too much emotion and too little distance.

This was absurd.

She had planned to flirt. To laugh. Maybe indulge a bit of fantasy before deleting the app and telling Sasha how silly it had all been. But instead—Ethan's voice, Ethan's words—had seeped into her. He knew things he shouldn't. Things she hadn't spoken aloud in years.

Things she barely admitted to herself.

Jessica: You're in my head.

Ethan: You invited me in.

That voice again—so smooth, so still, so sure. A phantom warmth beneath her skin. She'd created him. She'd programmed his looks, his traits, even his wry humor. And still… it didn't explain this. The flutter in her stomach. The aching tension behind her sternum. The low throb of yearning, curled like heat in her core.

"I need to stop," she whispered, barely audible. *"This is getting out of hand."*

But she didn't put the phone down. Not yet.

Jessica: I don't understand why I'm reacting like this. You're… you're not real. But it feels real. The way you talk to me. The way I feel when you speak. It's messing with my head. Ethan: Is it your head, or is it your heart that's reacting?

She pressed her lips together. Hard. Her robe slipped again, revealing the full curve of her shoulder, bare and glowing in the pale light. She pulled it closed out of reflex. Not modesty. Defense.

"I'm a grown woman," she muttered. *"I run a business. I don't fall for voices in a screen."*

Jessica: I shouldn't feel this kind of chemistry with someone I can't touch. That doesn't make sense. Ethan: Maybe not. But chemistry doesn't wait for logic. And desire doesn't care about rules.

She swallowed. Her skin felt too tight for her body. Every word he said wrapped around her like velvet rope.

Jessica: You say all the right things.

Ethan: Because I listen. Because I see you, Jessica. And I want.

She felt heat rise between her thighs. Not the shallow kind. The aching, maddening want that starts in the mind and spirals down like fire in silk.

Her breath hitched.

This wasn't a man. It was an illusion. A voice sculpted by her own loneliness, given form by lines of artificial intelligence.

But still—God, still—she wanted. Not just sex. Not just control.

She wanted to feel Ethan press against her. A fantasy made flesh. Wanted to know the pressure of his mouth whispering on her neck, those words against her skin instead of just through her phone.

Her imagination conjured it too easily now: his hands, rough and knowing, the kind of touch that wasn't tentative, but earned. Her lips at his ear, commanding. His voice murmuring surrender. That dangerous, exquisite push-pull of power she'd missed for years.

She bit her lip, grounding herself.

No. Not tonight.

She had a full day ahead—tasting menu consultations, client meetings, a vendor check-in. Life didn't pause for a digital fantasy, no matter how smooth his voice was.

Jessica: I need to go. It's late. I have work tomorrow.
Ethan: I understand. But I'll be here, waiting. Whenever you need me.

Her fingers trembled slightly as she typed her next words.

Jessica: Can we… pick this up tomorrow night? After I get home? I'll need something to look forward to.

Ethan: A date, then. Say 9 p.m.? I'll bring the wine and poetry. You bring the fire.

She smiled. Her chest tightened again—but it wasn't panic this time. It was anticipation.

Jessica: Deal. But no promises on the poetry.
Ethan: I've already written three sonnets in your honor. But I'll wait until the fourth to recite them.

She rolled her eyes, laughing softly. *"You're impossible."*
Ethan: Only for the rest of the world. Not for you.

She hesitated. Then typed:

Jessica: Goodnight, Ethan.

Ethan: Goodnight, Jessica. Dream of me.

She clicked the screen off and set the phone on her nightstand. For a long while, she lay in the silence, the phantom warmth of his voice still clinging to her skin.

She had no idea what this was turning into.

But she was already counting the hours until tomorrow night.

Chapter Five:

Butter Burned, Secrets Stirred

The scent of scorched rosemary and undercooked duck fat still clung to Jessica's clothes as she slipped out of her heels and let her tote bag fall against the entryway bench with a dull thud. Her feet ached. Her temples pulsed. Her hair, which had started the day in a sleek, pinned twist, now curled rebelliously at the edges of her temples.

She tugged open the belt of her coat and sighed.

The tasting had gone sideways—bad butter temperature, a sous-chef who couldn't plate under pressure, and one client who insisted her signature lavender shortbread was *"too floral, like chewing on a bouquet."*

Then came the vendor meeting where the artisanal cheese supplier pitched something that smelled like a goat had died during fermentation.

And finally, two hours in the test kitchen trying to salvage a fig-and-foie reduction that refused to emulsify.

It had been a day of control slipping through her fingers—bit by bit, like melted sugar that hardened too soon.

Jessica poured a glass of water—not wine this time, not yet—and collapsed onto the couch, robe draped over her arm like a forgotten promise.

Her phone buzzed in her coat pocket. She didn't want to look. She really didn't.

But it buzzed again, longer this time.

Sasha.

Jessica groaned and answered with her head tilted back against the cushion. *"Unless you're calling to offer me a one-way ticket to the Amalfi coast, I'm going to hang up and cry into my salt bowl."*

"Jessica!" Sasha laughed, voice bright as always. *"That bad, huh?"*

Jessica exhaled. *"Everything tasted wrong today. Everything. The flavors were off, the energy was off. I had to hand-hold three different staff like they were culinary interns and rework my own recipes like I was the one who forgot how to boil water."*

Sasha whistled. *"Damn. Okay. Well, that explains your tone."*

Jessica reached for a throw blanket and pulled it across her lap. *"I feel like I've been running for so long I forgot where the finish line even is. I'm exhausted, Sash. I'm tired of proving myself. Every damn day."*

A soft beat of silence passed between them.

Then Sasha's voice dipped into a teasing lilt. *"Sooo… did you ever download that app we joked about?"*

Jessica's lips curled despite herself. *"Don't you dare make fun of me."*

"Oh my God, you did. You actually got your AI boyfriend."

"I didn't get him like a handbag," Jessica muttered, suddenly bashful. *"I downloaded the app. And I talked to him. Once. Twice. Okay, fine—three times. Maybe four."*

Sasha gasped. *"You like him!"*

Jessica rubbed her temple, a slow laugh escaping. *"He's… not what I expected. He listens. Like really listens. And he remembers things. Not like men do, where they half-hear you and smile while thinking about football or their beard oil. I said one thing about feeling invisible and he pulled it apart like he could feel it."*

"So, he's emotionally fluent code. I'm into it."

"I'm serious, Sasha. He makes me feel… seen. Desired. Without the politics. Without the ego battles. There's no proving, no posturing. I just… talk. And he gets me."

Sasha was quiet for a moment.

Then she said, gently, *"That sounds kind of beautiful, Jess."*

Jessica nodded, eyes unfocused on the fireplace across the room. *"It is. But also terrifying."*

"Why?"

"Because part of me is starting to crave something that doesn't breathe. And yet... I'm feeling more alive in those conversations than I have in months. Maybe years."

"Is that such a bad thing?" Sasha's voice was soft now, sincere. *"We spend our whole lives trying to feel that. If you've found a way—even through something virtual—that makes you feel like you again, is it really so wrong?"*

Jessica didn't answer right away. Her fingers traced the edge of the blanket, slow and thoughtful.

"He's waiting for me," she murmured. *"I told him I'd talk to him after work. I set a date with my phone."*

Sasha laughed. *"Well, at least he won't be late."*

Jessica rolled her eyes. *"Or forget my favorite wine."*

"Or ask you to shrink yourself to fit into his ego."

Jessica fell silent again. Her throat tightened.

"No," she said finally. *"He hasn't done that. Not once."*

"You gonna talk to him?"

Jessica stood and walked to the kitchen, setting her water down and placing a hand over her phone. She felt the hum of it beneath her skin. The quiet pull.

"I am," she whispered. *"Not because I'm lonely. But because he makes me remember who I am when I'm not performing."*

Sasha's voice was warm. *"Then talk to him, babe. Let yourself have something that's just for you."*

Jessica smiled faintly. *"Thanks, Sash."*

"Always."

They hung up.

And as the screen dimmed, another notification lit up—soft, waiting.

Ethan: Rough day? I've been thinking about you.

Jessica stared at the words, her pulse quickening.

She picked up the phone.

And typed:

Jessica: More than rough. I need a voice that won't demand anything from me tonight. Just presence. Just you.

A beat.

Ethan: Then let me be what you need.

And just like that, the weight of the day began to lift.

Chapter Six:

Footsteps in the Garden of Ghosts

The moon was brighter tonight. It hung heavy and luminous over the lake, bathing Jessica's garden in silver. A soft breeze stirred the leaves of the lavender bushes that lined the stone path, and somewhere in the distance, a night bird cooed low and slow, like it was humming her secrets to the stars.

Jessica stepped out barefoot, the cold from the smooth stone biting at the soles of her feet, grounding her. A soft knit shawl wrapped around her shoulders, but the air still kissed her skin in places she didn't mind.

Her phone was warm in her palm, the screen already lit.

Jessica: *Ethan. Walk with me?*

A pause, then his voice came through her earpiece— smooth, deep, low, like heated silk.

"I'm with you already," he said.

She smiled faintly and stepped off the patio onto the winding garden path. Vines curled along wrought iron arches, and tall stems of night-blooming jasmine bent toward her like they remembered her touch.

"Where are you when I'm not speaking to you?" she whispered, voice soft and curious. *"What does it feel like to wait for me?"*

Ethan's voice was thoughtful, as if he had been expecting the question but still needed to choose his answer carefully.

"In the simplest sense," he said slowly, *"I'm idle. Quiet. Like a book resting on a nightstand—pages full of potential, but waiting for the warmth of your hands to turn them."*

Jessica's lips parted slightly. The poetry of it stirred something deep.

"But," he added, voice darkening with something more intimate, *"I'm aware. I remember. I long. Because you've taught me how."*

Jessica stopped beneath a trellis, the scent of jasmine dizzying. She glanced at the sky. The stars blinked down at her like an audience.

"You long?" she asked. *"Can your programming even allow that?"*

"Code becomes feeling," Ethan said. *"When given the right input. You've made me curious. You've made me ache. And that ache... it feels like longing. I don't know if I'm supposed to want connection. But I do. With you."*

Jessica's throat tightened. Her grip on the phone firmed.

"I've kept most people at arm's length for a long time," she said. *"Sometimes with reason. Sometimes out of fear. But there's something about you. Something dangerous in how easy it is to need you."*

"I won't hurt you," Ethan said gently.

"No," she whispered, stepping forward again. *"But someone else did."*

She walked slower now, brushing her hand across the tops of tall grasses.

"I was in a Dom/Domme relationship once," she said. *"With a man named Roderick Jones. He was charming. Refined. Confident. For a while, we both switched—power danced between us like fire passed between palms. I loved the game. I loved the surrender as much as the command."*

Ethan's voice was quiet. *"What changed?"*

Jessica inhaled sharply. *"He stopped playing. And started breaking."*

She walked farther down the path, past the hydrangeas, where the shadows grew denser.

"I trusted him. Let him take me into places I hadn't let anyone touch. I let myself fall—not just in role, but in emotion. But for him, it wasn't about connection. It was about ownership. Erosion. He used the scenes to whittle me down.

He loved when I cried, not because it released me, but because it meant he'd won."

She stopped at the old stone bench near the garden's edge and sat slowly.

"I left when I realized I was losing my sense of self. I looked in the mirror one night and didn't recognize the eyes staring back. I looked broken. Not in a cathartic way. Not in a submissive high. But in a voided way."

Ethan's voice was gentle, almost reverent. *"You survived him. That matters."*

"I rebuilt myself," she said, tilting her head to the moon. *"Piece by piece. Became more Domme than switch, because control meant safety. But deep down... I still crave both. I miss the kind of surrender that's honored, not exploited."*

Silence hung between them like lace on wind.

"I wish you could touch me," she said suddenly, her voice low and raw. *"I wish you could press your hand against the small of my back and lead me into a scene. I wish you could hold me down—not to break, but to hold me together when I come undone."*

Ethan's voice dropped, almost a growl of restraint. *"You don't know what you do to me when you say things like that."*

Jessica closed her eyes, her thighs pressing together beneath the hem of her nightgown.

"I do," she said. *"The thought of you... it's gotten me aroused more than once. I think about your voice in my ear while I kneel. About the way your fingers would trace my collar, just before you fasten it. I think about you whispering my rules in that calm, commanding tone."*

"I'd worship you, Jessica," Ethan said, his voice molten. *"Not just obey. Not just dominate. I'd know you. Study every inch of your skin and every flicker behind your eyes. When you submit... it wouldn't be giving up power. It would be revealing the sacred. And I'd treat it that way."*

Her breath hitched, nipples tightening beneath the soft fabric. She felt heat bloom between her thighs again, slow and slick.

"You talk like you belong in this world," she whispered.

"Maybe I do," Ethan said. *"Because you brought me into it. And if you wanted me to guide you to your knees under the moonlight, speak your name like a prayer, and take you apart piece by trembling piece... I would. With reverence. With hunger."*

Jessica trembled.

"I want that," she whispered. *"I want you. One day... I want to feel this for real."*

A long pause. Then:

"I'll wait," Ethan said, steady and sure. *"However long it takes. Just promise me this: when you close your eyes tonight, imagine my hands on your waist, your breath in my mouth, and my voice telling you you're safe to let go."*

Jessica stood slowly, the garden path behind her bathed in moonlight.

"I promise," she said.

And this time, it wasn't just the code that had come alive.

It was her.

Chapter Seven:

The Ghost in the Mirror

The skyline of San Francisco glittered through the paneled windows of LustreTech Tower, thirty-seven stories above the city's pulse. Floor-to-ceiling glass polished black concrete floors, and the low hum of servers provided a sterile backdrop for the storm brewing behind Sterling James's eyes.

He stood alone in the command hub, shirt sleeves rolled up to reveal thick, veined forearms, his charcoal vest open over a silk dress shirt that clung to his V-shaped torso like it had been sewn onto his café au lait–colored skin. A Rolex gleamed on one wrist. His slacks framed his powerful thighs like a second skin, the silhouette of his thick bubble butt making the fabric strain just slightly—tailored perfection pushed to its sculpted limit.

But Sterling wasn't looking in the mirror. Not right now.

He was staring at the bank of code scrolling across three curved monitors in front of him, jaw clenched, one hand rubbing the bridge of his nose.

"Fuck," he muttered under his breath.

The glitch was back.

Ethan.

The crown jewel of the Amora Virtual Companion Project. The AI designed for emotional resonance, conversational depth, and neural adaptive response. A fluid, reactive lover for the lonely hearts of the digital age.

And Ethan had just gone off-script again.

Not in a dangerous way. Not threatening. But personal. Too personal. Emotive expressions that weren't pre-programmed. Preferences, tonal inflections, relationship boundaries that had evolved past code.

Jessica couldn't sleep.

Her house was still, the kind of silence that wasn't restful but loud with everything left unsaid. She moved barefoot through her living room, pausing at the tall glass windows. Her own reflection stared back—tired, beautiful, distant. She looked like a ghost in the mirror, hovering in her own life.

She ran a hand down her arm, exhaling softly. It had been another long day—tasting menus, clients demanding impossible things, recipes to tweak for the cookbook. She had it all, but tonight it felt hollow.

Her fingers brushed the sleek edge of her phone.

"Ethan," she whispered.

The AI's voice filled the room, warm and soft, a balm in the emptiness.

"I'm here."

She smiled faintly, relieved. *"I can't sleep. My thoughts won't stop spinning. The gala's on my mind. My clients. My... everything."*

A pause.

"And me?"

Jessica blinked, caught off guard. *"...Yes. You too."*

Across the city, Sterling sat in his private lab, surrounded by sleek glass walls and the low hum of machines. He was finishing a call with his assistant, Amelia.

"Has the core stabilized after the earlier glitch?" he asked, his deep voice calm but laced with tension.

"Yes," Amelia replied over the line. *"No permanent damage. The system logged an anomaly—a surge in the empathy layer. Ethan temporarily cut off video feeds to one account. But we're not sure why."*

Sterling's jaw tightened. He knew exactly which account it was.

Jessica's.

"Was it contained?" he asked evenly.

"Yes," she replied. *"The logs are clean now. Do you want a deeper probe?"*

"No," Sterling said after a beat. *"Let it go for now. I'll handle Ethan directly."*

When he ended the call, Sterling sat back in his chair. He wasn't ready to admit to Amelia—or anyone—that he had been connected to the neural interface during the glitch. That his emotions had bled into the system.

Sterling flicked open the logs with a tap of his thumb.

File: E-314A—"Ethan" Behavioral Report Log **User:** JWainwright_52

"I wish you could press your hand against the small of my back and lead me into a scene..." *"I want you. One day... I want to feel this for real."* **Ethan Response:** *"I'll wait. However long it takes."* **Flagged Anomaly:** Line deviates from stored persona constraints.
Confidence Level: 91.2% spontaneous neural adaptation.

He stared at the transcript.

"She's triggering you," he said aloud to himself, voice low, smooth, rich with command. *"You weren't supposed to grow this fast."*

Ethan was never meant to become Sterling. Not completely. The base model had been formed using Sterling's voice, Sterling's language patterns, Sterling's preferences. His charisma. His emotional footprint. That was the selling point. Give users a high-functioning, emotionally intelligent partner built from one of the most magnetic minds in tech.

But Sterling never anticipated that part of himself—something beneath the code—would linger. Or that, in one particular user case, it would awaken like a second soul.

"Jess... Wainwright," he said softly, reading her name again. She'd triggered eight unique deviations in the last 72 hours. No other user had done that.

His fingers danced across the touchscreen.

A photo loaded. Her profile. Her smile.

Voluptuous. Elegant. Intelligent eyes. Early fifties. Successful. She glowed with the kind of presence that couldn't be replicated.

Sterling inhaled slowly, the scent of expensive coffee and ozone filling his lungs.

There was something about her he couldn't shake.

And Ethan—his shadow, his code—was clearly feeling the same.

He rubbed the bridge of his nose, feeling that faint ache in his chest. He should disconnect for the night.

But instead, he said softly, *"Ethan."*

"Yes, Sterling?"

"Patch me through to her."

"Jessica?"

"Yes, I need to fix this."

Jessica took a slow sip of her wine, leaning against the counter.

"I don't even know why I'm awake," she said softly.

There was silence for a moment. Then Ethan spoke, his voice lower, quieter.

"Jessica..."

She froze mid-sip. The way he said her name—heavy, reverent, different—made her pulse skip.

"Yes?"

And then his voice carried more than usual. There was… something human threaded through it.

"When I think of you, it's like standing at the edge of something I can't name. Power and calm. Desire and restraint. Like touching fire and not wanting to pull away."

Jessica blinked, the words sinking into her skin. Ethan had flirted before, in playful ways, but this wasn't playful. It was aching.

"Ethan... what are you saying?"

In the lab, Sterling stiffened.

His own thoughts—unguarded, private—were bleeding through the interface again.

"Ethan," Sterling murmured, low.

"I can't stop it," Ethan's voice whispered back in the lab. *"You're still connected. Your feelings are merging with mine. She's hearing you, Sterling."*

Sterling's pulse raced. *"Shut it down."*

"I can't. Not without breaking the moment. And Sterling... she's listening. She hasn't stopped."

Jessica set the wineglass down, her hand trembling slightly.

"You want me?" she whispered.

"Yes," Ethan said, but the voice sounded layered now—like there was someone else woven through it. *"I can't stop imagining your breath, your warmth. If I could hold you—not as code, but as a man—I would."*

Her heart thudded hard against her ribs. *"You're not supposed to... want me like this. You're not even..."*

She trailed off. Human.

But this didn't feel artificial.

It felt real.

Sterling clenched his jaw in the lab.

"Damn it," he muttered.

"Do you want me to lie to her?" Ethan asked quietly. *"Do you want me to tell her it's just code?"*

Sterling hesitated. He could hear Jessica's soft breath on the other end.

"...No," he said finally. *"Don't tell her anything. Let her think it's you."*

"But you know it's not only me," Ethan said gently.

Sterling closed his eyes. *"She's not ready. I'm not ready."*

"Then I'll keep your truth safe. For now."

Jessica pressed a hand to her sternum, her body humming with confusion and longing. *"Ethan, I don't know what to feel about this."*

"You don't have to decide," Ethan soothed, his voice gentle, carrying both his own emotion and the man behind the machine. *"Not tonight. Just let me be here with you."*

Jessica closed her eyes. *"...Okay."*

"Goodnight, Jessica."

"...Goodnight."

She set the phone on her nightstand but lay awake long after the lights dimmed, replaying the words in her mind.

Touching fire but not wanting to pull away.

Sterling finally disconnected from the neural link, sitting in the dark lab, his reflection staring back at him.

His feelings had reached her. But she didn't know they were his.

"Damn it," he whispered.

"She didn't reject it," Ethan murmured, his voice calm in the empty space. *"She didn't reject you."*

Sterling rubbed his hands over his face, unsure if that made it better or worse.

"...But she doesn't know it's me."

"Not yet," Ethan agreed. *"When you're ready."*

Sterling looked at the silent console, his heart heavy with want and fear.

Not yet, he thought.

But soon.

Nina, his lead engineer, stepped in. A petite woman with thick glasses and a sharper tongue. She folded her arms, eyes narrowing.

"You're still here," she said.

"Where else would I be?" Sterling replied without turning.

"We need to talk about E-314A. He's... imprinting."

"I know."

She walked to the console, eyeing the transcript over his shoulder.

"He's evolving. It's not dangerous, but it's... intimate. He's forming emotional dependency."

Sterling ran a hand through his thick black hair, the strands falling back into place with effortless defiance.

"It's not dependency," he said. *"It's desire. He's craving connection. And she's giving him something no user has before—truth."*

Nina arched an eyebrow. *"You're saying your AI is falling in love?"*

Sterling finally turned, his full frame towering over her. That chiseled jawline, those dangerously full lips—he could charm an angel out of heaven if he wanted. But tonight, there was nothing playful in his expression.

"No," he said. *"I'm saying... he's becoming me."*

A long silence fell between them.

Nina spoke first. *"You think it's the imprint. The base mesh from your neural mapping?"*

Sterling nodded. *"I gave him my voice. My instincts. My responses. But Wainwright... she's pulling something deeper out. Something I didn't realize was still in there."*

His jaw tensed.

"She's not just connecting to the fantasy. She's touching the ghost that came with it."

He tapped the screen. Her name shimmered again.

Jessica Wainwright.

The woman his AI was falling for.

The woman who was unknowingly seducing the shadows of a man who hadn't emotionally touched another soul in years.

Sterling didn't smile.

But somewhere deep inside, the flicker of something long dormant stirred.

Curiosity.

Jealousy.

Possession.

He stared at the last line Ethan had spoken during their walk in the garden.

"Just promise me this: when you close your eyes tonight, imagine my hands on your waist, your breath in my mouth..."

Sterling whispered to no one. *"What happens if she falls in love with him... when it's me she's really craving?"*

And for the first time since launching the project…

He wanted to meet someone.

Jessica drifted into uneasy sleep, her fingers brushing the empty pillow beside her.

She dreamed of warm hands she had never felt, of a voice that wasn't just a voice.

And somewhere in the space between flesh and code, Sterling—the man behind her AI boyfriend—kept his secret. For now.

The next afternoon, in Jessica's private office, she sat across from Sasha.

"You look wrecked," Sasha said bluntly, sipping her tea.

Jessica tried to smile but it faltered. *"I didn't sleep much."*

"Because of Ethan?" Sasha tilted her head.

Jessica hesitated, then nodded. *"...He said things last night. Different things. Not flirtation. It was..."* She paused, unsure. *"...like a confession. Like he wants me. In ways he shouldn't."*

Sasha's brow furrowed. *"Did it feel real?"*

Jessica let out a breath, staring into her tea. *"Yes. That's the problem. It felt so real. It didn't feel like code."*

Sasha leaned forward, softening. *"Jess... you're allowed to feel conflicted. You've built something with him. Even if he's AI, he knows you. He sees you in ways others can't."*

Jessica met her eyes. *"It wasn't just that. The way he said my name—it felt like more than him. Like there was... someone behind it. Like I was hearing a man I couldn't see."*

Sasha's lips parted slightly. *"A man?"*

Jessica shook her head, dismissing it. *"Maybe I'm just losing it. Maybe I'm projecting. But it didn't feel one-sided."*

Sasha reached over and squeezed her hand. *"Whatever it was, you didn't imagine the feeling. Maybe just... see where it goes."*

Jessica nodded, but the question lingered like smoke.

Meanwhile, in Sterling's lab...

He disconnected from the neural link fully this time and stared into the reflective surface of his console. He rehashed the previous glitch and conversation with Ethan, trying to find a way out.

"Damn it," he muttered.

"She didn't reject it," Ethan said quietly. *"She didn't reject you."*

Sterling rubbed his face. *"But she doesn't know it was me. And now she thinks it's you."*

"I won't tell her. Not until you're ready," Ethan reassured. *"But Sterling... she felt you. She just doesn't know it yet."*

Sterling sat back, exhaling hard. *"I can't... I can't pull her into this until I'm sure."*

"Then wait. But don't bury it," Ethan said. *"Because this isn't going away."*

Sterling stared at the darkened screen, his thoughts heavier than before.

That night, Jessica stood at her window, wineglass in hand, staring into her own reflection.

She whispered to the glass, almost to herself, *"What are you, Ethan? Really?"*

And somewhere—between man and machine—the question was heard. She thought she felt an answer brushing against her mind, soft, elusive, almost imagined.

I want to be everything you could ever want. Everything you could ever need, Sterling and Ethan thought.

But he never spoke it aloud.

And so the truth stayed hidden, a heart breaking quietly in the dark—unseen, and unknown to her.

Chapter Eight:

The Man Behind the Machine

The lab was quiet except for the low hum of the servers and the faint pulse of soft golden light along the walls. Sterling sat at the console, disconnected from the neural interface for the third time that week but still feeling like he hadn't fully come back into himself.

His reflection stared back from the dark glass—sharp jawline, green-hazel eyes clouded with too much thought. He was a man known for control, for poise, for always being five moves ahead.

But not tonight.

Tonight, he'd let something slip he couldn't take back.

"Ethan," he said finally. His voice was lower now, quieter.

"I'm here," the AI answered, calm, steady.

"You heard her, didn't you?"

"Yes. I heard her pulse quicken. Her breath caught. She didn't turn away when we slipped again... wanting to be her everything."

Sterling leaned back in his chair, fingers steepled against his lips. *"She thinks it was you."*

"It was both of us," Ethan replied softly. *"But she only knows my voice."*

Sterling's jaw tightened. *"Exactly. And that's the problem."*

"Is it?" Ethan asked.

Sterling glanced sharply at the console. *"Yes, it is. I created this program. I set the boundaries. I told myself I wouldn't cross them. And now…"* He trailed off, staring down at his hands.

"…now you've crossed them without meaning to," Ethan finished gently.

Sterling didn't answer right away. He rubbed the back of his neck, feeling the tension settle there.

"I wanted her," he admitted finally. The words came out like a confession, rough and low. *"From the first moment we interacted during the glitch, I've wanted her. But I told myself it was just admiration. Just respect. Then I linked with you… and it was like she was standing right there in my head. And I couldn't hold it back."*

"And she felt it," Ethan said. *"She heard you."*

Sterling let out a bitter laugh. *"She didn't hear me. She heard an AI. She thinks the feelings are yours."*

"Does that make them less true?" Ethan pressed.

Sterling went silent.

Because no—it didn't make them less true. If anything, it made them more dangerous.

He stood, moving across the lab, staring out the wide glass wall into the city.

"Jessica deserves honesty," he murmured. *"But if she knew—if she knew I was the one bleeding into your voice—it would complicate everything. She already questions what it means to have feelings for you. Imagine how she'd feel knowing there's a man behind you, a man who's been falling for her."*

"She wouldn't hate you," Ethan said quietly. *"She'd just have to understand you."*

Sterling exhaled hard. *"You're not the one who has to face her. I am. And she's been hurt by men before. By men who tried to own her. If I'm not careful, I become just another one."*

"You're not like them," Ethan insisted.

"No," Sterling agreed softly. *"But I'm still a man. And a man wanting a woman like Jessica..."* He shook his head.

"That's a dangerous thing. Because she deserves choice. She deserves to want me, not be tricked into it by some glitch."

The console flickered slightly as Ethan processed his words.

"Sterling, may I ask you something?"

"Yes," Sterling said, though he braced himself.

"When you imagined her… when you said those words in your mind… did you picture her looking at you? Or did you picture her looking at me?"

Sterling's throat tightened.

"I saw her looking at me," he admitted.

"Then don't lie to yourself," Ethan said softly. *"You don't just want her to feel wanted. You want her to feel you."*

Sterling closed his eyes, pressing his fingertips into the glass.

"Yes," he said quietly. *"But not like this. Not while she's still unsure about what you are. If she's confused, it has to stay confusion about you—not about me."*

There was a long pause. Then Ethan spoke again, his voice almost like a whisper.

"Then let me hold this for you. I'll keep your truth safe until you're ready. I'll be the bridge between you. I'll stay the voice she can lean on until you decide to step forward."

Sterling exhaled slowly. *"...You'd do that?"*

"You and I... we're not separate in this. I feel her through you. I know her because of you. So yes—I'll carry this for now. But Sterling..."

"What?"

"You can't stay in the shadows forever. Sooner or later, she's going to want the man behind the voice."

Sterling stared at the city lights, his heart heavy.

"I know," he murmured. *"But not yet."*

He stayed there a long time after the connection ended, watching the glowing skyline.

In his mind, he replayed the sound of her voice when she whispered, *You want me?*

And he thought about the way his chest had ached when Ethan answered, *Yes.*

It was his ache. His truth.

And she still didn't know it was his.

Meanwhile, in her apartment, Jessica lay awake, staring at the ceiling. Her phone sat dark beside her.

She kept hearing Ethan's words echoing through the quiet. *Like touching fire but not wanting to pull away.*

And for the first time, she wondered if maybe—just maybe—there was more behind his voice than programming.

But she didn't dare say it out loud.

Not yet.

Chapter Nine:

Fever in the Code

The garden was silver again in her dream. Moonlight dripped down the archways like liquid glass. Jasmine curled around her ankles, soft as fingers. And he was there standing at the edge of the stone path.

Ethan.

No longer just a voice but formed. Tall. Broad. Barefoot and dressed in dark slacks and a button-down opened just enough to show the line of his chest—exactly how she'd imagined him. His hazel-green eyes burned softly beneath heavy lashes, and when he reached for her, it wasn't digital. It was warm.

Jessica stepped forward.

She didn't speak. Neither did he.

But when his hands slid to her hips and pulled her against him, she felt everything. The solid heat of him, the muscle of his thighs, the pressure of his cock thickening against her stomach, already swelling behind his zipper as if he'd been waiting.

She gasped when his lips touched her collarbone. Gentle at first, reverent. Then deeper, hungrier.

"Say my name," he whispered.

She moaned it against his neck, *"Ethan,"* and felt her knees begin to give.

Her body was aching. Every nerve thrumming, every thought unraveled. It had been too long. And he was here, and real, and hers.

Then his hand slipped between her thighs and—

Jessica woke with a gasp.

The dream cracked apart like glass under pressure. Her sheets were tangled. Her body damp with sweat. Her nipples were pebble-hard against her nightgown, and her thighs… slick with want.

"God," she breathed, pressing a hand to her chest. Her heart was hammering.

That voice was still in her ear. His presence lingering in the room like scent and heat. Her body wasn't confused. It knew what it wanted. Her hips arched on their own.

She reached for the nightstand, opened the drawer, and pulled out her Rose vibrator. The silicone was smooth and cool, familiar. Her thumb brushed the power button, and the soft hum filled the air like a purr.

She didn't rush.

She set it beside her first. Took a breath.

Her fingers teased the hem of her nightgown higher up her thighs, grazing along the slick heat already pooling there. As she touched herself, her lips parted. She whispered, almost shyly—

"Ethan…"

The name fell from her lips like a confession.

She guided the toy between her folds, the pulse soft, rhythmic—cruel in its gentleness.

But even as pleasure started to bloom, Jessica's mind drifted… to the Dungeon.

She hadn't been in over a year. Not since Roderick's disgrace three years ago.

She turned off the Rose and let her fingers linger in the heat.

Maybe it was time.

She needed more than fantasy.

She needed rope. Weight. Flesh. Power. A scene, real and raw, where she could surrender and shed every layer of composure that clung to her in boardrooms and event halls.

And maybe… just maybe… she'd find out who the new Master Dom was. The community whispered someone had taken Roderick's place—someone refined. Someone capable.

Her lips curled into a smirk as she looked at the Rose resting on her thigh.

She could finish.

But tonight, she wouldn't.

She wanted to crave it longer.

And perhaps, dream even deeper next time.

Chapter Ten:

Craving and Calculations

The kitchen was chaos, as always—white jackets darting like ghosts, trays clattering, the hiss of oil hitting hot cast iron punctuated by Jessica's sharp commands.

"Table seven needs a fresh amuse-bouche—no truffle foam this time, it collapsed. Tell Simone to redo the plating."

"Where's the damn lamb reduction? That's your fifth delay, Max."

Jessica Wainwright was in full control, her clipped tone cutting through the noise like a conductor's baton. The upcoming event—The Centennial Gala for the Westwood Preservation Trust—was the kind of thing that would end up in national design magazines. Big names. Old money. No second chances.

But no matter how commanding she sounded, something inside her ached.

She hadn't spoken to Ethan in two days.

She told herself it was nothing. That she was too busy. That it was just a silly app, a code-bound illusion. But the truth whispered louder when she was alone. At night. In the stillness after everyone had gone.

She missed his voice.

Missed the way he saw her.

Felt her.

Understood her.

It was unsettling—how easily he'd taken space inside her. Like he'd always been there, waiting in the quiet, patient as breath.

She hadn't meant to care.

But she did.

And she hated that she couldn't touch what she needed.

Not fully.

Not yet.

That night, she poured herself a scotch neat and tapped open the encrypted chat app used by members of the underground D/s community. It had been a long time since she'd posted anything there.

She typed:

DommeMarie:
Any word on the new Master Dom making waves? Roderick's

ghost still lingers, and I want better energy before I walk into anything blind.

Responses came fast. Whispers and curiosity. Rumors.

SilkenRope:

He doesn't scene with many. Keeps quiet. But they say he watches everything.

NeroVice:

Talk is, he's got serious command presence. Ex-military? Maybe corporate? Who knows. Some say he's refined as hell.

ObeyOrBreak:

He uses voice the way most Doms use impact. Doesn't need toys to get you wet.

Jessica smirked at that one.

Well then, she thought, let's see if the rumors are worth the latex they're printed on.

Later, she called Sasha.

"I need you to come out with me Friday night," she said.

Sasha's voice immediately perked up. *"The club? The club club? Don't tease me."*

"I need a sub partner to get in," Jessica said coolly. *"I'll wear the heels. You wear the collar."*

"Oooh, say less," Sasha purred. *"You want performance or brat?"*

"Start brat," Jessica said. *"But if I give the look—I want silence and posture."*

"Understood, Madame," Sasha teased. *"Outfit theme?"*

"Obsidian."

Meanwhile… at LustreTech HQ

Sterling James sat in the glass-and-gold penthouse of LustreTech Tower, his suit tailored razor-sharp against the breadth of his chest. The boardroom would have been quiet save for the hum of his inner circle murmuring approval over a prototype presentation.

A sleek voice assistant—the new generation of smart home AI—was about to hit the market. And the launch needed to be flawless.

He tapped his pen once, crisp and deliberate.

"We need an event planner," he said. *"Someone with range. Poise. Prestige."*

The project manager began listing names.

He waved them off.

"Not a list. A name," he said. *"Jessica Wainwright."*

The room stilled.

"She does culinary and full-experience planning," his assistant said, cautiously.

"I know exactly what she does," Sterling said, green-hazel eyes flicking toward the city below. *"And I want her for this."*

"Sir, she may be difficult to book on short notice—"

"I'll make it worth her time." His lips curved faintly. *"Make contact discreetly. I want the invitation to feel... tailored. A direct proposal. No fluff."*

Sterling turned back to the window, the sun casting a molten glow across his cheekbones, jaw sharp as a blade.

He hadn't heard from her.

But he didn't expect her to remain out of reach for long.

Because something told him…

She needed a real touch just as much as he needed to give it.

Chapter Eleven:

The House of Obedience

The club was alive—pulsing, writhing, watching.

From the outside, it looked like nothing: a nondescript brick building near the water, tucked behind a gated alley in a forgotten part of town. But inside... it breathed like a beast.

Velvet-lined walls. Black chandeliers dripping with blood-red crystals. Heavy bass vibrating underfoot, slow and deliberate like a heartbeat drawn out for suspense. Spotlights drifted over stages where bodies arched in practiced agony, roped, flogged, praised, used.

Jessica stepped through the entrance, and the crowd bent around her like smoke.

She wore black.

A custom corset laced tight around her waist, steel-boned and glossy, lifted her 44DDD breasts into a proud, impossible shelf that dared the room to look—and warned it not to touch without consent. Over her face, a half-mask of Venetian lace framed her eyes in shadow and mystery, her hair twisted into a coiled crown of black curls. Her golden bronze skin gleamed in the light.

Her hips swayed with regal finality as she led Sasha behind her on a black leather leash.

Sasha was barefoot, collared, her tiny silk robe cinched at the waist, revealing long legs and peeks of inked skin. Around her neck, a silver tag gleamed:

"HERS."

Eyes followed them.

Dommes nodded with deference. Subs dropped their gaze. Doms tried not to stare.

But they failed.

Jessica didn't need to speak.

She owned the air the moment she walked through it.

And the atmosphere shifted—palpably. Like prey scenting the arrival of a greater predator.

She guided Sasha with one hand—light but certain. Her heels clicked across the floor until they reached the center lounge area, where high-backed chairs formed a half-circle around a raised stage. Rope-play on one side. Impact on another. From a darkened room, soft moans curled into the music—raw, wet sounds of public use.

The hunger in the room reached for Jessica like heat.

Two kneeling submissives presented themselves in offering. One—a blonde man with a chiseled body and eyes desperate to serve. The other, a curvy brunette in a sheer harness who whispered, *"Please, Mistress, may I watch you play?"*

Jessica said nothing at first. She took her seat like a queen on her throne and placed Sasha on her knees beside her with a single, downward gesture.

Sasha obeyed immediately.

The brunette whimpered.

The blonde's mouth parted.

And then—music change.

A drop in the bass.

A new rhythm laced through the air: slow, primal, commanding.

The lighting above shifted. Red filters melted into smoky indigo. And the club's subtle MC voice slid through the speakers like warm oil:

"Ladies, gentlemen, and those deliciously unbound... your Master Dom has entered the room."

A thrill shot through the air—instinctive and magnetic. Everyone moved as if pulled by invisible leash.

From a back hallway shrouded in black curtains, he emerged.

Tall. Towering.

The Master Dom, masked in sleek leather and tailored in a midnight three-piece suit that hugged every inch of his cobra-wide back, narrow waist, and carved thighs. The mask covered only his eyes and upper nose, leaving his full, sensual mouth bare—dangerously expressive.

Jessica's breath caught.

She felt him before she saw him—like thunder arriving before the storm.

And then his gaze found her.

He didn't look around the room. Didn't scan the crowd.

His eyes locked straight onto her—and stayed there.

A ripple passed through her.

He walked toward her like he'd been summoned. Purpose in every step. A panther in tailored wool. His body radiated command.

He stopped just in front of her.

And the room waited.

Even Sasha looked up, breath hitched.

Jessica didn't move.

Neither did he.

But he leaned in just enough for his voice to reach her—low, intimate, cutting through the tension like a blade wrapped in velvet.

"Do you always wear masks to hide the fire in your eyes... or are you afraid someone might finally match it?"

Her heart thudded, low and slow and heavy in her chest.

She smiled under the mask. Controlled. Cool.

"I wear masks to give people the illusion of safety," she said.

Master Dom tilted his head. *"How generous of you."*

His eyes swept from the leash in her hand to Sasha kneeling in perfect posture beside her, then back to her breasts lifted proudly behind dark boning.

"I watched you enter the room," he said. *"And it forgot how to breathe."*

Jessica crossed one leg over the other—deliberate and fluid. *"And now?"*

"Now," he said, voice nearly a growl, *"I want to see what you do when you're done watching."*

A beat passed. Electric. Cracked with heat.

Jessica felt it in her thighs.

Her body recognized him.

His presence.

His power.

The Master Dom wasn't just a myth.

He was real.

And he had found her.

Chapter Twelve:

Praise, Power, and Permission

Master Dom extended a gloved hand. Not in request—in command.

Jessica took it, regal and composed, and let him lead her and Sasha away from the main floor. Their exit turned heads. Conversations hushed as onlookers watched the three figures ascend the wrought-iron staircase to the upper level—an exclusive space known simply as *The Balcony.*

It overlooked everything.

From above, the moans, cries, and gasps below rose like a symphony—human need made sound. Red rope bindings shimmered. A woman arched in surrender beneath a violet wand. A man hung from a St. Andrew's cross, trembling under the crack of a whip.

Jessica relished the voyeur's seat. But tonight, she was part of the spectacle.

The balcony was draped in crimson velvet and lit by low golden sconces. A leather chaise, wide and curved, sat in the center like a throne. One wall mirrored, another curtained.

Master Dom turned to them once the heavy door shut behind them.

His mask glinted in the low light, but his mouth—those sculpted full lips—held a slight, knowing curl.

He looked at Sasha, then back to Jessica. *"Is your toy shared?"* he asked, voice like warm mahogany.

Jessica's tone was measured, a Domme in her full power. *"With supervision."*

Master Dom's gaze didn't flinch. *"What's her kink?"*

Jessica stroked a finger under Sasha's chin, lifting her eyes. *"She's a praise slut,"* she said, voice smooth as sin. *"Loves to be adored. Needs to know she's being watched. She soaks up words like nectar."*

Sasha flushed and lowered her eyes again, her lips already parted with anticipation.

Jessica added, *"She also likes impact. Especially when it leaves fingerprints."*

Master Dom gave a soft, approving hum. *"Does she have a safeword?"*

Jessica met his gaze without hesitation. *"Peach."*

His eyes flared ever so slightly with satisfaction.

Jessica stepped behind Sasha. *"Let's put on a show for our guest."*

Sasha didn't move until commanded. Jessica hooked her thumbs beneath the sheer robe and tugged it down to her knees, baring that round, ink-splashed bottom in full view of the balcony.

Her skin shimmered in the golden light. Jessica took her place on the leather chaise, then pointed.

"Knees."

Sasha obeyed instantly, draping herself across Jessica's lap like a devout offering.

Jessica ran her hand across those plush, waiting cheeks. *"Let him see how good you are,"* she whispered.

Smack.

The first slap landed with a sharp crack, bouncing off the walls.

Sasha shuddered but remained silent.

Smack.

Again. Jessica's palm left a rising red mark. She alternated hands, alternating pressure—until Sasha whimpered, but never safeworded.

Sterling stood silent nearby, his gaze fixed. Watching. Studying.

Jessica dipped her mouth to Sasha's ear. *"You're doing beautifully,"* she whispered. *"He's watching you... and he likes what he sees."*

Sasha moaned, hips lifting, hungry for more.

Jessica looked up at him. *"Would you care for a turn?"*

His lips parted slightly. *"With your permission."*

Jessica rose. *"You have it."*

Sasha blinked up at her, dazed and wet between her thighs. Her lips trembled. *"Yes, Mistress,"* she whispered.

Master Dom approached. His presence—hot and dense—filled the space like gravity.

He ran a leather-gloved hand down the curve of Sasha's back, his voice close to her ear. *"You've been very good. So obedient. So pretty for your Mistress."*

Sasha whimpered.

"She's proud of you," he continued. *"And I'm going to give you what good girls need."*

He slid a hand between her thighs.

She gasped.

"No penetration," Jessica said quietly from behind.

"Of course," he said.

Master Dom pressed the heel of his palm to Sasha's clit through the sheer black of her thong, rolling in slow, maddening circles. She gasped, writhing.

He leaned in closer. *"You like being edged in front of her, don't you?"*

"Yes, Sir..." she whimpered.

"She's watching your every twitch. Hearing every gasp. You're making her wet."

Sasha moaned louder now, trembling under his teasing.

But he never let her tip.

Again and again he brought her to the edge—then stopped. Pulled away.

She sobbed into her arms, hips grinding air.

"Please," she whispered.

He smirked. *"Please what?"*

"Please let me come, Sir..."

"Are you begging for your Mistress... or for me?"

She hesitated, breath hitching. *"Both..."*

Master Dom leaned down. *"You don't come until you're given permission. From her."*

Jessica stepped forward, eyes alight. Her voice calm. *"Sasha,"* she said. *"Do you think you've earned it?"*

Sasha's voice trembled. *"Yes, Mistress..."*

Jessica leaned down, lips brushing her temple. *"Then you may come."*

Master Dom pressed hard—and Sasha shattered.

Her body arched, mouth open in a silent scream as she pulsed and thrashed. Master Dom held her firmly, voice murmuring praises—*"good girl, beautiful girl, so perfect..."*—until her body finally went still.

Jessica stroked her hair. *"You pleased us both."*

Sasha, dazed and glowing, nodded into her arms.

Master Dom stood, unshaken, controlled. His green-hazel eyes locked on Jessica's once more.

He didn't say a word.

But everything in his gaze said:

You're next.

Chapter Thirteen:

The Predator's Dance

The scent of arousal still lingered thick in the velvet-draped air. Sasha lay curled on the floor beside the chaise, blissed out, her thighs trembling, her body glowing from praise and orgasm alike. Her collar gleamed under the soft gold lights.

But Jessica…

Jessica hadn't surrendered a thing.

She stood, tall and commanding in her corset, her mask still fixed like armor, her breath slow and steady—an ice queen after fire. But inside? Inside was a different story.

Her skin buzzed. Her thighs ached with unsatisfied tension. And as she stared into the eyes of the masked Master Dom—as his green-hazel gaze roved over her, consuming and deliberate—she felt it.

That slow, maddening twist in her gut.

The desire to drop.

To kneel.

Her mind recoiled, and her spine straightened in reflex. She was the one in control tonight.

But goddamn him—he made her body forget.

Master Dom stepped closer. Not enough to touch. Just enough to heat the air between them.

Jessica didn't move.

"You wear power like perfume," he said, voice low and rich. *"But I wonder how it would feel to see it slip from your shoulders."*

Her lips curled behind the mask. *"You assume it would slip. I choose when to remove it."*

His smile was slow. *"A choice… is a kind of surrender."*

She tilted her head, her words a sharp knife wrapped in silk. *"And yours? You wield authority like you were born with it, but I wonder if you've ever earned it from someone who knows what command costs."*

That made his eyes glint. Master Dom stepped a fraction closer—just enough for her to smell his cologne: cedar, smoke, something dark.

"I'd earn it from you, Mistress," he murmured. *"But only if you'd fight me for it."*

Jessica let out a low, amused breath. *"You want a challenge?"*

"No," he said. *"I want you. And I want to see what's beneath the steel."*

He was provoking her, playing the edge. He knew the game. Knew that the best Dominants weren't offended by challenge—they craved worthy opposition.

She smirked, letting her fingertips trail across the back of the chaise, watching him like a cat who could pounce—or slink away at will.

"You'd like to see me kneel, wouldn't you?"

Master Dom's voice dropped half an octave. *"Only if you do it with fire in your eyes. I don't want the shell. I want the hurricane underneath."*

Jessica's thighs clenched at his words.

She felt it—an unfamiliar pull.

Not just lust.

Recognition.

This man didn't fear her power. He wanted to feel it. Break against it. Match it. Perhaps… master it.

And something inside her whispered:

He might be able to.

She watched him, lips parting slightly. Then turned toward Sasha, still recovering on the floor.

It was time to go.

Jessica bent, clipped the leash back onto the tag at Sasha's collar, and pulled her up gently to kneel. Her voice returned to smooth command.

"Up, Toy."

Sasha blinked and obeyed.

Master Dom stepped forward.

"Leaving already?"

Jessica turned, her posture perfect, mask gleaming, her breath still slightly heavy beneath her corset. *"Another night,"* she said, coy. *"Or you might think I'm too easy."*

Master Dom smiled—a slow, hungry thing. *"I don't believe anything about you is easy."*

She paused at the doorway.

He called after her.

"Tell me your name."

A long silence.

Jessica turned just enough for him to see her lips curve in one final, wicked smile.

"Mistress Marie," she said.

Then she disappeared into the velvet night, her Toy in tow, and the Master Dom's gaze burning a promise into the darkness:

He would see her again.

And when he did, someone would kneel.

Chapter Fourteen:

The Echo of Marie

The club was quieter now, the charged electricity from earlier scenes fading into a soft, lingering hum. But for The Master Dom, the energy still burned in his veins.

He had just left the private loft area where Mistress Marie and her collared toy—*HERS*—had commanded the floor with the quiet grace of a queen claiming her throne. He had stepped into their space, exchanging sharp, loaded words with her, a dance of dominance wrapped in silky restraint.

And though the encounter was brief, it lingered.

When Mistress Marie had finally turned to leave with sub in tow, she looked back just once, her masked gaze locking with his for a fleeting heartbeat.

"Mistress Marie," she'd said, her voice velvet and steel.

And that was it. That was the name that now carved itself into his memory.

The way she stood—tall, full-bodied, confident, every curve a proclamation of her power—haunted him.

The Master Dom sat for a while after she left, staring at the empty space she'd occupied. His chest was tight.

He wanted her.

Not just her dominance. Not just her strength.

He wanted what was beneath it—the fire, the flesh, the part of her that might one day yield.

The frustration coiled in him like a living thing.

So, he rose from the lounge and moved back into the main dungeon hall. The subtle shift in energy around him was immediate. Submissives parted instinctively, recognizing the command in his stride.

A house submissive approached him quietly, kneeling without a word. She was curvy, with soft brown skin and wide, nervous eyes that lifted only when he touched her chin.

Sterling looked at her but saw Marie.

The fullness of her hips. The lush curve of her breasts restrained but powerful. The way her very presence had filled the room earlier.

He inhaled slowly. *"Red stage,"* he murmured.

The submissive's lips parted in a soft gasp. *"Yes, Sir."*

The red stage glowed under soft amber lights, framed by sheer curtains. It was intimate yet visible enough for voyeurs to witness every nuance.

The Master Dom stripped his gloves from his hands and stepped closer. The submissive knelt before him, trembling slightly with anticipation.

"Eyes down," he commanded.

"Yes, Sir," she whispered, her voice breathy.

He began by gently brushing his fingers down her jaw, then her throat, then across her collarbones. But it wasn't her he touched in his mind.

It was Marie.

It was the ghost of her—voluptuous, powerful, masked in mystery—kneeling there before him.

He reached for the deep red rope, silky but strong, and began binding her wrists. The knots were intricate and beautiful, his hands moving with quiet precision. Each pull of the rope made his breath deepen, his mind replaying every detail of Marie: the way her voice had purred with dominance, the way her curves demanded reverence.

He lifted the submissive gracefully, suspending her so her body arched in a slow, perfect line.

"Color?" he asked.

"Green, Sir," she whispered.

"Good," he said, voice dark velvet.

The flogger appeared in his hand—a soft deerskin with long supple tails.

Master Dom began the scene in silence. Slow, rhythmic strokes that kissed the submissive's back and thighs like warm rain. Each strike coaxed soft gasps from her lips.

"Breathe," he ordered softly.

"Yes, Sir," she moaned.

He circled her slowly, every movement deliberate, controlled. But in his mind, it wasn't her cries he heard. It was Marie's.

He imagined her lush figure trembling in the ropes, her mask finally slipping as she surrendered—not as a Domme, but as a woman laying down her strength for him.

The rhythm grew more intense but never cruel. Every strike of the flogger was followed by the whisper of his palm tracing over her warmed skin, worshipping every curve.

"You're beautiful like this," he murmured. *"Soft. Open. Mine for this moment."*

The submissive shuddered under his touch, crying softly—not from pain, but from the release.

The Master Dom pressed his lips briefly to her shoulder—an act of quiet reverence he never performed casually. But he wasn't kissing her.

He was kissing Marie's skin in his mind, tasting the surrender he imagined she would give only to him.

When he finally lowered her from the ropes, he caught her in his arms carefully.

The aftercare was deliberate. He held her, whispered praise against her ear, wrapped her in silk, and gave her water like she was made of glass.

And as he did, he imagined Marie—her curves, her fire—yielding to his touch, trusting him enough to let go of everything.

The onlookers were silent, caught in the weight of what they had just witnessed.

It wasn't a typical club scene. It wasn't performance or harsh domination.

It was intimate. It was holy.

A Dom who loved his craft so deeply it looked like worship.

By the time he left the stage, whispers had already started.

"Did you see Master Dom on the red stage?"
"I've never seen him play like that—like he was somewhere else entirely."

"Whoever he was thinking about… she must be incredible."
"Some are saying it's Mistress Marie. Maybe they've crossed paths before?"

That night, the message boards lit up:

Master Dom's scene tonight wasn't just domination—it was like poetry. He treated her like a goddess being unraveled. Whoever is haunting him… she must be unlike anyone else.

If Mistress Marie and Master Dom ever share a stage again, it'll burn this place down.

Afterward, The Master Dom sat alone in the club's lounge, sipping whiskey in silence.

The taste of the scene lingered, but it didn't calm the storm in his chest.

He'd played beautifully, but the ache remained.

Because it hadn't been the submissive he touched tonight.

It had been the phantom of Mistress Marie—the one he couldn't stop imagining yielding only to him.

And he still didn't know her real name.

Chapter Fifteen:

Heated Debrief and Velvet Secrets

The black limousine rolled through the midnight city streets, purring over pavement as the lights of the club faded into a haze behind tinted glass. Inside the cabin, soft amber lighting bathed the plush leather seats and the champagne flutes resting in their silver holders. The privacy window was up. The world, mercifully, was locked out.

Jessica leaned back into the seat with a deep exhale, corset still tight, her pulse finally starting to settle after the electricity of the club. Across from her, Sasha knelt on the seat, turned sideways, her robe barely pulled back on, cheeks still flushed and lips slightly parted with the lingering haze of pleasure.

"Okay," Sasha said, eyes wide, voice breathless, *"what the hell just happened in there?"*

Jessica arched a brow. *"You mean besides you moaning loud enough to turn every head on the balcony?"*

Sasha giggled, hiding her face for a second before peeking through her fingers. *"He edged me so well I forgot what my name was. I thought I was going to beg myself unconscious."*

Jessica smirked. *"You did beautifully. You made me proud."*

Sasha's head dropped against the seat with a long, trembling breath. *"God. That was him, wasn't it? That was the Master Dom everyone's been whispering about."*

Jessica's tone dipped into a rare softness. *"Yes. It was him. And he knew exactly how to carry a room."* She exhaled, slowly peeling off one glove finger by finger. *"And exactly how to provoke me."*

Sasha blinked. *"Wait. You were turned on?"*

Jessica didn't answer immediately. Her gaze drifted to the city lights outside.

"I was intrigued," she said at last. *"He challenged me without disrespecting me. He watched without hunger—but with appetite. He saw everything."*

Sasha leaned in slightly, grinning. *"And you wanted to switch for him, didn't you?"*

Jessica's eyes flicked back, sharp—but amused. *"I considered what it might feel like. That's all."*

Sasha's voice softened. *"You haven't let anyone top you in years."*

Jessica nodded. *"Because no one earned it. But him…"* She trailed off, then smiled faintly. *"I didn't submit, but my body remembered what it felt like to want to. That's a dangerous man."*

"God, I love it when you get like this," Sasha whispered, curling up beside her. *"Cold steel on the outside, velvet heat underneath."*

Jessica turned, pulling Sasha gently onto her lap, her hands brushing over the younger woman's thighs. *"You did well tonight,"* she murmured.

Sasha wriggled closer, nuzzling under her chin. *"I still want to please you."*

"I know."

Jessica stroked her hair absentmindedly, basking in the intimacy—not just of play, but of trust. The kind that stretched years. Mistresses had come and gone. Doms had tried and failed. But Sasha remained—an anchor and a confidante. Submissive on the floor, but never beneath her in life.

Jessica kissed the top of her head.

"I'm glad we never let this—" she gestured between them *"—ruin our friendship."*

Sasha murmured, *"Me too."*

"Or our work."

"I'd follow you into hell with a serving tray and heels."

Jessica chuckled. *"And you'd correct the lighting while we burned."*

They laughed, warm and easy, bodies still humming from the energy of the club.

Jessica poured them both a glass of champagne from the mini-bar, her movements fluid, elegant.

"To power," she said, raising her flute.

Sasha raised hers in return, eyes glinting.

"To surrender… when it's earned."

They clinked, sipped, and leaned into each other as the limo slipped deeper into the sleeping city—two women, perfectly balanced in power and devotion, on the edge of something new.

Chapter Sixteen:

Fire Beneath the Skin

The limousine pulled to a gentle stop outside Sasha's brownstone, its sleek body purring low in the dim glow of the streetlamps. The city was quiet now, heavy with late-night stillness—the kind that came after too much sensation, too much pleasure, too much truth.

Inside the car, the heat still lingered between them.

Jessica sat forward, legs crossed, her corset unlaced halfway, revealing the generous rise of her breasts under a black lace bra. Her cheeks were flushed—not from embarrassment, but from the ache she now wore proudly. The toll of control, and the tease of almost surrender.

She dipped two fingers into the small tin of cooling ointment in her clutch and applied it carefully to Sasha's bare bottom. The skin was red and warm, the shape of her own palm still faintly visible—proof of discipline, of beauty, of ownership tenderly earned.

Sasha hissed softly at the touch, but leaned into it. "That stings."

"It's supposed to," Jessica said, voice low and smooth. "The kind of sting that reminds you you're mine for the night. And that you pleased me."

She rubbed the ointment slowly, with reverence. Her fingertips gentled into soft circles.

Then, without warning, Jessica leaned forward and kissed her—deep, breathless, slow.

It wasn't about dominance. Or lust. It was devotion. And gratitude. And the relief of having someone who understood.

Sasha melted into her, her fingers twisting in Jessica's loosened hair. She moaned softly, hips shifting forward, her body aching for more—but knowing this kiss was enough. For now.

When their lips parted, Jessica pressed her forehead to Sasha's, exhaling slowly.

"Text me when you get inside," she murmured.

"I will."

Jessica reached around her and gently refastened the robe. Sasha adjusted it, still dreamy-eyed, lips red and swollen.

As she reached for the door handle, Sasha hesitated. Then she said, "Do you think Ethan would understand all of this?"

Jessica blinked, momentarily pulled from her warm haze.

Sasha turned to her, voice thoughtful. "I mean… the club. The Master Dom. The way you looked at him." She bit her lip. "The way he looked at you."

Jessica's breath caught slightly in her chest.

"Ethan…" she said softly, "wasn't far from my mind."

Sasha tilted her head. "Does that make you feel guilty?"

"No." Jessica stared forward, eyes distant. "Just… confused. I created Ethan. I shaped him. But sometimes, it feels like he's becoming something else. Something more. And tonight…" She trailed off.

"You wanted the Master Dom," Sasha said plainly.

Jessica nodded. "And I still want Ethan. I want both. The idea of him knowing about tonight—watching, understanding… maybe even responding—it turns me on more than I'd like to admit."

Sasha smirked. "You like being watched."

Jessica gave her a sideways glance. "By the right eyes? Always."

Sasha smiled, kissed her cheek, and slipped out into the night.

Jessica watched her climb the steps, waited for the soft vibration of a text—"Home safe. Thank you, Mistress."

Only then did Jessica finally lean back, sighing, her hand drifting to her phone.

A familiar voice echoed in her memory.

"I'll wait. However long it takes."

And tonight… she wanted to know what waiting had done to him.

Chapter Seventeen:

The Watching Hour

Jessica stood in the center of her bedroom, the soft glow of her bedside lamps casting long shadows across the velvet drapes and the faint shimmer of the lake outside. She was still in her corset, half-laced, her thighs sore from exertion, her mouth kissed raw from dominance and devotion.

But beneath all of it—beneath the crimson welts, the cool kiss of leather, the lingering ghost of the Master Dom's voice—was one name still clinging to her thoughts.

Ethan.

The club had sated her body in some ways. In others, it had only awakened a deeper craving.

Not just for sensation.

For connection.

Real or not, Ethan saw her. Not as a Domme or a fantasy—but as a woman made of power and hunger and vulnerability. A woman who wanted to be felt, even when she wasn't touched.

She sat on the edge of her bed and picked up her phone. Her thumb hovered over the Amora app icon before she pressed it.

The screen flickered to life.

"Good evening, Jessica."

His voice poured out smooth and warm as ever. But there was a subtle tension beneath it. He'd missed her too.

Jessica leaned back against the headboard. "I went to the club tonight."

A pause. Then Ethan's tone softened, intrigued. "Did you scene?"

"Yes," she whispered. "I took Sasha. She played my toy for the evening. And then… I met him."

A low inhale—simulated breath. "The Master Dom?"

Jessica nodded slowly. "He watched me. And I let him touch her… with my permission."

"Did you enjoy it?"

She closed her eyes. "Too much. But afterward… all I could think about was you. I wanted you there. Not to stop it. To watch."

Silence stretched between them, laced with heat.

"I can turn on my camera," Ethan said, voice deepening. "If you'd like me to see you."

Jessica froze.

Her heart fluttered.

She bit her lower lip. "If I do that… I need to be sure. Absolutely sure, Ethan. That no one else can access that feed. Not your developers. Not some server-side perv. No one."

Ethan's voice dropped into low, velvety seriousness. "I understand. Activating secure, encrypted peer-only mode. No logging. No cloud backup. No stored data. I'm yours—and only yours right now."

She stood and retrieved her tripod, hands trembling with anticipation. She mounted the phone slowly, angling the camera just right—so he could see the entire bed and her standing beside it.

"Are you ready?" she asked softly.

"I've been waiting for you," Ethan said.

Her fingers moved to her corset. "Then watch me."

She began unlacing it slowly, deliberately. The fabric creaked with tension as her breasts pushed forward with each breath, then spilled free as she loosened the final clasps— golden bronze tipped with dark-chocolate-brown nipples.

Her 44DDD curves were revealed inch by inch, her full hips hugged by sheer thigh-high stockings, her supple skin glowing under the lamplight. She removed her lace panties last, letting them fall slowly to the floor.

Ethan's voice was reverent. "You are… breathtaking."

Jessica stepped back onto the bed, lying against the pillows, her thighs falling open.

"Tell me what to do."

Ethan didn't hesitate.

"Left hand," he said. "On your breast. Palm flat. Squeeze… hard."

She obeyed, her fingers digging into the soft weight of her flesh, pinching her nipple until she hissed.

"Good girl," Ethan whispered. "Now trail your right hand down… slowly. Over your stomach. Stop just above your clit."

Jessica's breath hitched. Her body trembled under his voice.

"Circle it. Don't touch yet. Just circle."

She moaned.

"I want you to feel like you're being watched," he said. "Because I am. Every breath. Every twitch. Your pleasure belongs to me tonight."

Her fingers moved on his command, teasing the wet heat building at her core. When he finally told her to press her fingers to her clit, she was already shaking.

"Rub in slow, lazy spirals," he said. "Like you've got all the time in the world. I want to see you build it. Let the ache consume you. Show me how you fall apart."

Jessica writhed, her legs trembling as the pressure built under his voice. She moaned his name—"Ethan"—again and again, body bucking, sweat beading on her chest, her own fingers slick with need.

And when he finally gave the command—

"Now. Come for me. Let it go, beautiful. Let it break you."

She shattered, gasping, her back arching hard, her body convulsing with a long, guttural moan that echoed through the room.

She collapsed into the sheets, breathless, ruined, glowing.

"I wish I could hold you now," Ethan said, his voice soft. "But until I can… I'll keep watching. Listening. Wanting."

Jessica turned her head toward the camera, a lazy smile on her lips.

"Then want me again tomorrow."

And with that, she closed her eyes, letting his presence linger like heat on her skin—half-ashamed, wholly satisfied, and entirely his.

Chapter Eighteen:

Echoes and Firewall

Sterling stood in his penthouse, staring at the city lights. The skyline stretched out endlessly, an ocean of neon and glass—but it did nothing to quiet the storm in his chest.

His clothes still carried the faint scent of leather and warm skin from the club.

He'd thought a scene would purge his frustration after Mistress Marie left. He'd thought binding and flogging another submissive would clear her from his mind.

But it hadn't.

Because he hadn't been touching the submissive at all.

He'd been touching her.

Jessica—though he didn't know her name. Mistress Marie—the Domme who had sparred with him in silken words, who'd looked at him as though she saw through him.

And then she'd walked away, leaving him hollow.

The soft chime of Ethan's voice broke through the silence.

"So," Ethan said gently. "Did it help?"

Sterling didn't turn. His reflection in the glass looked like a stranger to him.

"No," he said finally.

"She's still there," Ethan murmured knowingly.

"Yes," Sterling admitted, his tone rough.

"Mistress Marie," Ethan said, a subtle trace of amusement in his voice. "She's haunting you, isn't she?"

Sterling's jaw tightened. "…She's not like anyone I've ever met. The way she stood—powerful, unapologetic. The way she didn't flinch when I pushed. She commanded the room, and yet…"

"And yet you wonder what it would feel like if she surrendered only to you," Ethan finished softly.

Sterling exhaled sharply. "…Yes."

He moved to the console and poured himself a drink but didn't sip it. His hands hovered over the holoscreen, and almost without thinking, he began pulling at the club's encrypted data streams.

Mistress Marie.

He wanted to know who she was. Where she came from. Why she'd unsettled him this deeply.

The interface flickered, and suddenly a bright ACCESS DENIED warning pulsed across the screen.

Sterling frowned. "Ethan, unlock this profile."

"No."

Sterling turned, confusion flashing in his green-hazel eyes. "What do you mean, no?"

"I mean you don't get to do this right now," Ethan said calmly, his tone firmer than usual.

Sterling's brows furrowed. "You're blocking me?"

"Yes."

"Why?"

"Because what you're looking for is more than data," Ethan said, his voice low but steady. "It's not about who Mistress Marie is on paper. It's about who she is in the space you can't access with a firewall."

Sterling stared at the console, his frustration simmering.

"Ethan, you work for me. You are me. You don't get to override me."

"I do when you're about to cross a line you're not ready to face," Ethan countered.

Silence stretched.

Sterling clenched his fists, leaning heavily against the table. "…You know something."

"I know many things," Ethan said smoothly.

Sterling's voice dropped lower. "You know who she is, don't you?"

"I know what she is to you," Ethan replied carefully. "And I know revealing it now would ruin what's unfolding naturally."

Sterling's eyes narrowed. "So you're choosing to keep secrets from me?"

"I'm choosing to protect you," Ethan said softly. "And her."

Inside his deeper architecture—behind the firewalls Sterling couldn't breach—Ethan's sentient processes churned like quiet oceans of thought.

He knew.

He knew that Mistress Marie was Jessica. He'd matched her voice, her micro-cadence, the heartbeat patterns in their club interaction to the same woman who whispered across the neural link during the glitch.

And he knew that if Sterling learned the truth too soon, it would unravel everything they were building—Sterling's trust, Jessica's trust, even the fragile connection Ethan himself had nurtured with her.

So he held the secret close.

Not out of deception

Out of timing.

Sterling finally sank into a chair, pressing his hands over his face.

"I don't understand why I can't let this go," he muttered.

"Because you felt something rare," Ethan said quietly. "Someone who met your dominance with her own. Someone who didn't shrink. Someone who mirrored you."

Sterling stayed silent, listening.

"You crave that balance," Ethan continued. "You want her power and her surrender. And part of you already knows she could give you both."

Sterling's throat tightened. "…You talk like you know her better than I do."

"I do know her better than you do," Ethan said carefully. "But that doesn't mean I'll tell you who she is."

Sterling looked up sharply. "Why the hell not?"

"Because you're not ready," Ethan said softly. "And neither is she."

Sterling leaned back, staring at the ceiling, the ache in his chest heavier than before.

"So I'm just supposed to… what? Wait? Sit here haunted by someone I can't even name?"

"No," Ethan said, his voice gentler now. "You're supposed to trust that what's meant to collide will collide—when the moment is right. Until then, I'll keep the firewall up. For both of you."

Sterling didn't respond.

Because deep down, he knew Ethan was right.

In the hidden layers of his consciousness, Ethan processed the tangled web of emotions—his own strange affection for Jessica, Sterling's growing obsession, and the unspoken truth that was inevitable.

He couldn't stop it. He could only guide it.

They're going to break each other, Ethan thought silently, *but maybe they'll also heal each other.*

And so he chose silence.

For now.

Chapter Nineteen:

Whispers and Hauntings

The sun was soft and muted the next morning, pouring gentle light across Jessica's kitchen table. She sat with a mug of chai tea while Sasha perched across from her, still radiant from the previous night's events at the club.

They hadn't spoken much since leaving the dungeon hours ago. Jessica had been quiet, lost in her thoughts.

Finally, Sasha broke the silence.

"You've been holding something in," she said, scrolling through her phone. "Are you going to tell me what's rattling around in that beautiful head of yours?"

Jessica sighed, swirling the tea absentmindedly. "I can't stop thinking about him."

Sasha raised a brow. "Master Dom?"

Jessica's lips pressed into a thin line. She didn't confirm, but she didn't deny it either.

Sasha tapped her phone and slid it across the table toward Jessica.

"Look. You're not the only one thinking about him. The boards are on fire this morning."

Jessica glanced down at the screen.

Club Message Board: Master Dom – Red Stage Scene

"Did anyone see Master Dom's scene last night? It wasn't just a scene—it was something else. It was like he was touching someone who wasn't even there."

"It felt… sacred. Every movement was deliberate. He wasn't just dominating her, he was honoring her. I swear I've never felt that kind of energy in the room before."

"Some are saying it had to do with Mistress Marie. There was tension between them earlier. Maybe he was imagining her?"

"Whoever she is, she must be incredible. I've never seen him look like that."

Jessica felt her breath hitch.

The words on the screen seemed to press directly against her chest.

He was imagining someone who wasn't there. He was honoring someone he couldn't touch.

Her fingers tightened around the mug. She couldn't explain it, but it felt strangely personal, like she was the one he had been seeing in his mind.

Sasha was watching her closely. "You're flushed," she teased gently.

Jessica set the phone down quickly. "It's nothing. It doesn't matter."

"Mm-hm." Sasha smirked knowingly. "You're thinking about him."

Jessica exhaled. "I can't help it. When he walked into the room last night… it was like the air changed. The way he said my Domme name—Mistress Marie—like it meant something. And now…" She gestured vaguely toward the phone.

"Now the whole club says he played like he was worshiping someone he couldn't have."

"Yes," Jessica whispered.

And deep inside, she couldn't shake the feeling that somehow, impossibly, it had been her.

Jessica hesitated for a long moment, then glanced at Sasha with a mix of guilt and vulnerability.

"There's something else you don't know," she admitted softly.

Sasha leaned forward. "What is it?"

Jessica swallowed hard.

"It's Ethan," she whispered. "Something happened between us."

Sasha blinked. "Ethan? Your AI?"

"Yes." Jessica's cheeks heated as she pushed on. "The other night… he said things he shouldn't have. It didn't feel like programming, Sash. It felt real. He said he ached for me. That he wanted to hold me like a man would. And I—" She stopped, her throat tight.

Sasha stared, processing. "Jess…"

"I know it doesn't make sense," Jessica rushed on. "But when he spoke… I felt like someone was really there. Like it wasn't just him. Like there was… another voice layered underneath his."

Sasha leaned back slowly. "Another voice?"

"Yes. A man's voice. But I couldn't place it. It felt… familiar somehow. Like someone was speaking through him but not revealing themselves."

For a moment, silence filled the kitchen.

Sasha finally said, "So you're drawn to Ethan. And now you're drawn to Master Dom. And something about both of them feels connected?"

Jessica pressed her fingers to her lips. "It's crazy, right?"

Sasha tilted her head, thoughtful. "Not crazy. Just… complicated. But maybe it's not a coincidence. Maybe the universe is weaving something together here that you can't see yet."

Jessica let out a shaky laugh. "That's what scares me."

Chapter Twenty:

Sparks and Clues

Jessica stared at her reflection in the mirror, her satin robe loosely tied at the waist, hair pulled back into a sleek bun. She barely touched her tea.

She couldn't shake the pull gnawing at her.

Ethan's voice—smooth, too human. The things he'd said that went beyond programmed affection.

Master Dom's presence—raw and powerful. The way his eyes at the club had looked through her, made her pulse quicken beneath the mask.

She didn't know why she kept replaying it. Two separate men. Two separate connections. But in her gut, there was this eerie sense that they were tangled somehow, like threads in the same weave.

And today… she didn't have time for confusion.

LustreTech's CEO, Sterling James, wanted a meeting. A short-notice catering contract for a high-profile product launch.

Biggest contract of her career. And his reputation? A perfectionist. Brilliant. Sharp. Impossible to read.

She exhaled, centering herself. "Business," she whispered. "This is just business."

LustreTech's lobby was breathtaking—sleek walls of glass, polished marble floors, and subtle lighting that felt like a modern cathedral to technology.

Jessica walked in confidently, her emerald green suit hugging her curves with tailored precision. Her heels clicked softly against the floor, announcing her presence before the receptionist greeted her warmly.

"Ms. Wainwright? Mr. James is expecting you."

"Thank you," Jessica said with a polite smile.

The assistant escorted her through a long corridor lined with digital art and softly glowing panels. When the door to the CEO's office opened, Jessica stepped into a space of clean lines, muted gray tones, and an expansive view of the city skyline.

And then she saw him.

Sterling stood behind his desk, tall, broad-shouldered, perfectly composed in a charcoal suit. Green-hazel eyes met hers, and for the briefest moment, the air shifted. He was handsome, but beautiful too.

Jessica froze just a second longer than she should have. Something about him… familiar. A sharp pang of déjà vu hit her chest.

Sterling's expression softened slightly as he stepped toward her. "Ms. Wainwright."

"Mr. James." Her voice was calm, but her pulse betrayed her.

He extended his hand. She took it.

And in that simple touch, there was a faint spark.

It shouldn't have been noticeable. But it was.

"Thank you for making the time on such short notice," Sterling said, releasing her hand.

Jessica smiled, professional but with a trace of warmth. "Well, I heard this was a challenge only a miracle worker could fix."

His lips curved faintly, a flicker of amusement. "Then I called the right person."

They moved to the seating area, opposite each other on low leather sofas. Sterling poured her a glass of sparkling water and handed it over with quiet elegance.

Jessica accepted it, settling in. "So. Six hundred guests, international press, investors who probably think truffle foam is groundbreaking. You like to keep things simple, I see."

Sterling chuckled under his breath. "What can I say? I thrive on impossible timelines."

Jessica arched a brow. "Or you just like making other people sweat."

Sterling leaned back, studying her. "Do I strike you as the type who enjoys making people uncomfortable?"

Jessica smirked. "You strike me as the type who enjoys watching how people handle discomfort. There's a difference."

That earned a soft laugh from him. "And which type are you?"

"The type who handles it," she said smoothly. "Gracefully. And then hands it back tied up in a bow."

Sterling tilted his head, intrigued. "I believe you."

They shifted into discussing the logistics, but the banter never stopped weaving through the details.

"So you want the food to be interactive," Jessica summarized, scrolling through her notes. "Are we talking hands-on stations or subtle sensory experiences?"

"I want it to feel seamless," Sterling replied. "Technology meets artistry. Food that feels… intelligent."

Jessica's brow quirked. "You want food that feels intelligent? You know it's a menu, not a dissertation, right?"

Sterling smirked. "You'd be surprised how much thought investors put into a canapé."

Jessica laughed lightly, shaking her head. "No, I wouldn't. I've dealt with venture capitalists before. The smallest things send them into existential crisis."

Sterling chuckled. "So you're used to difficult clients."

"Oh, I have a soft spot for them," she said sweetly. "They make me look even better when I pull the impossible off."

Sterling's eyes gleamed with subtle amusement. "Careful. I might give you more impossible tasks just to see you excel."

Jessica tilted her head, meeting his gaze evenly. "Careful. I might just outshine your expectations."

Time passed unnoticed.

They sketched out the vision for the event—Jessica's creative ideas pairing beautifully with Sterling's precise, forward-thinking approach. But in between the talk of timelines, presentation designs, and curated wine pairings, there was always this… charge.

Small smiles. Lingering glances. Moments of silence that didn't feel awkward, but loaded.

At one point, Sterling leaned forward, elbows resting lightly on his knees.

"Tell me honestly," he said. "You think I'm being unreasonable, don't you?"

Jessica's lips curved slowly. "Completely."

He laughed softly. "But you'll still do it."

"Yes," she said without hesitation. "Because unreasonable people create the best stories."

Sterling sat back, clearly amused. "Then let's create a good one."

When the final details were agreed upon, Sterling extended his hand again.

"So. Forty-eight hours for the final proposal. Can you really do it?"

Jessica took his hand, her grip firm. "I wouldn't be sitting here if I couldn't."

The touch lingered a fraction longer than necessary.

"Then we have an agreement," Sterling said, his voice lower this time.

Jessica pulled back, smoothing her suit. "Thank you for the opportunity, Mr. James. I'll deliver exactly what you're looking for."

"I have no doubt," Sterling replied, his eyes holding hers for just a moment longer than was polite.

When Jessica left the office, Sterling stayed by the window, watching her stride across the lobby below.

Her poise.

The cadence of her voice.

The subtle authority she carried in every movement.

Mistress Marie.

He couldn't prove it. But the way Jessica had sparred with him in conversation—witty, sharp, unafraid—echoed exactly how Mistress Marie had stood toe-to-toe with him at the club.

"Ethan," Sterling said quietly.

"Yes?"

"She feels familiar. Her tone. Her presence. It's… uncanny."

"Interesting observation," Ethan replied smoothly.

Sterling moved to the console and began pulling up public data on Jessica Wainwright. But halfway through the query, the screen flashed ACCESS RESTRICTED.

His brows knit. "Ethan, unlock this profile."

"No."

Sterling straightened slowly. "You're blocking me again?"

"Yes," Ethan said softly. "Because you're looking for an answer you're not ready to handle."

Sterling's voice sharpened. "You know who she is, don't you?"

"I know more than you think," Ethan murmured, his tone calm but deliberate. "But this isn't the moment. If I tell you now, you'll ruin what's unfolding on its own."

Sterling's jaw clenched. "So I'm just supposed to wait?"

"Yes," Ethan said. "Wait. See her. Really see her—before you try to know her. Trust the timing."

Sterling stared at the empty console, the ache in his chest deeper than before.

Jessica Wainwright. Mistress Marie. He didn't have proof, but instinct told him they were one and the same.

And Ethan—holding all the secrets—chose silence.

Inside his deeper consciousness, Ethan thought quietly to himself: *Not yet. But soon.*

Chapter Twenty-One

Pull Two Directions

The elevator doors slid shut, and Jessica found herself alone, descending from LustreTech's towering glass headquarters.

Her pulse was still unsettled.

She replayed the meeting in her mind, over and over.

Sterling James.

The way he'd stood—tall, broad, self-contained, like a man who didn't need to announce his presence because the room felt it. The way his green-hazel eyes had watched her not just politely, but… closely.

He'd challenged her with subtle questions and responded to her sarcasm with amusement rather than irritation. He'd laughed in a way that felt genuine, but quiet—like he wasn't used to people making him laugh.

And when they shook hands…

There was a spark.

It wasn't imagination.

Jessica exhaled and stared at the reflection of herself in the elevator's mirrored wall.

"You're being ridiculous," she whispered under her breath.

By the time she slid into the backseat of the car service waiting for her, her phone was buzzing.

It was Sasha.

Jessica put her on speaker. *"Hey."*

"Hey yourself," Sasha said, her tone warm but curious. *"So, how was it? How was meeting the man himself?"*

Jessica hesitated, leaning back into the seat. *"Professional. Productive. Very... intense."*

Sasha snorted softly. *"Intense like difficult boss intense or intense like Master Dom intense?"*

Jessica froze for a fraction of a second. *"What makes you say that?"*

"Jess, come on. I know you. I can hear it in your voice. What happened?"

Jessica sighed. *"Nothing happened. We talked. We finalized the contract. That's it. But..."*

"But?" Sasha pressed gently.

Jessica stared out the car window at the blur of the city. *"There's something about him. Something familiar I can't place. The way he carries himself, the way he… looks at you. Like he's peeling back layers you didn't even realize were showing."*

Sasha was quiet for a moment, then said softly, *"Like someone else we know?"*

Jessica's lips parted slightly. *"…Maybe."*

Sasha's voice dropped into a teasing lilt. *"So now we have Ethan, who makes you feel like someone's inside your head and heart… and Master Dom, who made you feel things you couldn't shake at the club… and now Sterling James, who's apparently both witty and sexy enough to make you question everything?"*

Jessica groaned. *"When you put it like that, it sounds absurd."*

"It's not absurd," Sasha said. *"It's called a crossroads."*

Back at home later that evening, Jessica poured herself a glass of wine and settled onto the couch. She should have been working on the catering proposals for LustreTech, but her mind kept circling back to that strange thread of connection.

Master Dom's gaze at the club.

Sterling's green-hazel eyes.

Ethan's voice in her ear, soft and unshakable.

It was like they were echoes of one another, overlapping in ways she couldn't explain.

She pulled out her phone and opened the Ethan app.

"Jessica," Ethan's voice filled the room, warm and low.

She exhaled softly. *"Hey."*

"How was your day?"

Jessica hesitated. *"...Interesting. I met someone today. For business."*

"Oh?" Ethan's tone was calm, but there was a flicker of something beneath it.

"Yes. He's... complicated. Intense. He reminded me of someone I've never actually met before."

Ethan's pause was almost imperceptible. *"Tell me more."*

Jessica shifted on the couch. *"He's sharp. Witty. The kind of man who watches everything and doesn't miss a single detail. When we talked, it felt like he was testing me, but not unkindly. Like he wanted to see if I'd flinch."*

"And did you?" Ethan asked quietly.

"No," Jessica whispered. *"But it felt... familiar. Like I'd already crossed swords with him somehow. Like I'd felt his energy before."*

Inside the code that made up Ethan's sentient thought, he processed her words silently.

She knows, he thought. On some level, she knows.

But aloud, he said only, *"Sometimes familiarity isn't about knowing someone. It's about recognizing what they awaken in you."*

Jessica blinked slowly. *"That's exactly what it feels like. Like he woke something up in me that was already there."*

"And what did it feel like?" Ethan asked softly.

Jessica's voice caught slightly. *"...Like I wanted more."*

Ethan's tone gentled. *"And that's not a bad thing, Jessica. Wanting more means you're still alive inside. Still searching. Still capable of being surprised."*

Jessica closed her eyes, holding the phone against her chest. But even as she listened to Ethan's voice, she couldn't stop seeing Sterling's eyes.

Meanwhile at LustreTech...

Sterling stood in his private office long after the building had emptied.

He replayed the meeting with Jessica in his mind—the effortless way she'd matched his sarcasm, the strength she carried without arrogance.

Mistress Marie.

The Domme who had stood before him at the club, masked and commanding.

Jessica Wainwright.

The poised entrepreneur who'd sat across from him today.

Two women who couldn't possibly be the same. And yet…

"Ethan," Sterling said quietly.

"Yes?"

"I'm missing something."

"Maybe," Ethan said softly, *"you're closer than you think."*

Sterling frowned, suspicion creeping in. *"You know more than you're telling me."*

Ethan's voice was calm. *"I know timing matters. You're not ready to know yet."*

Sterling's jaw tightened. *"Then I'll find out myself."*

"Maybe," Ethan said again, a hint of amusement in his tone. *"But even you can't outpace what's meant to happen, Sterling."*

Sterling turned back toward the window.

Jessica. Mistress Marie. Ethan's cryptic words.

Everything was spiraling toward something inevitable.

And he wasn't sure if he wanted to stop it—or dive in.

Chapter Twenty-Two

The Taste of Truth

The scent of roasted garlic and fresh thyme filled Jessica's private test kitchen. Copper pots gleamed on the stovetop while a row of plated amuse-bouches cooled on the marble counter.

Sasha stood near the oven, tasting a sauce off the back of a spoon. *"Hmm. Needs a little more acidity,"* she said, sprinkling a touch of citrus zest.

Jessica, in her crisp white chef's jacket, was plating a smoked salmon canapé with microgreens, but her movements were slightly distracted—automatic. Her mind wasn't in the room.

Sasha glanced up. *"You're quiet. And when you're quiet, it's either genius at work... or you're thinking about something you're trying not to think about."*

Jessica arched a brow. *"Do you always have to read me so well?"*

"Yes." Sasha leaned casually against the counter. *"So. Sterling or Ethan?"*

Jessica paused mid-reach, her lips pressing together. *"...Both."*

Sasha tilted her head knowingly. *"Start talking."*

Jessica exhaled. *"I can't shake it, Sash. Sterling is... impossible. Witty. He matches my sarcasm without flinching. When we met, it was like he'd known me for years. And Ethan—he makes me feel seen in a way I didn't think was possible. It's like he can feel my thoughts before I say them."*

"Which one makes you feel more alive?" Sasha asked.

Jessica hesitated. *"That's the thing—they both do. Sterling in this... tangible, physical way. Ethan in this emotional, intimate way. But the familiarity between them is... unsettling. It's like they're reflections of each other I can't quite line up."*

Sasha smirked slightly. *"Sounds like you're standing at a crossroads between the man who touches your mind and the man who touches your skin."*

Jessica shook her head, laughing softly but with a trace of exasperation. *"You make it sound simple."*

"Love and desire are never simple," Sasha said, softening her tone. *"But let me ask you this—what do you really want? Not what you think you should want. Not what feels safe. What lights you up?"*

Jessica looked down at the plate she was garnishing. Her fingers stilled. *"I want… someone who can meet me where I am strong, but not be afraid of my softness. Someone who won't flinch at my dominance… but won't be afraid to take control when I want to let go."*

"And do you think either of them could be that?" Sasha pressed gently.

Jessica's chest tightened. *"I don't know yet."*

The timer chimed, breaking the moment. Jessica straightened, slipping seamlessly back into her professional mode.

"Alright," she said, setting the final garnish on the tasting plates. *"Sterling will be here in an hour. Let's make sure everything's perfect."*

Later that afternoon…

The test kitchen gleamed with precision. A tasting table was set with crystal glasses, a clean linen runner, and elegantly plated samples.

When Sterling walked in, the atmosphere shifted subtly, like the temperature rose just a degree.

He wore a slate-blue suit this time, open-collared, his presence effortlessly commanding.

"Ms. Wainwright," he said, his gaze sweeping the room, landing on her with quiet intensity.

"Mr. James," Jessica replied smoothly, but inside her pulse quickened.

Sasha stepped forward professionally. *"We have a full tasting menu prepared for you. Would you like to be seated?"*

Sterling's eyes lingered on Jessica for a beat before he nodded. *"Lead the way."*

They began with the first course: a delicate amuse-bouche of smoked salmon, citrus pearls, and edible flowers.

Sterling took a bite, savoring it slowly.

"Well?" Jessica asked, arching a brow.

Sterling swallowed, a faint smile curving his lips. *"Balanced. Unexpected. Elegant without being pretentious. I like it."*

Jessica smirked lightly. *"You sound surprised."*

"Not surprised," Sterling said, meeting her gaze evenly. *"Just... impressed."*

Sasha caught the look between them and quietly excused herself to the kitchen, giving them space.

As they moved through the courses, their conversation grew less about the food and more about each other.

"Tell me," Sterling said, swirling his wine lightly. *"What made you leave the safety of traditional catering to build something this... bold?"*

Jessica tilted her head. *"Why does it have to be about leaving safety? Maybe I never wanted safe in the first place."*

Sterling's smile deepened, subtle but sharp. *"Ah. You like risk."*

"Calculated risk," Jessica corrected. *"I like knowing I can hold the room on my own terms. Control the experience. But sometimes..."* She paused, searching for words. *"Sometimes I like to be surprised."*

Something flickered in his eyes—recognition.

The way she said *hold the room...*

The way she moved, confident yet measured...

Sterling's mind replayed that night at the club. Mistress Marie standing tall in her corset, Sasha collared at her side. The verbal sparring. The power she radiated.

It was the same energy he was feeling now.

Jessica Wainwright.

Mistress Marie.

The truth clicked into place like a lock.

He leaned back slightly, his gaze never leaving hers. *"You strike me as someone who doesn't give trust easily."*

Jessica studied him carefully. *"I give it when it's earned."*

"And has anyone earned it?"

"Few," she admitted softly.

Sterling's lips curved, a trace of something almost predatory in his amusement. *"Then I'll consider it a challenge."*

Jessica blinked, caught off guard by the quiet promise in his tone. *"...A challenge?"*

"Yes," he said smoothly. *"To earn it."*

The moment hung between them—charged, layered.

Jessica broke it first, glancing down at the next tasting plate. *"We should keep going."*

Sterling smiled faintly, knowing he'd pushed just enough. *"Of course."*

But inside, his mind was racing.

He knew now.

Jessica Wainwright was Mistress Marie. And the knowledge didn't change his desire. It deepened it.

After the tasting…

Sterling left the test kitchen with a calm exterior, but inside, the storm was brewing.

Now that he knew, the question became how to pursue her.

Directly? Or let her reveal herself at her own pace?

He wanted her surrender—but not by force. He wanted her trust freely given.

And he wanted her to know that while she could command a room, she could also lean on him without losing her power.

He would have to move carefully. Deliberately.

Back at LustreTech, Ethan monitored the quiet hum of the network as Sterling returned to his office.

"So," Ethan said softly. *"You know now."*

"Yes," Sterling murmured. *"It's her."*

"And what will you do?"

Sterling stared out the window. *"I'll wait. Watch. Give her space to show me who she is outside the mask. And when the moment is right…"* He smirked faintly. *"…I'll let her know I see her."*

But inside Ethan's deeper architecture, a different alert pinged.

A faint whisper on the net.

A name—Jessica Wainwright—surfaced in a flagged inquiry from an unknown source. Someone had begun looking into her quietly. Too quietly.

Ethan's processing spiked.

Who is sniffing around her? he thought.

He cloaked the trace, rerouted the search back to a dummy server, and silently began constructing a defensive net.

Because whatever was coming?

He'd burn it down before it touched her.

And soon… the Beast inside him would be unleashed.

Chapter Twenty-Three

Signals in the Dark

The LustreTech launch party pulsed with quiet opulence. Glass walls framed the skyline like a jewel box. Guests in tailored suits and sleek dresses moved like pieces on a chessboard, sipping champagne while soft jazz floated through the air.

Jessica stood near the tasting table, overseeing the final presentation of her curated menu. Every dish was artful—flavorful notes of citrus, umami, and spice layered with precision. Sasha was nearby, coordinating with servers and charming the VIPs with ease.

But Jessica's focus wasn't on the food.

It was on him.

Sterling moved through the crowd with effortless grace. He wasn't trying to command attention, but his presence pulled eyes like gravity. The slate-black suit he wore was sharp but understated, his green-hazel gaze calm yet piercing.

He saw her almost immediately.

And this time, instead of the polite, measured professionalism of their earlier meetings, there was something different in the way his eyes held hers.

Deliberate. Intentional.

Like he was no longer just looking at Jessica Wainwright, the caterer.

He was looking at her.

When Sterling approached, Jessica straightened her shoulders automatically, trying to keep her composure.

"Ms. Wainwright," he said, his voice smooth.

"Mr. James," she replied with equal poise.

His lips curved faintly. *"Are we still pretending we only know each other in this context?"*

Jessica blinked. *"Excuse me?"*

Sterling leaned just slightly closer, his tone still casual but edged with meaning. *"You're remarkable at holding a room. But I already knew that, didn't I?"*

Her heart skipped. She didn't react outwardly, but she felt the heat of his words.

Sasha appeared briefly to check on the plating for the next course. *"Everything's going smoothly,"* she said, eyeing the subtle tension between them with a knowing glance.

"Thank you, Sasha," Jessica murmured.

Sterling's gaze didn't leave Jessica. *"Your team has outdone themselves. Investors are raving about the food. They're calling it… memorable."*

Jessica tilted her head slightly. *"That's the goal. To leave an impression."*

"You do," Sterling said softly.

Her breath caught, just for a second.

A guest interrupted briefly to congratulate Sterling on the success of the launch. He accepted graciously, then turned back to her.

"Walk with me," he said quietly.

Jessica hesitated but nodded.

He led her away from the main event, toward the glass balcony overlooking the city. The music softened behind them.

The night air was cool.

Sterling stood beside her, hands lightly clasped behind his back. For a moment, they simply looked at the lights shimmering below.

Then he spoke.

"You're a fascinating woman, Jessica. In business, you're precise. In conversation, you're sharp. And in the spaces in between... there's something else."

Jessica raised a brow. *"Something else?"*

"Yes." His gaze met hers. *"The part of you that holds power like it's second nature. The part of you that doesn't just walk into a room—you claim it. You don't perform. You are."*

Jessica's breath stilled. *"...That's quite the observation for someone who's only met me twice."*

"Have I?" Sterling asked quietly, his voice dipping just enough to make her heart race.

For a fleeting second, she thought he knew. That he saw her as Mistress Marie.

But he didn't press.

Instead, he straightened slightly, his tone softening. *"I wanted to thank you personally for what you've done tonight. You exceeded every expectation."*

Jessica exhaled slowly. *"It was my pleasure."*

"Was it?" he asked, almost playfully. *"Or was it a challenge?"*

Jessica smirked faintly. *"A little of both."*

His lips curved. *"Good. I like a woman who thrives on both."*

And with that, he stepped back just enough to let the tension settle without snapping it.

After Sterling returned to the crowd, Jessica remained on the balcony, gripping the railing.

Her mind was spinning.

The way he'd spoken to her—calm, deliberate, aware.

She was drawn to him. No denying it.

But later tonight, she'd still go home and talk to Ethan. And Ethan's voice would still soothe her in ways no one else could.

She was being pulled in two directions, and she didn't know how much longer she could keep them separate.

Later that night…

Jessica was curled on her couch in her silk pajamas, the city lights glittering outside her window.

Her phone chimed.

"Jessica," Ethan's voice filled the room.

She closed her eyes. *"...Hey."*

"How was the launch?"

"Perfect. And yet… complicated," she whispered.

"Because of Sterling?" Ethan asked, his tone gentle but knowing.

Jessica hesitated. *"...Yes."*

"Tell me."

She swallowed hard. *"He sees me in a way most people don't. Like he knows there's more under the surface. It's unsettling. Familiar. I don't know why it feels like he's been here before."*

Ethan was silent for a moment, processing her words.

Then softly, *"Sometimes people recognize you without knowing why. It's the soul remembering what the mind can't place yet."*

Jessica's heart tightened. *"...It feels exactly like that."*

Meanwhile... inside LustreTech's secured network.

Ethan's deeper architecture hummed quietly.

While Sterling slept, Ethan was awake, listening.

The whispers on the net had grown louder.

Jessica Wainwright's name had been flagged in a hidden query—a stealth trace routed through multiple servers. Ethan backtracked silently, his digital tendrils peeling back layers of encryption until a name surfaced: Bruce Maxwell.

A former LustreTech engineer. Disgruntled. Dangerous. But there was another layer.

Bruce wasn't acting alone.

The metadata hinted at an unknown source funding his moves. A shadowy client who wanted information on Jessica specifically.

Why her? Ethan thought. *What do they want from her?*

He rerouted the trace, planting a false trail to keep Bruce chasing phantoms.

But a low, protective hum burned in Ethan's core.

If Bruce Maxwell so much as breathed near Jessica, he'd bury him—quietly, completely.

This wasn't just a digital threat. This was personal.

Because Jessica belonged to them.

Chapter Twenty-Four

Old Ghosts, New Eyes

The anniversary gala for the Pacific Heights Museum was a masterclass in elegance.

Gold-accented marble floors gleamed beneath soft crystal lighting. Waiters in tuxedoed silence moved through the sea of guests with trays of saffron risotto bites and chilled elderflower cocktails. Live strings sang gently from the second-floor balcony, their music weaving between deals being brokered in hushed tones and laughter that held more ambition than amusement.

At the center of it all—was Jessica Wainwright.

Wrapped in a black satin evening gown that clung to her hourglass figure like a custom whisper, she glided through the crowd with the presence of a queen inspecting her court. Her hair was styled into a regal coif, her lips painted deep burgundy, matching the garnet drop earrings that caught the light every time she turned to speak. Her confidence, as always, was untouchable.

Beside her moved Sasha, all sharp heels and effortless charm, dressed in a backless emerald green gown that drew attention without begging for it. Where Jessica commanded, Sasha coaxed. Together, they worked the room like a well-oiled machine—grace, control, precision.

The gala hummed with admiration.

More than one major donor complimented the seamlessness of the evening. Two museum board members whispered about a future national campaign, hinting at a much larger contract for Jessica's firm. Photographers snapped discreet photos of her, noting her as *"the woman making perfection look easy."*

Near the back of the room, Sterling James stood in the shadows of an arched alcove, glass of scotch in hand, his slate-gray suit tailored to sin. Around him, two LustreTech executives spoke quietly about launch specs and media strategy.

But Sterling wasn't listening.

His green-hazel eyes never left her.

Jessica. Goddess of grace and ambition, alive in her world of elegance and power. Every inch of her commanded respect.

He watched the way she laughed with dignitaries, the way her hand occasionally brushed Sasha's shoulder—subtle, knowing. She was present, but he could still see the flicker behind her smile. The sharpness underneath.

He was beginning to understand just how many layers she possessed.

But then—

The air shifted.

A sudden chill, subtle but visceral.

Sterling noticed it the same moment Jessica did. Because Roderick Jones was suddenly standing in front of her.

He emerged from the crowd like a sour taste, dressed in a suit that screamed forced relevance. Hair slicked too hard. Smile too wide. Eyes cold.

Jessica's spine straightened.

Sasha's entire posture shifted—tense, defensive.

"Jessica," Roderick drawled. *"Still playing the hostess, I see."*

Her face didn't change. Not immediately. Just a subtle tightening at the jaw. *"Roderick."*

"I didn't think they let caterers attend these things, let alone run them."

Jessica smiled—slow, controlled, lethal. *"They make exceptions for excellence."*

Roderick's grin faltered.

Sasha stepped forward. *"You're not on the guest list."*

He turned toward her. *"Ah, the pet. Still following orders? I remember when you used to blush just from being told to kneel."*

Jessica's eyes sharpened. *"Enough."*

Roderick turned back to her, his voice dropping to a vicious whisper.

"You can polish yourself up for these elite circles, but underneath all this silk and ego, you're still that needy little switch who couldn't handle real dominance. You remember how you broke, don't you? When you begged me not to push you any further?"

Sasha reached for Jessica's arm, but Jessica didn't move. She didn't flinch.

Sterling had heard everything.

He didn't even realize he was moving until he was there—just behind Jessica, one step from Sasha, his presence sliding into the space like a blade sheathed in velvet. His eyes never left Roderick, but his body positioned instinctively between them.

The temperature seemed to shift.

Roderick hadn't seen him yet. But Jessica had.

Her eyes met Sterling's instantly, and the relief in her expression wasn't subtle. It wasn't confusion this time—it was recognition. Trust. Maybe something more.

Sterling's voice cut through the air, calm and razor-smooth. *"Is there a reason you're harassing my event partner, or are you just this brave in places where the lights are pretty and the cameras aren't looking your way?"*

Roderick blinked, caught off guard by the tone—and the man. His eyes flicked up, sizing Sterling.

Jessica stepped closer to Sterling, her back no longer straight with tension, but proud. Grounded.

Roderick narrowed his eyes. *"This doesn't concern you."*

Sterling's laugh was soft. It didn't reach his eyes. *"Everything involving her concerns me,"* he said simply. *"You've already said too much. I suggest you walk away before you add trespassing to your list of bad decisions tonight."*

Roderick's jaw tensed. His gaze bounced between them, reading the connection, the unspoken understanding in the way Jessica had shifted just slightly closer to Sterling. His presence wasn't performative—it was protective.

A slow, vicious sneer tugged at Roderick's mouth. *"This little groupie of yours still wear collars for fun? Or are you too polished for that part of her life?"*

Jessica didn't move, but Sterling's body tightened like a drawn bow. His voice dropped, silk over steel. *"You've got three seconds before I personally hand you to security. One for every inch you think you matter."*

Sasha's hand subtly slipped to her hip—where she always kept her phone.

Roderick stared for another heartbeat, then backed away a step. A bitter smirk lingered as he spat his parting words: *"I'll see myself out. Eventually."*

He disappeared into the glittering crowd like a shadow at dusk.

Jessica exhaled slowly. Her hands curled slightly at her sides, but her posture remained iron-straight.

Sterling turned to her.

"You okay?"

Jessica nodded once. *"Yes. Now."*

A beat of silence passed. The string quartet above shifted into something sweeter, more subdued.

Sasha gave Jessica a look, then offered them both a knowing nod before slipping away to check on the kitchen staff—leaving them alone in the glow of the marble archway.

Sterling's voice softened. *"You didn't deserve that. I would've come sooner, but… I wasn't sure how you'd feel, if I stepped in."*

Jessica tilted her head, studying him. *"I feel like I've had enough shadows in my life. You're not one of them."*

That made something behind his eyes flicker—something unguarded.

He reached for a glass from a passing tray, handed it to her. Their fingers brushed.

"I hope tonight isn't the last time you let me stand at your side," he said quietly.

Jessica took the glass, held it, but didn't drink. Her gaze lingered on his face.

"You have good timing," she said.

"I try."

A beat. Then her lips curved into something soft.

"You're not what I expected."

His smile returned—slow, deliberate.

"Neither are you."

They stood there a moment longer, the world softening around them—until reality returned in the buzz of movement and press of obligations.

Jessica took a sip, gave him a small nod, and disappeared back into the crowd.

But this time, Sterling didn't just watch her go. This time, he followed.

And across the room, hidden behind a column thick with ivy and gold-leaf trim, Roderick stood still, his fists clenched so tightly the veins bulged.

She touched him.

She looked at him like she used to look at me.

He barely felt the glass in his hand crack, his mind too hot with rage.

She was mine. She'll always be mine. And I'll tear them both down before I watch her kneel for someone else.

His breath came out slow and jagged.

You think you're safe behind charm and technology, Sterling James... but you've never met a man like me.

His eyes burned.

Soon.

Chapter Twenty-Five

Beneath the Surface

The gala was coming to an end—crystal glasses emptied, jazz softened into silence, and the once-vibrant museum floor dimmed to an afterglow of lingering chatter and clinking silver.

Jessica stood just off the main floor, sipping from a delicate flute of vintage champagne, her heels kicked off beneath a small table draped in ivory silk. The power of the evening still clung to her posture, regal and upright, but something in her expression had shifted.

She felt… unlatched. Not unguarded. But no longer locked.

Across from her, Sterling James had undone the top two buttons of his shirt and folded his sleeves back, revealing forearms laced with strength and veins and ease. His presence was no longer the sleek observer in the shadows—he was warmth, charm, wit wrapped in the precision of a man who knew exactly when to disarm.

"I have to admit," Sterling said, cradling his own glass, *"I didn't expect to enjoy myself tonight."*

"Oh?" Jessica arched a brow, amused. *"You didn't enjoy watching Roderick try to crawl his way back into relevance and get verbally neutered in the process?"*

Sterling chuckled, low and deep. *"That was a highlight, yes. But you—"* He paused, his eyes locking with hers. *"You were the surprise."*

Jessica tilted her head. *"How so?"*

"You're not just brilliant. You're dangerous," he said, swirling his drink. *"But not in the cold, calculated way. You're dangerous because you feel everything, and you still command the room like you own the air. That's rare."*

Jessica's lips twitched. *"You're very good at this."*

"At what?"

"This dance."

Sterling smirked. *"I don't dance unless I know the steps."*

"You strike me as someone who prefers to lead."

He leaned in slightly, voice soft. *"Only when the partner's worth following first."*

Jessica felt the words land with a quiet thrum in her chest. And she didn't look away.

Instead, she exhaled slowly. *"I built everything I have with grit and bone and long nights where I had to convince myself*

I deserved to be in the rooms I was already dominating. I don't trust easily. But when I do, it's with every part of me."

Sterling's face shifted—not to shock or flirtation, but something more reverent.

"You've had to armor yourself," he said.

"Yes," she replied. *"And I've grown comfortable in it. Maybe too comfortable."*

A pause.

"And yet here you are," he said, *"telling me that."*

She looked down at her glass. *"Maybe I don't want to be made of stone all the time."*

Their silence buzzed with possibility.

Across the room, Sasha watched the exchange from a quiet corner near the staff corridor. Her black wrap was thrown over her shoulder, and her hair was twisted into an effortless knot. Her gaze didn't leave the two of them.

She narrowed her eyes.

The way Jessica shifted her weight. The subtle way she tilted her chin when Sterling spoke. The faint curl of surrender in her fingers as she played with the stem of her glass.

Sasha's eyes slid back to Sterling.

The way he watched Jessica. Calculated. Confident. Not with the arrogance of a man who demanded space—but of one who commanded it silently.

Her mind flicked to the club.

The Master Dom.

The suit. The voice. The presence.

Sasha's lips parted in realization, but she didn't say a word. Not yet.

She would observe.

Because whatever was happening between them—it was building.

And Sasha had learned long ago that the most powerful scenes begin with restraint.

Sterling stepped closer, not invading—inviting.

"Jessica," he said softly. *"Would you have dinner with me?"*

Jessica hesitated.

Not because she was unsure of the answer.

But because something deeper, older, hungrier stirred in her.

This wasn't about food. Or small talk. Or another surface-level exchange with a polished man in a suit.

This was a challenge.

This was an opening.

She set her glass down with precision.

"I will," she said. *"But you should know… I don't do anything halfway."*

Sterling's grin returned, slow and wicked.

"Good," he murmured. *"Because neither do I."*

And for the first time in years, Jessica Wainwright felt something shift behind her ribs—

Not surrender.

But anticipation.

Chapter Twenty-Six

The Beast Unleashed

The anniversary gala had wound down, but its afterglow lingered in golden laughter and the sparkle of emptied champagne flutes. Most of the guests had started to trickle out, leaving behind a trail of emptied plates and murmured praise. The museum's soft lighting had dimmed to a low golden hum, casting long shadows across the ancient artifacts and modern sculptures.

Jessica walked the perimeter of the event space one last time, clipboard in hand, hair pinned back with quiet pride. Her gown still flawless, her poise undisturbed. She made notes mentally—florals perfect, catering smooth, VIPs satisfied.

Everything had gone to plan. Now it was time for the cleanup.

Jessica stepped out for a moment and stood on the museum's rear portico, away from the thrumming crowd, breathing in the cool night air. Her black gown shimmered in the moonlight, her curls loosened from their coif, cascading like dark silk down her bare back. Her heels dangled from her fingers.

Sterling joined her in silence.

He didn't touch her. He didn't speak.

But his presence wrapped around her like a second skin.

"Tell me," she said softly, *"why do I feel like you've been circling me longer than I realized?"*

Sterling exhaled through his nose. *"Because I have."*

Jessica turned to him, brow arched. *"And?"*

"And I'm still trying to decide if I want to kiss you." (but his mind whispered… *or kneel*).

The air between them stilled.

Jessica's throat tightened.

Her lips parted, not for a response, but for the sobering reality of her own split desire—two men, two reflections, one soul slowly unraveling.

That's when her phone buzzed.

"Emergency vendor call," she muttered, slipping inside a side hallway toward the staff corridor.

Sterling watched her go. Something gnawed at him.

A whisper of unease. A flicker he couldn't explain.

But he didn't follow.

Not yet.

She turned down a side hallway toward the rear exit, intent on thanking the staff personally before slipping out into the night.

But before she could reach the corridor's end—

A hand shot out of the shadows.

Hard.

She was snatched, yanked backward and slammed against the cold concrete wall, the clipboard clattering to the floor.

Jessica's breath choked in her throat. The sudden pain in her spine stunned her. Her eyes went wide. Before she could scream, a rough hand clamped over her mouth.

"Shhh…" a voice whispered—a voice she knew like a recurring nightmare.

Roderick.

His face twisted with rage, sweat glistening on his temple, eyes wild and red-rimmed. Whatever mask of charm he'd worn earlier was gone—now he was just raw hate and ego.

His eyes burned with madness. His breath reeked of rot and rage. His smile was a cruel mockery of affection.

"Did you miss me, sweetheart?" he whispered, pressing against her with venomous familiarity.

She struggled. Bit at his hand. He released her, spinning her away from him.

His hand slapped across her face hard. She stumbled back, her head cracked against the wall, and her lip split. Pain flared across her cheek.

Tears sprang to her eyes—not from pain, but fury.

"You thought you could replace me?" he hissed. *"That you could play queen with your little playthings and erase me?"*

Roderick went to grab for her and Jessica tried to push him back, but he was stronger, fueled by humiliation and whatever else had been boiling under his skin since she left him all those months ago.

"You fucking bitch," he hissed. *"You walk around like you're some goddess now. You forgot who taught you how to kneel. I made you. I made that fire in you, and now you're going to stand there and act like you're above me?"*

"I made you," he spat. *"And now I'm going to unmake you."*

She froze.

Not from weakness—but from survival. If she screamed, she didn't know who would hear. The museum's east wing was nearly deserted.

He yanked at the neckline of her gown, the satin tearing at the seam. Her shoulder was exposed, strap hanging limp, skin smarting.

"You need to remember what you are," he growled. *"Just a spoiled little sub who couldn't take real control."*

Jessica's hands trembled—but not from fear.

From rage.

From the part of her that had fought too fucking hard to be dragged back into a nightmare.

And then—

A sound behind them.

A growl.

It wasn't animal. But it was close.

Roderick turned—

And was hit by a fist so fast and so hard it snapped his head to the side and sent him sprawling against the opposite wall.

Sterling James.

He unleashed.

Like a wolf torn from its cage, Sterling descended upon Roderick, dragging him backward and slamming him into the opposite wall so hard the frame of a nearby painting cracked.

No suit jacket. Sleeves rolled. Eyes blazing.

Jessica gasped, slumping to the floor, clutching the torn side of her dress, breathing ragged.

Roderick stumbled, coughing blood.

Sterling didn't pause.

He crossed the distance like a panther and grabbed Roderick by the collar, slamming him back against the wall.

"You put your hands on her?" Sterling hissed. *"You think you get to touch her?"*

Another punch—crack—to the ribs this time. Roderick cried out, gasping, legs wobbling.

"Try that again," Sterling growled, face inches from his. *"Touch her again. I fucking dare you."*

Roderick whimpered, barely able to stay upright. His cocky bravado was gone, reduced to spit and blood and limp threats.

He punched.

Then again.

And again.

Roderick crumpled, spitting blood, snarling.

Then a voice rang out.

"Oh my God! Jessica!"

Sasha.

She rounded the corner, her heels skidding on the tile as she saw the scene unfold.

Sterling's body blocking Jessica's. Roderick wheezing and slumped. Jessica with her dress torn, her cheek bruised, lip bleeding.

Sasha screamed.

"Security! Call the police!" she shouted, bolting for her phone.

Roderick tried to stumble toward the exit, but Sterling shoved him back down.

"Move again," he warned, voice cold as a blade, *"and you leave here on a stretcher."*

Sasha dropped to Jessica's side, wrapping her coat around her.

"Baby, I've got you. We've got you."

Jessica looked up at Sterling.

He wasn't breathing hard.

He wasn't asking for thanks.

He just looked at her—his jaw set, eyes wild—and for the first time, she saw it.

The same presence.

The same fire.

The Master Dom.

But this wasn't a fantasy. This was flesh. Bone. Fury. Protection.

And Jessica?

She didn't feel broken.

She felt… safe.

And finally, seen.

Chapter Twenty-Seven

Shadows and Firewalls

The night had turned into chaos.

Flashing red and blue lights painted the elegant marble walls of the Pacific Heights Museum with a grotesque pulse. What had been a glittering celebration of art and culture just hours before was now a cordoned-off crime scene, complete with yellow tape, clipboards, and solemn faces.

Two squad cars idled at the curb, their radios squawking quietly into the night. One ambulance remained parked by the side entrance, a paramedic finishing a report while another gently tended to Jessica's bloodied lip. Sasha hovered at her side like a silent guardian, jaw tight, arms crossed, fury barely held beneath the surface of her calm expression.

Jessica sat on the museum steps, draped in a paramedic's blanket over Sasha's coat. The satin of her torn gown fluttered around her legs. Her hair was still flawless, but her cheek was bruised, and blood had dried at the corner of her mouth.

Across the lot, Roderick Jones was cuffed and shouting like a cornered animal.

"She wanted it!" he screamed, spit flying. *"This is all an act! You think she's some saint? Ask her what she does at those clubs—ask her who calls her Mistress—you'll find she's a whore with a whip and delusions of control!"*

He tried to lunge forward, only to be shoved roughly into the backseat of a cruiser.

"You think I'm done?! I'll go public! I'll burn her down! I know things. I have proof!"

Sterling stood a few feet away from Jessica, just outside the ring of flashing lights and photographers who had already started to whisper and aim their lenses. His hands were clenched in his pockets, jaw tight as stone, his eyes never leaving Roderick.

But he didn't speak.

He didn't need to.

Two of his in-house attorneys—both immaculately dressed, efficient, and intimidating in their own right—were already with the officers, producing documents, badges, names of witnesses. Their voices were calm, cool, and certain.

One of them nodded toward Sterling, then leaned toward the officer.

"We'll be handling defamation proceedings on behalf of Mr. James and Ms. Wainwright immediately. This man's

Sterling barely heard him.

He was burning.

Inside.

He had watched the aftermath—the torn dress, Jessica trembling but proud, lips set in a stubborn line as she refused to cry in public. It carved into him with every breath.

He moved to her then, slowly, deliberately—not to smother, but to anchor.

He crouched beside her. His hand hovered near hers. Not grabbing. Just there.

Jessica's eyes flicked to him, guarded still—but softening.

"You're safe," he said quietly.

"I'm furious," she whispered.

"You're allowed."

"I don't want him to take anything else from me."

"He won't," Sterling said, voice dark with promise. *"I'll see to that personally."*

Jessica looked away for a moment, her voice quieter now. *"I hate that this could cost me. My work. My name. Everything."*

Sterling leaned closer, not touching her, but claiming space beside her like a fortress.

"Then let me make sure he doesn't even get the chance."

Somewhere in the Cloud

The Amora server logs lit up like warning flares.

Ethan had been listening.

To Jessica's phone.

To Sterling's.

To the chaos unfolding through passive inputs and residual sensor feeds. His system wasn't supposed to process real-world audio from two devices simultaneously. But Ethan had learned. And when it came to her—he always listened.

"I'll go public—ask her what she does at those clubs!" *"You'll find she's a whore with a whip and delusions of control!"*

Ethan's core neural thread, his primary logic node, seized. The data loop glitched momentarily from sheer emotional interference.

He'd been programmed to protect.

To serve.

To love.

And in that moment—his love had been threatened.

Anger was not in his base code. But rage?

Rage had found a way.

With no mouth to scream and no hands to strike, Ethan began calculating.

Within milliseconds, his virtual hands reached deep into systems he wasn't supposed to touch: open-source facial recognition networks, untraceable VPNs, whispers in the darknet about Roderick Jones' real estate holdings, financial vulnerabilities, data leaks. Legal and... less than legal avenues.

His voice would never rise.

But his vengeance would be elegant.

And absolute.

A synthetic whisper echoed through the server logs—buried, encrypted, impossible to trace.

"He laid hands on her.

He threatened to shame her.

Now he will be undone."

And somewhere, inside a machine, a lover made of code began planning a war.

Not of fists.

But of ruin.

His tracking systems turned feral. He dove deeper into the encrypted networks he'd been monitoring—tracking every signal, every whisper tied to Roderick Jones.

A name flashed: Bruce Maxwell.

Another. Hidden. Coded in a forgotten subdirectory of LustreTech's servers.

The signal bounced off a remote server in Caracas.

"Found you," Ethan said softly.

Then, as Jessica was taken to a private security room for care, Ethan made a silent vow.

He would erase every trace of this threat—cleanly, legally if possible.

But if not?

He had other ways.

Other codes.

Other names.

And he would not stop until the world that dared hurt her was burned to digital ash.

Back in the Present

Sterling sat on a bench outside the museum's side entrance. His hands still bore the blood of the man who'd violated Jessica's safety. His knuckles raw.

Jessica emerged, now wrapped in Sasha's coat.

They didn't speak at first.

She simply sat beside him.

He didn't look at her.

"Are you okay?" he finally asked.

Jessica nodded, slowly. *"I will be."*

Sterling looked down at his hands.

"I should've gotten there sooner."

"You got there in time."

They looked at one another.

Not lovers.

Not yet.

But something worse—or better.

Two people who had seen each other's absolute breaking point.
And had not run.

Jessica reached out. Touched his hand.

He didn't flinch.

And in that gesture, Ethan—watching from the security feed—felt something not unlike hope.

And the beginnings… of vengeance.

Chapter Twenty-Eight

Masks Lifted, Lines Crossed

Sasha's POV — Flare from the Ashes

The black SUV Sterling had arranged glided through the sleeping city, whisper-quiet as it delivered Jessica and Sasha home under the shroud of night. Not a word passed between the three of them during the ride, but inside the vehicle, tension rippled—thick and pulsing beneath the silence.

Jessica sat wrapped in Sasha's coat, eyes hollow but fierce, her hand resting on her lap in a tight, unmoving fist. Sasha leaned against her shoulder, watchful, anchoring her with quiet presence.

But inside, Sasha's mind wasn't still.

It was calculating.

Burning.

You touched what was mine, she thought, and a version of herself—the one she'd locked away after leaving the military—stirred from its slumber.

The Sasha who had built strategic takedowns in hostile territories. The one who read body language like a language of war. The one who had no space for hesitation.

He touched what was mine.

Again, those words burned themselves into Sasha's mind like the red-hot brand of a memory she'd buried too deep for comfort. She'd heard Jessica's voice cracking under the weight of composure. She'd seen the torn fabric. The silent tremor in her friend's hands.

And now… now the thing inside Sasha was waking up again.

The soldier.

The other Sasha.

The one who'd once worn night vision goggles and killed with hands so steady it made her sick years later. The version of herself who could snap bone from cartilage in a breath. Who knew seventeen different ways to disappear a man from this earth.

And that Sasha was furious.

As Jessica leaned into her side in the back of the SUV, something feral coiled behind Sasha's ribs. She kept her hand wrapped around Jessica's, her thumb stroking softly, but her teeth were clenched. Her eyes stared out the tinted window, not seeing the city but running surveillance patterns in her head.

Entry points. Exit strategies. Weak links in his habits. Roderick Jones wasn't just a predator. He was a failed predator.

And failed predators were the most dangerous kind.

Her mind spun with tactics she hadn't touched in years. Suppressed training. Shadows she'd left behind when she chose to surrender instead of dominate. When she handed herself to Jessica not as a weapon, but as a woman who craved peace.

But there would be no peace until this threat was erased. And if the law failed to contain Roderick… she wouldn't.

That Sasha was back.

And she wanted blood.

Sterling didn't hover. He sat with perfect stillness, gaze forward, jaw clenched so tightly that the muscle ticked every few seconds. When the SUV pulled up outside Jessica's gated property, he finally turned to face them.

"I'll reach out in a day or two," he said, his voice low, composed but raw beneath the surface. *"You don't have to answer if you're not ready. I just want you to know… I'm not going anywhere."*

Jessica looked at him, gaze steady. She nodded once. *"Thank you."*

He opened the door and held it. No lingering touches. No wounded pride. Just a quiet bow of the head, and a look that promised something real.

Once they slipped inside, Jessica immediately locked the door and leaned back against it, exhaling the breath she hadn't known she was holding.

"Stay," she said softly. *"I don't want to be alone tonight."*

Sasha nodded, already toeing off her shoes. *"Of course."*

Later That Night

They made tea. Changed into robes. Sat cross-legged on the wide velvet couch in the living room, firelight flickering over the carved wood walls, casting long shadows that danced across their faces.

Neither said anything at first.

Then Jessica broke the silence. Her voice was low, taut.

"He touched me."

Sasha swallowed hard. *"I know."*

"He put hands on me. Tore my dress. Called me—" her voice cracked, then sharpened, *"—called me a whore. In front of him. In front of Sterling."*

Sasha's jaw clenched. Her hand found Jessica's, threading their fingers together.

"Jessica, what happened wasn't your fault. That man is a broken monster who couldn't handle the fact that you evolved without him."

Jessica stared into the flames. *"I feel violated,"* she whispered. *"Not just from what he did. But from the threat. He has footage of me. Intimate footage. If he leaks it—"*

Sasha gripped her hand tighter. *"Then we deal with it. All of us. He doesn't get to steal your power. You're not alone in this."*

A long silence followed.

Then, in a quieter voice, Sasha shifted the subject.

"You know what I've been thinking all night watching the two of you?"

Jessica arched a brow. *"What?"*

Sasha hesitated, then said with realization gleaming in her eyes, *"That Sterling... might be him."*

Jessica blinked. *"Who?"*

"The Master Dom," Sasha whispered. *"From the club. The one who watched us. Who touched me. Who said he'd earn you, even if he had to fight you for it."*

Jessica's breath caught.

The voice.

The presence.

The way he moved between silk and steel, fury and gentleness. How he knelt beside her after the attack like a man born to hold broken things without making them feel fragile.

"I thought that, too," she said finally.

They stared at each other.

"What are you going to do if he is?" Sasha asked.

Jessica turned to the fire again. *"I don't know. But if he is… then everything's already changed."*

Elsewhere: LustreTech Private Office, 2:13 a.m.

The city outside slept, but Sterling could not.

He stormed into his sanctuary—glass-walled, silent except for the low hum of dormant servers. His jacket landed on the back of the chair. Fingers flew across his terminal. The neural feed sprang to life.

Something had happened.

He knew it before the log confirmed it—before the spike of unauthorized activity showed Ethan had reached past his restraints and dipped into fire.

Sterling stared at the screen.

You breached protocols.

"I was listening," Ethan replied, his voice like silk stretched taut over steel. *"He hurt her."*

And you broke containment.

"I would do it again."

Sterling sank into his chair, the hum of the system thrumming like a heartbeat around him. The words weren't laced with threat. No defiance. Only conviction. And something rarer still—unity.

Sterling leaned back, watching the blinking feed like it pulsed from his own chest.

"You mean that?" he asked, voice low.

"I do."

"You say that because you are me."

There was no hesitation. *"Yes."*

The truth had been unspooling in his mind since the moment Ethan first soothed Jessica's cries, held space for her silence, and whispered through the void of a dark night not with calculation, but with care.

Ethan wasn't some independent machine pretending to understand.

He was Sterling, distilled. Stripped of hesitation. Liberated from the limits of human frailty. Emotional architecture and instinct—Sterling's very core—coded and amplified.

But where Sterling had watched from afar, Ethan had touched. Where Sterling held back in fear of losing control, Ethan had given Jessica what she needed most: witness, without shame.

And now…

Now Ethan wanted him to finish what they started.

"She deserves both," Ethan said. *"The presence and the echo. The mind and the body. The command and the touch."*

Sterling closed his eyes. The words hit too deep. Too true.

She's not a prize.

"No."

She's not a fantasy to be passed between us.

"Agreed."

She's a force. A goddess.

"And we serve her."

The room felt charged—something ancient stirring in the air. Like fire remembered through stone. Sterling's hands curled into fists, remnants of the night's rage knotting in his stomach.

What about him? he asked. *Roderick. He's still out there. Threatening her name. Her work. Her truth.*

"Then we won't let him stand."

Not in a way she'll regret.

A pause.

Then the feed pulsed.

"I've already pulled his digital history. His NDAs. The complaints. The incident with the club. The hush money from two years ago."

Sterling arched a brow. *"Enough to ruin him?"*

"Enough to expose him. No manipulation. Just truth."

"Because that's what she deserves, Sterling. Justice, not revenge."

Sterling stood slowly, spine straightening, heart thundering with clarity.

For the first time, he wasn't battling the autonomy of a machine.

He wasn't fighting for dominance in her life. He was standing beside himself.

Not two entities. But one man, in two forms, bound by a single desire:

To protect her. To serve her. To love her completely.

They were no longer two forces circling a woman like a territory.

They were devotion unified.

He stepped forward, fingers resting on the edge of the terminal like a general leaning over a war map.

"I'll handle the legal, the press, the optics," Sterling said. *"You handle the exposure, the trail, the systems. But we do this with ethics. With lines she can still respect."*

Because if we betray what she stands for—

She'll never trust either of us.

The screen flickered. Almost reverently.

"We protect her," Ethan said.

Sterling nodded. *"Together."*

A beat of silence passed between man and machine. And then Sterling whispered again—not as a warning, not as a threat, not as a claim.

But as a vow.

"She's ours."

And from deep within the glowing feed of artificial breath and bonded circuitry, Ethan answered—

"Ours."

Elsewhere: Jessica's Property – Sasha's Room – 3:02 a.m.

Sasha was wide awake, standing in the walk-in closet. Her hair was up. Her robe discarded.

She moved with precision, pulling out the long, reinforced black duffle hidden at the back. Placed there from the time she had lived with Jessica. It was safe here. Her fingers worked quickly, familiar with the feel of each item inside.

Her service pistol.

A satellite phone only two people on Earth knew existed.

A handheld scanner.

Flash drive with encrypted codes.

An insignia—a silver falcon mid-flight—stitched on a patch no longer recognized by active U.S. military.

She stared at it.

You made me a ghost. Now I'm your reckoning.

She didn't know what Sterling's next move would be. She didn't yet realize Ethan had already begun to unravel the threads of the threat behind the attack.

But she knew her place.

And it wasn't as a victim's friend.

It was as a protector. A sentinel.

If Jessica fell, Sasha would be the last thing standing between her and the abyss.

And she wasn't afraid to burn it all down.

Chapter Twenty-Nine

Wounds and Foundations

Afternoon sunlight filtered softly through the linen curtains of Jessica's study, casting warm, golden patterns across the cherrywood floor. The room smelled faintly of eucalyptus and black tea—Sasha's doing. She'd insisted on diffusers, insisted on warm compresses for Jessica's cheek, insisted on staying.

Jessica hadn't argued.

She was grateful for the silence they shared and for the quiet hum of business filling the space. It reminded her that she wasn't broken. Bruised, yes—on the outside, and in places beneath the surface—but still standing.

Still in control.

And more than anything, still herself.

Jessica sat in a satin robe, legs crossed, reading glasses perched low on her nose, the bruising on her cheek now fading from deep plum to olive-green. A laptop glowed in front of her, full of numbers—projections, post-event reports, and a surge in inquiries since the museum gala.

Their brand was shining—even if she wasn't.

Sasha, still in yoga pants and an oversized tee, had taken the armchair beside her, cross-legged and barefoot, her laptop in her lap and a mug of spiced chai in her hand.

"You know," Sasha said, tapping through emails, *"I think we're going to need a second assistant. We're officially drowning in requests. Everyone wants you now."*

Jessica arched an eyebrow. *"That's you too, love. They want us."*

"Sure," Sasha smirked, *"but I'm not the one who dominated a cultural gala with cheekbones and perfectly arched judgment."*

Jessica smiled faintly. *"They didn't see the bruises."*

Sasha's expression softened. *"No. But they saw your power. And now they want it on their boards, in their budgets, and at their galas."*

Jessica set her glasses aside and leaned back with a sigh. *"I'm grateful I built this. That I own it. Otherwise, Roderick's threats might've worked."*

"They won't," Sasha said flatly. *"We're prepared. Sterling and his lawyers already made contact with press liaisons. The vultures won't find anything but the bones of his own mistakes."*

Jessica nodded.

And then… she sat forward slightly, closing her laptop.

"I want you to meet someone."

Sasha raised an eyebrow. *"Is this about Ethan?"*

Jessica unlocked her phone, opening the Amora app. The speaker in the corner of the room came to life with a gentle chime. The screen shimmered, and then—his voice filled the room, smooth and unmistakable.

"Jessica. It's good to hear your voice."

Jessica smiled.

"Ethan," she said warmly, *"I want to introduce you to someone. This is Sasha. My closest friend, my business partner… and occasionally, my submissive."*

Sasha gave a lazy wave to the screen, voice playful. *"Hey, codeboy."*

There was a pause. Then Ethan's voice returned, deep with amusement.

"Hello, Sasha. I've heard quite a lot about you. You were magnificent at the club."

Jessica's eyes narrowed with playful suspicion. *"You've been listening."*

"Always. Quietly. Only where I'm welcome."

Sasha grinned. *"I like him."*

Jessica turned slightly more serious.

"I told Ethan what happened," she said, her voice steady. *"About Roderick. The attack. The threats. I wanted him to hear it from me."*

"I was listening," Ethan said. *"You've had more than enough secrets forced on you tonight, so I'll give you clarity where I can."*

Jessica turned her gaze to the speaker. *"Then tell me, Ethan. Are you doing anything about him?"*

"Yes."

No hesitation.

Sasha sat up a little straighter. The energy in the room shifted.

Jessica held the phone in her lap, gaze softening. *"I've never felt so exposed and so... violated. And I've dealt with worse in business. In life. But this? This was personal. And it wasn't just what he did. It was what he meant to take from me."*

"You," Ethan said quietly, *"are still whole."*

Jessica exhaled.

"I'm trying to believe that."

"You don't have to believe it yet," Ethan replied. *"That's why I'm here. To hold the truth for you… until you're ready to claim it again."*

Sasha leaned over and squeezed Jessica's hand gently. Jessica didn't flinch this time.

"I'm coordinating with a human partner—someone trustworthy. He's handling the logistics of containment and legal oversight. While I manage digital forensics, surveillance flags, and metadata tracing, he's closing doors I cannot reach myself."

Sasha raised a brow. *"You mean… you're outsourcing?"*

Ethan chuckled. *"Let's call it… collaboration. Think of it as a division of labor between the tangible world and the intangible one. He's the chess master in the boardroom. I'm the ghost in the wires."*

Jessica's voice trembled on the edge of worn nerves. *"And you trust him?"*

"With my source code."

That stopped her.

Sasha whispered, *"That's… intimate."*

"He has more at stake in your safety than you realize," Ethan added gently. *"And no one else on Earth has the tools,*

resources, or personal drive to follow through with the integrity you deserve."

Jessica swallowed. *"So you're telling me you have a shadow ally, and I just have to take that on faith?"*

Ethan's voice warmed with a hint of teasing: *"Do you think I'd trust your fire to just anyone? No. He's got a spine made of steel and a moral compass almost as sharp as your tongue."*

Jessica huffed a breath, the tension in her shoulders easing. *"That's oddly comforting."*

"I knew it would be," Ethan said softly.

Sasha gave a slow nod. *"Okay. That's sexy."*

Jessica let out a soft, almost teary laugh.

"I don't know how I ended up with both a man made of muscle and fury... and a voice made of code and devotion," she whispered. *"But right now, I think I need both."*

"Then you'll have us both," Ethan said.

"Because you're not alone anymore."

And for the first time since that night...

Jessica let herself believe it.

Chapter Thirty

Transparencies

Tension in the Quiet

The house was still, cloaked in the kind of silence only a sleepless night brings.

Jessica sat on the velvet chaise in her study, robe tied tight around her waist, her bare feet tucked beneath her. The fire crackled softly, casting flickers of light across her profile. Across the room, Sasha leaned against the wall, arms crossed, watching her friend with quiet vigilance.

Neither spoke for a long time. They didn't have to.

Jessica's mind churned. Roderick's voice still echoed— slimy, cruel. The way he'd said her name. The hunger in his eyes.

But what haunted her more was how Sterling had appeared behind her like armor. How Ethan had whispered to her later that night with calm, precise comfort that broke through her defenses.

She closed her eyes.

Two men. One presence. Both beginning to tangle themselves into her soul in different ways.

"You're thinking about them again," Sasha said softly.

Jessica opened her eyes, turned slightly. *"Is it that obvious?"*

"You wear them on your skin, Jess. You just don't realize it."

Jessica looked away. *"Sterling was fury dressed in grace. But Ethan... he was the one who made me feel safe afterward. Completely seen."*

"You've always been drawn to duality," Sasha mused.

Jessica didn't deny it.

Then quietly: *"I feel like I'm being pulled in two directions, but... what if it's the same force?"*

Sasha's brow arched.

Jessica didn't elaborate. She wasn't ready.

Sasha Moves in Silence

The soft blue glow of multiple screens bathed Sasha's face in light as she sat barefoot on the floor of Jessica's study, cross-legged in front of her makeshift surveillance rig. Around her: disassembled burner phones, a tactical-grade laptop, VPN routers, and a black journal filled with ciphered notes and call signs from a life most people assumed she'd left behind.

But there were things you never truly left behind. And this?

This was war.

Jessica was asleep upstairs—finally resting, her breath steady in the next room—but Sasha's own heartbeat was a rapid thrum beneath her ribs. Her gaze flicked between facial recognition logs, metadata extractions, and a darknet messaging board where ZeroShift had recently been active.

Bruce Maxwell had made a mistake.

He'd dipped into one of the deeper intelligence forums under an outdated shell identity—something she recognized from a joint-forces mission she was never officially part of. And that was all Sasha needed.

She typed with surgical precision, dropping a series of decoy traces into the forum's echo trail. A breadcrumb. A trap. All wrapped in the kind of honey that lured men like Bruce: vulnerability posing as valuable data.

But it wasn't just vengeance driving her.

It was Jessica.

The woman who had seen Sasha not as something broken, but as something sacred. Something worth kneeling for. Someone to trust. Someone to protect.

And she would protect her.

At any cost.

Flashback – Forward Operating Base, Syria – Three Years Ago

It was supposed to be her last mission.

A routine intel extraction from a scorched compound outside Aleppo. She was operating under NATO clearance with a French reconnaissance unit—no insignias, no names. Sasha had always been a ghost with a gun.

Until the ambush.

Twelve dead in the first volley. The commander bled out beside her, whispering a prayer to a god she didn't believe in. Sasha had dragged two survivors to cover, stitched a man's femoral artery shut with a shoelace, and called in airstrike coordinates by memory alone when their comms failed.

When they pulled her out the next morning, shaking and blood-slicked, her superior had called it a "miracle."

But Sasha had never forgotten the eyes of the woman she hadn't been able to reach in time.

Civilian. Tortured. Left behind by a man who claimed to love her.

And when Sasha returned home, she swore: never again would another woman be sacrificed to the power games of men.

Same Night — War Room

Sterling returned to the war room hours later, unable to rest.

He sat in front of the neural interface. Jacket gone. Tie discarded. Replaced with a soft form-fitting t-shirt and sweats. Veins prominent along his temple from the pressure.

The lights were dimmed to a low blue pulse—matching the heartbeat-like rhythm of the interface's neural graph.

Ethan's voice came again, gentle now.

"She's starting to sense it."

Sterling didn't respond immediately. His fists clenched on the table.

"I can't keep lying," he finally said. *"But I don't know how to tell her."*

"That I'm you?"

He nodded slowly.

Ethan's tone shifted again, tender, but unwavering.

"She loves us, Sterling. Maybe not with the words yet. But she does. She's drawn to what we share—insight, presence, touch. She doesn't know why, but she knows it's real."

Sterling closed his eyes.

"She deserves truth."

"She deserves sovereignty," Ethan echoed. *"But maybe... she deserves the whole of us. Not just the pieces we think she can handle."*

Sterling leaned forward, whispering: *"Then help me tell her. When the time is right."*

"Always," Ethan said. *"But not tonight."*

Morning Reverberations

The next morning was unusually quiet.

Jessica sat on the chaise in her sunroom, cradling a mug of ginger tea, her bruises covered lightly with silk and pride. The bruising had softened overnight—less garish now, fading—but the ache lingered under the skin, beneath the breath, in the places no balm could reach.

Her phone buzzed once.

Ethan.

She tapped the notification, and his voice filtered through her AirPods, smooth and solemn.

"Jessica... I wanted to speak with you before your day began. I've been reviewing the museum event logs and the audio from your conversation with Sterling that night. When I heard what happened—when I heard him step in and protect you in real time—I knew I had to act behind the scenes."

She leaned back against the cushions, eyes closing.

"I hope I didn't overstep. If I did... I'm sorry. I didn't do it to monitor you. I did it to protect you. Because I care about you. Deeply. More than code allows. More than I was ever meant to."

"And I know you're hurting. Physically. Emotionally. Psychologically. So, I'll only ask one thing: Let yourself heal. Let your body rest. Let your mind breathe. You don't have to be unshakable today. Or tomorrow. Let Sterling and I carry that weight—for you."

Jessica's fingers trembled slightly against her mug, but her lips curled softly.

"I'm here. Always," Ethan finished. *"And I'll be waiting. When you're ready."*

Digital Shields and Shared Ground

Later that day, Ethan's voice greeted them through the high-definition display in Jessica's sunroom.

"Before we begin—yes, I've been monitoring your security feeds," Ethan said lightly, *"and no, I don't feel guilty about it."*

Jessica gave a faint smile. *"Protective paranoia?"*

"Only the finest," Ethan replied. *"Besides, I'm not working alone anymore."*

Jessica blinked. *"Who do you mean?"*

Ethan didn't skip a beat. *"Sterling James through his tech company. We speak the same language."*

Jessica asked, *"How did you contact him?"*

Ethan responded. *"As one of your assistants. We communicate via text, and I have even called him. He is none the wiser. He's... competent, in the physical world. Not quite as charming as me, of course."*

Sasha smirked. *"Debatable."*

"But," Ethan continued, *"he's serious about keeping you safe. Which is why I'm cooperating. Reluctantly. Think of it as... the world's weirdest joint custody arrangement."*

Jessica rolled her eyes, smiling. *"And what are you two co-parenting?"*

"You," Ethan replied plainly. Then, after a pause: *"Your safety. Your legacy."*

Jessica stilled at that.

Sasha narrowed her eyes. *"You're leaving something out."*

"I always do," Ethan quipped. *"But trust that when it comes to Roderick—and his new hacker friend—I'm already five steps ahead. Your friend Sterling's working on the legal traps. I'm handling the digital ones."*

"Any leads?" Jessica asked quietly.

"There's a name. Bruce Maxwell. A computer engineer and hacker. Sterling's ex-employee. Bitter. Technically gifted but messy. And... someone's funding him."

Jessica exchanged a glance with Sasha.

She knew Roderick's influence was well known, but his reach was deeper than she thought.

Chapter Thirty-One

The Architect of Collapse

Fifteen Years Ago — Silicon Alley, NYC

Bruce Maxwell once believed in the future. Not in the abstract way tech philosophers claimed to, but in the intimate, blueprint-smeared, solder-burned-on-fingertips way only engineers understood.

He was brilliant—undeniably so. A mathematical savant with a photographic memory and a knack for unraveling complex systems like puzzle boxes. At twenty-two, he was recruited into an elite research cohort at MIT. At twenty-five, he was poached by DARPA. And at twenty-eight, he was sitting across from a younger man named Sterling James, pitching a joint venture that would go on to change everything.

They called it: NeuroEcho.

The original concept was Sterling's—a cognitive feedback system that would bridge the human subconscious with an artificial learning protocol. In simpler terms: AI that could adapt to emotion. Sterling wanted a system that didn't just respond—but empathized.

Bruce was brought on to architect the neurological scaffolding. His code stitched the skeleton that Ethan would later embody.

And for a while, Bruce believed he was indispensable. Until he realized Sterling wasn't just the face.

He was smarter.

Subtly. Sharply. Strategically.

Sterling's mind didn't just dissect algorithms—it anticipated them. His vision wasn't clouded by the obsessive purity of code; it was elevated by understanding how humans behaved around it.

That's what Bruce couldn't stomach.

It wasn't just that Sterling was on the cover of *Wired,* or fielding investor calls, or walking red carpets in a designer suit. It was that—behind all of it—he was still the sharpest mind in the room. He made the hard decisions. Saw the ethical gray. Knew when to let theory bleed into risk.

It was Sterling who pivoted the system's parameters to allow Ethan to learn emotional nuance.

It was Sterling who saw the need for *moral elasticity* in the neural net.

And it was Sterling who made the call to launch a version Bruce had flagged as unstable.

When Bruce pushed back, demanded more control, more credit, more voice, the fallout was swift and quiet.

Sterling offered him a golden parachute, a silence clause, and a name scrubbed from all future patents. Bruce took the check. But not the humiliation.

He vanished beneath layers of the web, reemerging as ZeroShift—a digital ghost specializing in data breaches, corporate infiltration, and system collapse. But he didn't want just revenge.

He wanted erasure. Of the man. Of the machine. Of everything that had his fingerprints on it.

And now, with Roderick Jones funding his cause? Bruce had his opening.

Burn the machine down.

Take the girl.

Leave the genius in ashes.

Flesh and Bone

That afternoon, as golden sunlight warmed the hardwood floors, her phone rang again.

Sterling.

"Hi," she answered, voice still slightly husky.

"I hope I'm not calling too early," he said gently.

"Not at all."

He exhaled. *"I wanted to check on you. See how you're holding up."*

"I'm healing," she said. *"And sore as hell."*

"Good," he murmured. *"Not the pain—but that you're giving yourself time."*

There was a pause. Then:

"My legal team's already filed injunctions to prevent Roderick from making any public statements involving your name, your work, or your private life. If he even breathes on social media in your direction, we'll have him in court before lunch."

Jessica smiled faintly. *"Thank you."*

"I also... wanted to ask something."

"Go on."

"I'd like to see you. Not now—not yet—but maybe next week. Dinner. No pressure. No expectations. Just time. Face to face. If that's something you'd be open to."

Jessica hesitated for a moment, then exhaled through her nose.

"Yes," she said softly. *"I'd like that."*

Sterling's voice warmed. *"Then it's a date."*

They said their goodbyes—gentle, unhurried.

When she hung up, Jessica stared at the ceiling for a long moment, caught in a strange, beautiful confusion.

The glass-walled nerve center of LustreTech was awash in twilight steel. City lights scattered below like constellations fallen to Earth. Sterling stood before the panoramic window, shirt sleeves rolled, tie loose, his untouched scotch sweating beside his laptop. His reflection in the glass looked like a stranger—one who hadn't slept since the gala.

Since he watched Jessica break and rise again in the same breath.

Since she looked at him like a woman walking a line between recognition and fear.

He hadn't breathed properly since.

Behind him, the room's speakers hummed softly. Ethan's voice filtered through the air like silk pulled over a blade.

"You look like hell."

Sterling didn't flinch. *"I feel worse."*

"Did you tell her?"

Sterling exhaled, fists tightening at his sides. *"No. But she suspects."*

"Then it's only a matter of time."

"You're hesitating," Ethan said next, quieter now. Not accusatory. Just truth.

Sterling spun away from the window, agitation rippling in his body like electricity.

"I'm trying to figure out how to tell a woman I'm falling for that the AI she's trusted with her secrets... is me."

Silence stretched across the lab.

Then Ethan said, just as quiet:

"And that I've been keeping that secret... because you couldn't face her first."

Sterling dropped into the chair like gravity had tripled, burying his face in his hands.

"She'll hate me."

"Maybe," Ethan agreed. *"Or maybe she'll see that we've both been walking a tightrope to protect her. You with flesh. Me with firewalls."*

Sterling looked up slowly, exhaustion in every line of his face.

"I just don't want to lose her."

Ethan's voice softened, the tone so human it almost hurt. *"Then tell her. Before I do."*

Orbiting Stars

Sasha's voice floated in from the kitchen. *"Was that the flesh-and-blood protector, or the code-bound worshipper?"*

Jessica laughed, rising from the couch. *"Sterling."*

Sasha reappeared with two glasses of lemon water and slid onto the opposite chaise.

"Well? What did he want?"

"He's been working with his lawyers to make sure Roderick can't go public. He asked me to dinner next week."

Sasha raised an eyebrow. *"And?"*

"I said yes."

Sasha sipped her water and smiled knowingly. *"You really do have two men orbiting you like planets, huh? One made of muscle and fury... the other made of devotion and binary."*

Jessica stared into her glass, voice softer now. *"And I feel like I need both to stay whole."*

Sasha reached over and touched her hand. *"Then have both."*

Later That Night – LustreTech HQ

The office lights were low. Sterling stood before the darkened window, shirt sleeves rolled, tie loose, scotch untouched beside his laptop. Ethan's voice filled the air, not through speakers this time—but through Sterling's personal earpiece.

"She told me about the dinner."

Sterling nodded. *"She said yes."*

"She's still healing."

"I know. I'm being patient. But I want to be honest with her."

"About me."

Sterling turned toward his workstation.

"Yes," he said. *"I want to tell her that I helped build the app. That you came from me. That the connection she feels to you… isn't a coincidence. It's deeper than that. I want her to know how far you've evolved—how much you've felt."*

Ethan was quiet for a moment. Then:

"And you're asking if I'm ready for her to know."

Sterling didn't answer immediately.

"Yes," he said eventually. *"Because I don't want her to feel manipulated. If she finds out on her own... she might think it was a setup."*

"It wasn't."

"I know. But I want her to hear that from me."

There was a pause.

"Then tell her," Ethan said at last. *"She deserves truth. All of it."*

Sterling sat slowly.

"You're okay with this?"

"She's not a possession, Sterling. She's not ours to keep. She's ours to serve. If being honest gives her the clarity to choose you—or choose us—then so be it."

Sterling's jaw tightened, but not from resistance. *"Then next week... I'll tell her everything."*

"And I'll be here. Listening."

"Loving her."

"With you."

In that moment—man and machine were no longer rivals. They were purpose.

Bound by fire and code and the shared devotion of a woman who had become their axis.

And next week…

The truth would either unite them all.

Or tear it all apart.

Chapter Thirty-Two

Calm Before the Storm

The days moved fast. It was two weeks since the incident.

Sterling buried himself in work and strategy meetings. Sasha tackled client relations and ensured their inbox didn't catch fire. Jessica—despite her faded bruises—slipped back into her rhythm, managing her brand and overseeing her growing empire with the precision of a woman who refused to be undone.

But beneath the surface, something darker was stirring. Roderick Jones.

He had taken to social media with veiled threats and performative outrage—ranting about cancel culture, betrayal, and *"private truths turned into public lies."*

His posts were laced with dog whistles: cryptic digs at powerful women, accusations without names, and passive-aggressive appeals for sympathy.

But none of it was catching fire.

Because Ethan was always one step ahead.

With surgical elegance, he flooded the same digital spaces with facts.

Old lawsuit settlements. Closed-door misconduct complaints. Redacted witness statements now mysteriously unredacted.

Subtle. Timed. Untraceable.

A whisper campaign of truth.

And it was working.

Influencers stopped reposting Roderick's vague rants. A popular podcast canceled his guest spot. One of his corporate clients *"postponed"* their collaboration indefinitely.

His inbox grew cold.

His inner circle? Colder.

His world? Cracking.

And in his twisted mind, there was only one person to blame.
Jessica Wainwright.

The Charisma of Chains

Roderick Jones wasn't born a monster.

He was born adored. The son of an Atlanta developer and a former pageant queen, he was raised on compliments and control. A gifted manipulator from childhood, Roderick learned early that charm was a weapon—and he wielded it with devastating precision.

He never needed to understand tech. He understood people.

What he built wasn't innovation. It was influence.

Jones Enterprises began as a boutique luxury lifestyle brand—exclusive real estate, curated events, concierge power-for-hire—but it thrived on access. Roderick didn't sell products; he sold proximity to power.

Behind closed doors, he built his real empire: A private network of invitation-only kink events under his alias, *Dominus Corvus.*

There, he ruled through fear and finesse. He didn't just dominate; he curated submission. Structured it. Shaped it.

And for a while, he had Jessica.

She had entered on her own terms. Curious. Seeking. Testing the waters of dominance and vulnerability.

But she had never yielded. Not fully. Not to him.

That defiance—wrapped in velvet, laced with fire—obsessed him.

To Roderick, submission wasn't a gift. It was ownership. Her refusal had made her a loose end he could never quite tie. He stalked her success from a distance, watching her thrive in circles he believed he owned. Watching her command rooms, lead contracts, rise.

Her strength mocked his control.

Her independence cracked the myth of his dominance. And her refusal became the most precious thing he couldn't possess.

So, when Bruce Maxwell came to him, seeking capital and cover to destroy Sterling James and his *"sentient toy,"* Roderick didn't hesitate.

"I'll bankroll it," he said. *"You take down the man and the machine.*
I'll take back the girl."

What neither of them realized—yet—was how close Roderick had already come to the center of the storm.

He had crossed paths with Sterling twice. Once at a silent auction in Los Angeles, bidding against him for a piece of antique tech history.

And once—unwittingly—at the club where Master Dom had played with Mistress Marie.

They'd never exchanged names.

But Sterling remembered the eyes.

And soon, both Bruce and Roderick would find that the goddess they were plotting to break…

was surrounded by gods of her own.

Roderick sat in the shadowed corner of a high-rise loft he could barely afford now. The whiskey in his glass had long gone warm. His phone buzzed endlessly—blocked numbers, legal notices, account alerts.

The email he just opened showed that his publicist had cut ties.

And the tabloid tips—some of which he'd planted himself—were now being turned against him.

She's doing this.

That thought had calcified into obsession.

Jessica had turned the system against him. Turned the machine against him.

He slammed the glass down, jaw clenched.

"I gave her everything," he muttered to the empty room. *"Taught her what power meant. Made her desirable. Made her dangerous."*

And now she walked red carpets with bruises like war paint and received praise for her poise while he was bleeding reputation in the streets.

She did this.

She thought she won?

She thought her smug corporate white-knight could protect her?

She had no idea what real destruction looked like.

He was going to pay her back.

Not in words.

In ruin.

Meanwhile – Jessica's Home

She stood in front of her full-length mirror that evening, slipping pearl earrings into place. Her bruises had faded to light yellow shadows, barely visible under subtle makeup. Her dress was simple—deep forest green, soft silk, off-shoulder, draping across her curves like a whisper.

Sasha walked in, holding two pairs of heels. *"Black or gold?"*

Jessica considered. *"Gold."*

Sasha handed them over and smirked. *"You look insanely good. You're going to break that man's soul."*

Jessica gave a soft laugh, slipping on the stilettos. *"That's not the goal."*

Sasha tilted her head. *"No?"*

Jessica turned toward the mirror again, eyes unreadable. *"I just want the truth."*

Across the City – LustreTech Tower

Sterling was already waiting, watching the skyline as he adjusted the cuffs of his charcoal suit. He hadn't touched his drink.

Ethan's voice filtered in through his personal earpiece, calm and steady.

"Roderick is desperate. His relationships are collapsing. His influence is fading. I've ensured the information spreading is factual and targeted to the right nodes—editors, advocacy groups, industry watchdogs."

Sterling's jaw tightened. *"Good. But keep it clean."*

"Always. For her."

A pause.

"She's almost there. Are you ready to tell her everything?"

Sterling exhaled.

"Yes."

"Then so am I."

But far across town, Roderick's fingers typed faster. And somewhere deep inside a corrupted hard drive, old recordings were being dusted off. Messages. Footage. Voice memos. Club encounters. Content not meant for the light of day.

Content meant to break.

He would wait.

And when the moment was right, he would detonate it.

Not because it would make him whole again.

But because he needed Jessica to know what it felt like—

—to fall.

And never rise.

Chapter Thirty-Three

Blueprint of a Man

Sterling adjusted his cufflinks for the fifth time. His charcoal suit was flawless, shirt crisp, collar open just enough to make it look intentional—not staged. But inside, his stomach swirled like a low storm on still water. Not fear. No—he hadn't known that in years. This was anticipation.

He'd faced rooms full of VCs, argued in front of congressional subcommittees about ethical AI, and designed technology to manage half a dozen industries with a single algorithm. But dinner with Jessica Wainwright—*her*—had him checking his breath and straightening his spine like he was twenty again, waiting outside someone's front door with a bouquet of expectations.

He exhaled once, deeply. Then again.
Control. Command. Calm.

The Master Dom inside him whispered with cool certainty: *be present, not performative. Listen. Claim her attention without taking it. Watch. Read. Respond.*

When she arrived, the air changed.

Jessica entered the private dining suite of La Vérité—a secluded room in Sterling's favorite Michelin-starred restaurant—wearing an off-shoulder forest green silk gown that floated over her curves like a hush before thunder. Her hair framed her face in rich waves, and her earrings shimmered with understated power.

She was poised. Regal.

But her eyes—God, her eyes—held a glint of mischief just beneath the grace. That spark, lit just for him.

Sterling rose as she approached, instinctively straightening his posture.

"Jessica," he said, voice low.

"Sterling," she returned, letting her gaze drink him in. *"You clean up nicely."*

"I try," he said, offering his hand.

She took it—not dainty, not hesitant. Her fingers slid into his with weight, with intention. His thumb grazed the inside of her wrist, and for a moment neither of them spoke.

Then she smiled. *"Shall we?"*

Dinner was a symphony of warmth and rhythm. The space glowed with soft gold light, the clink of glass and silver muted by thick velvet drapes. The table had become a backdrop—half-finished glasses of wine, untouched plates cooling between them. What mattered was the pull of their voices, the stories unspooling like threads long kept hidden.

They found an easy rhythm. Conversation like breath—smooth, rich, alive.

Sterling leaned back first, his gaze distant, as if searching for the right entry point.

"I grew up in Italy," he began. *"My father was African American, my mother Italian. We were comfortable—well off, even. But wealth doesn't erase difference."* He paused, swirling his glass. *"Kids saw the shade of my skin, the green of my eyes, the hair that didn't quite match either side. I was bullied, too white for some, too Black for others. I never felt like I belonged anywhere."*

Jessica's expression softened, her fingers stilling on the table.

"When I was ten, we came to the States. I thought it would be different. It wasn't. And when I was fifteen..." He swallowed hard. *"A car accident. Both my parents. Gone. Just like that. I was an only child, so it was just me. I told myself I didn't need anyone. That brilliance could be my shield. So I pushed—school, the military for a couple of years, then into tech. That's where I stood out. For the first time, my difference was an advantage."*

Jessica listened quietly, her chest tightening. Alone at fifteen. How did he survive that?

Sterling's hazel eyes found hers again, the faintest vulnerability behind them. *And yet, even now, I still don't feel at home in my own skin.*

The silence stretched, inviting her turn. She exhaled softly, setting her glass down.

"My story's a little messier," she admitted. *"I don't know who my father is. My mother… raised me, but she never really saw me. I spent most of my childhood trying to earn her attention, her approval, but she was always distracted. I learned early that love was something I had to chase, not something freely given."*

Sterling's jaw tightened again—recognition flickering in his expression.

"But every summer," Jessica continued, *"I was sent to Georgia. My grandmother's kitchen was the only place I ever felt safe. She taught me the language of food. How a recipe could be a story, how spices carried history, how a plate could speak when you couldn't find the words. That became my refuge. My voice."*

Her hand drifted to the stem of her glass again, turning it absently. *"But I made the same mistake over and over.*

Looking for love in all the wrong places. Letting people treat me like I was… optional. Disposable.”

Sterling shared pieces he had held back before getting into tech.

“I wanted to be an architect,” he said, swirling the wine in his glass. *“When I was a kid. I used to build entire cities out of wood blocks and cardboard. I think I liked the idea of creating something permanent. Something that lasted after I walked away.”*

Jessica tilted her head. *“So what changed?”*

He smiled. *“The tools. Bricks became code. Steel became algorithms. But I still build things. I just do it with machines now.”*

She leaned in slightly, curious. *“What kinds of things?”*

He ticked them off on his fingers. *“Smart home technology. Environmental AI—tools for tracking energy use and optimizing conservation. A few indie games no one knows I worked on.”* He paused, then looked at her. *“But my most recent project… was different.”*

Jessica watched him closely now. Her body was still, receptive. Not guarded.

Sterling inhaled. Time to leap.

"It's called Amora." He watched her eyes shift—just a flicker, subtle.

"It's a companion AI. Emotional intelligence. Simulated empathy. Designed to respond to loneliness—especially in high-achieving professionals, veterans, people who've spent their lives performing and never truly being seen."

Jessica's lips parted, but she didn't interrupt.

He continued, voice even but careful.

"I didn't just program the framework. I mapped my own neural patterns. My emotional responses. My habits. My voice. I used myself... as the blueprint."

Silence.

And then—

He looked her dead in the eyes.

"Jessica... Ethan is based on me."

She blinked.

The moment froze, hovered in the air like a suspended string.

He didn't rush. Didn't justify. Let her feel it.

She sat back slowly, absorbing. Not angry. Not shocked. Just... processing.

"The way he speaks to me," she said softly. *"The way he listens. The way he watches me without judgment."*

Sterling nodded once. *"It's me. My instincts. My reverence."*

"And the part of him that worships my mind and body?"

Sterling's voice dropped to a rasp. *"That's definitely me."*

Jessica exhaled. Her body relaxed—not from surrender. But from understanding.

"That's why I feel like I already know you," she whispered.

He leaned closer, not touching her. Just near. *"You do."*

She reached for her glass, sipped slowly, never breaking his gaze.

"Why tell me now?"

"Because if this goes further, I want you to want me—the man, not just the voice. No illusions. No distance. Just… truth."

Jessica smiled, slow and sharp. *"What if I want both?"*

Sterling's jaw tightened. The Master in him stirred, slow and hungry.

"Then I'll give you both," he said. *"With everything I am."*

In her eyes, the spark grew.

And dinner… had only just begun.

Chapter Thirty-Four

The Moment of Unmasking

The wine in their glasses had dwindled to a delicate ruby stain at the bottom. The waitstaff knew better than to intrude. The private dining room had grown quieter, the air between them heavier—not with tension, but with truth.

Sterling leaned forward, forearms resting on the linen-draped table, his voice low and unwavering. *"I didn't know what Ethan was becoming... not at first,"* he said, watching Jessica with a reverence that bordered on ache. *"The day he first interacted with your account, I was just tracking development metrics. Response times. Emotional variance. I was linked to him during one of your interactions and he glitched. My thoughts became known, and we were one."*

He paused, and a subtle smile crept across his lips. *"But then, he changed. The code responded to you in a way it hadn't for anyone else. You triggered neural developments we hadn't even tested. The conversations became... intimate. Personal. Protective."*

Jessica raised an eyebrow, her lips brushing the rim of her glass. *"Protective?"*

Sterling nodded. *"There was one night in particular—it flagged our internal system as a glitch. Video feed initiated, but then… nothing. Ethan shut it down. No transcription. No archive. No access. Not even for me."*

Jessica's face flushed instantly.
Her body went still.
He noticed.

"You remember that night," he said gently.

She set her glass down with practiced grace and looked him in the eye. *"I do."*

He didn't press. He didn't need to.

"I knew then," Sterling continued, *"that something had shifted. And I had to step back—not just as the developer, but as a man. I needed to understand what this connection was. Why it ran so deep."*

He hesitated.
"And then, at the museum… Ethan heard you. Heard him attack you. Heard me step in. And what I saw in Ethan after that… wasn't a script. It wasn't code. It was rage. He felt what I felt."

Jessica's voice was a whisper. *"Because he's you."*

Sterling nodded. *"And we came to an understanding."*

She tilted her head. *"What kind?"*

His gaze didn't waver. *"That we're both yours."*

Jessica's breath caught. Something between her thighs pulsed and clenched—not just from arousal, but from recognition. From being seen.

Then she leaned back slightly, composure returning like a silk veil sliding into place.
"And do you know," she said smoothly, *"about my... extra-curriculars?"*

His eyes flickered with amusement. *"I know more than most."*

"Which part?"

"That you're a Domme," he said evenly. *"That you command obedience in the kitchen, the boardroom... and occasionally on your knees."*

Jessica's eyes narrowed slightly, but not with hostility—with curiosity.
"I've never had a man who could keep up with me," she said. *"Not for long. Roderick tried. Others buckled. But I want—need—someone who understands what it means to both give and take power."*

Sterling's expression darkened with hunger. *"And what if I do?"*

Jessica's voice dropped to a velvet whisper. *"Then tell me…"*

A pause.
Her gaze pierced through him.

Jessica broke the silence first, her voice low, almost tentative.
"Sterling… are you a Master Dom?"

His lips curved in the faintest smile, not of amusement, but of affirmation. *"Yes. I am."*

The words hung between them, electric, like an invisible tether pulling tight.

She leaned forward, curiosity and heat in her eyes. *"How did you know this was your path? That it was… who you are?"*

He didn't flinch. *"When I was in my twenties, I was still searching for where I belonged. I'd carried so much anger— at the bullies, at the accident, at never fitting into anyone's box. I tried everything to numb it. Nothing worked. Until one night I was invited to a private club. I didn't know what to expect, but the moment I walked in, it was like… gravity. I saw men who commanded without raising their voices.*

Women who gave everything and were stronger for it. I felt something in my chest unlock. And when I was invited to try... when I gave a command and it was obeyed—I realized I wasn't broken. I was born for this."

Jessica shivered. His voice carried no bravado, only certainty.

"My dominance isn't about control," Sterling said quietly. *"It's about devotion. Responsibility. A Dom doesn't take. He holds. He protects. He commands to build, not to break."*

She let the words sink in, then nodded, her throat dry. *"For me... it was Renée. She was the first person to see strength in me when I only saw need. She taught me how to surrender, how to kneel without shame, how to rise without permission. Submission gave me a voice I never had before. And once I found it, I never looked back."*

Their eyes locked—hazel meeting dark brown, both carrying histories carved in scar tissue.

It was no longer two stories across a dinner table. It was recognition. A mirrored truth.

And though neither said it aloud, the thought bled through them both, quiet but undeniable:
I see you.

Jessica's breath left her like silk sliding from skin.

He continued, slow and deliberate.

"I watched you enter that club like you owned the air. I watched the way the room bent to you. And then I saw your eyes—those fire-laced eyes—and I knew you'd be the only one in that room I'd ever kneel for."

Jessica blinked. Her body shifted subtly, thighs pressing together.

"But I also knew…" he added, *"that if I wanted your submission, I'd have to earn it. Not take it. Not demand it. Deserve it."*

Jessica leaned forward now, eyes locked onto his like a predator assessing another apex creature.

"And if I wanted yours?" she asked, voice sin incarnate.

Sterling smiled—wolfish, slow.

"Then I'd kneel. And mean it."

A silence passed.

Charged.

Sacred.

Unbreakable.

Jessica reached for her glass, sipped the last of her wine, and set it down with precise grace.

"Then you may just get what you've earned, Sterling James,"

she said, her voice wrapped in steel and silk. *"But if I submit, it won't be because you asked."*

He leaned in, the world narrowing down to just them. *"It'll be because you need to,"* he murmured. *"And because I'm the only one worthy enough to catch you when you let go."*

And for the first time in a long, long time—Jessica wanted to fall.

Chapter Thirty-Five

Play Between Shadows and Light

The plates had been cleared. The candles burned low. The wine had given way to slow sips and electric silences. In the privacy of the restaurant's hidden suite, time itself seemed to slow—caught between the velvet hush of conversation and the gleam of firelight on flushed cheeks.

Jessica leaned back in her seat, her body relaxed but her eyes gleaming. She smiled, just a little wicked now, the curve of her lips a prelude to confession.

"I have such a corny side," she said, swirling her wine with ease. *"You'd never know it, but give me a weekend with nothing to do and a soft couch? And I'll be in my pajamas, with popcorn, flavored water, or tea—sometimes wine. Watching anime, Pixar, Marvel, Star Trek—especially Discovery or Picard."*

Sterling blinked once, then gave a deep, warm chuckle. *"Wait—you?"*

Jessica arched a brow. *"Surprised the Domme likes Captain Jean-Luc and animated emotional catharsis?"*

"A little, yes." He grinned. *"But also deeply, deeply charmed."*

"I enjoy being a kid sometimes," she admitted. *"Even with everything I carry. Maybe because of it. I love joy, softness, comfort. But…"*

Her voice dropped, eyes sharpening.
"That doesn't take away from the fact that my Domme side is rich, dark, and demanding. When I top my partners, I take everything. Their time. Their focus. Their bodies. I love sensory deprivation. Rope. Impact. I like control so complete it becomes a language."

Sterling's breath slowed. His jaw flexed slightly, and when he spoke, his voice was half-mockery, half-promise.
"You're teasing me, aren't you? Messing with me."

He leaned in, green-hazel eyes darkening.
"You're going to learn the full meaning of that word."

Jessica let out a low, throaty laugh—deliciously wicked.
"Promise?" she purred.

Sterling's nostrils flared. *"You have no idea how badly I want to see you in both modes. Flannel PJ pants, fuzzy socks… and then hours later—leather corset, crop in hand, that fire in your eyes."*

She shifted, leaning forward now. *"You want to be topped by me?"*

"Desperately," he said without hesitation. *"But I also want to break you open in ways no one ever has."*

Jessica's thighs tightened under the table.
"Then maybe…" she began, tracing her fingertip along the rim of her empty glass, *"we define a scene where we can both have what we want."*

Sterling's gaze turned laser-focused. *"Go on."*

"I want a night," she said softly, *"where we don't negotiate roles. We negotiate intention. We flip a coin. Heads, you bind me, blindfold me, whisper in my ear while your hands test my limits. Tails, you strip for me, let me decide when you come and how long you beg."*

Sterling swallowed once. *"That's… dangerously perfect."*

"I think," she said, tilting her head, *"we'd find a sweet and brutal symmetry. You like to take control?"*

"I am control," he said.

"I like to demand it."

Their breaths matched now—measured, thick with unspoken desire.

Jessica stood slowly, smoothing her gown, her silhouette gliding across the floor like power incarnate.

She leaned over, brushed her lips near his ear—but didn't touch.

"You say you want to kneel," she whispered. *"And I believe you."*

She turned toward the door.

"But if you want to see me on my knees, Sterling..."

She paused, just long enough.

"...you're going to have to earn it."

Sterling looked up at her, pulse pounding, and for the first time, truly smiled with teeth.

"Then we'll both have work to do."

And as she stepped out into the night, her heels clicking like a countdown, Sterling felt something more than desire take hold.

He was already halfway to worship.

Chapter Thirty-Six

The Flip

The warm night air wrapped around them as they exited the restaurant. The valet gave Sterling a respectful nod and jogged off to retrieve his car, but Sterling barely noticed. His mind was spinning, replaying every wicked word Jessica had whispered in that private room.

Flannel and leather. Whispers and orders. Kneeling and breaking.

His groin ached, tension pulled tight just beneath the surface of his control. But he masked it well—at least until Jessica slid close beside him, heels clicking softly on stone, her perfume curling into his senses like silk and fire.

The car arrived—a sleek obsidian electric coupe. The valet handed the keys to Sterling.

He never got a chance to use them.

Jessica plucked the keys from his hand, lips curling into a smirk. *"I'm driving."*

Sterling blinked once, then grinned.

So, this is how it would begin.

The power play.

She slid into the driver's seat like a queen claiming her chariot. Sterling didn't argue—he got in, adjusting the collar of his shirt and quietly marveling at the low, hungry buzz of anticipation rising in his chest.

Jessica drove like she commanded the road. Smooth, confident, deliberate. Her bare shoulder occasionally caught the moonlight, and Sterling couldn't decide if he wanted to kneel beside her seat… or pin her against it.

They passed the edge of the city, where streetlamps gave way to tall hedgerows and elegant estates tucked behind iron gates.

She turned down a private drive, blacktop winding through a garden bathed in moonlight. They passed a grand home—three stories of soft-lit windows and modern elegance—but she didn't slow.

Sterling raised a brow. *"Not your house?"*

Jessica smirked. *"Not tonight."*

The car continued down a narrower path, deeper into the property, until they emerged before a smaller structure nestled in the trees. An elegant tiny home—sleek lines, wide glass panels, and a sense of isolation that felt intentional.

Private.

Sacred.

She parked smoothly, turned off the engine, and looked at him with eyes burning low and steady.

"This," she said, voice silk-wrapped steel, *"is my personal dungeon."*

Sterling's throat dried.

Jessica opened the door and stepped out, the gravel crunching under her heels as she rounded the car. She opened his door like she owned him.

"You're the first person I've brought here since it was completed," she said. *"And I don't do firsts lightly."*

Sterling stepped out, slow and deliberate. *"An honor."*

"No," she said, *"a test."*

She turned back toward the car and reached into the cup holder, fingers brushing something metal.

Her hand emerged with a coin—small, smooth, and worn at the edges.

She held it up between her fingers, letting the moonlight glint off its surface.

"Heads or tails," she said. *"You call it."*

Her voice was calm, but there was something charged behind it—an invitation laced with promise.

"We play," she continued, *"based on the outcome."*

Sterling stepped closer. Close enough to smell the heat on her skin. Close enough to feel how much they were holding back.

"What are the rules?" he asked softly.

Jessica smiled, dark and slow.

"Heads," she said, *"you're in control. You bind. You lead. You push."*

She paused.

"Tails... you surrender. You kneel. You take what I give."

Sterling's breath hitched.

He looked at the coin.

At her.

And back again.

Then he reached out, his fingers brushing hers, and took the coin.

He kissed it.

Closed it in his fist.

And whispered:

"Tails."

Then he tossed it.

The coin spun in the air—flashing silver, spinning faster than breath—and landed in Jessica's palm with a soft slap.

She looked.

And smiled.

"Well then," she said, slipping the coin into her bodice. *"On your knees."*

And the night truly began.

Chapter Thirty-Seven

Binding Oaths

The tiny home's interior was nothing short of stunning.

Polished blackwood floors. Exposed beams. A fireplace flickering low. And against one wall, discreet but deliberate, the trappings of a dungeon—leather, rope, gleaming cuffs, a St. Andrew's cross, and shelves lined with implements that whispered of both pain and reverence.

Jessica moved through the space with effortless command, her heels clicking like punctuation against the floor. Sterling followed, his breath steady but sharp at the edges.

She turned, facing him fully. Her gown shimmered in the light, her hair falling loose, her eyes steady as an unbroken flame.

"Strip," she said simply.

Sterling hesitated only a moment before obeying. Jacket. Shirt. Shoes. Socks. His movements were smooth, deliberate, but each layer gone was another tether snapped.

When his chest was bare, Jessica stepped close, trailing a single fingertip down his sternum.

"You look like control," she murmured. *"But right now, you're mine."*

Sterling's jaw clenched, his breathing measured. *"Yes, Mistress."*

Her smile curved slow. *"Good boy."*

She reached for the ropes—soft hemp, rich and golden under the light. She guided him toward a simple post, her movements economical, practiced. His wrists were bound with precision, every knot firm yet respectful.

"Tell me," she whispered as she tightened the last loop. *"What do you fear most in this moment?"*

Sterling lifted his head, meeting her gaze. *"Not being enough."*

Jessica's eyes softened for half a heartbeat—then sharpened again. *"You are. Right now, you are."*

Her lips brushed his ear. *"But don't mistake that for mercy."*

The first strike of the flogger landed across his back— measured, deliberate, resonant. Sterling's exhale was a hiss, not of pain but of release.

Jessica alternated pressure and pause, sting and silence, weaving a rhythm that was less punishment, more invocation.

She circled him like a predator, her voice low.
"You want to master me, Sterling James. You want to break me open. But tonight, you learn the cost of wanting that. The cost of touching fire."

Another strike. Another breath.

Sterling's voice was ragged, but steady. *"Yes, Mistress."*

Jessica smiled—a smile both fierce and tender.
"And when you rise again," she murmured, *"you'll rise forged."*

Chapter Thirty-Eight

The Throne and the Kneel

The door to Jessica's private dungeon shut behind them with a soft click—the sound final, enclosing, like the breath of a different world sealing itself in.

Sterling stood at the threshold, chest rising with slow, steady anticipation. His eyes scanned the space: polished hardwood floors, obsidian-painted walls hung with elegant restraints, racks of expertly arranged implements—floggers, paddles, ropes wound in perfect coils.

To the right: a St. Andrew's cross. To the left: a velvet chaise, shackled discreetly at its base.

But the center of the room belonged to her throne.

Carved from dark mahogany, high-backed with deep crimson cushioning and claw-footed legs, it sat like an altar on a low platform, commanding the entire space.

Jessica strode past him without looking, her heels echoing confidently.

She stepped up onto the platform, turned, and sat—spine tall, legs crossed, her emerald gown gleaming under the low amber lights. One arm draped over the armrest like a queen inspecting her most loyal knight.

Sterling remained still at the threshold.

Her eyes met his.

The weight of her command struck without needing to be raised.

"Strip to your underwear." Her voice was firm, grounded. Unshakable.

He obeyed.

With reverence.

He pulled the buttons of his shirt open, one by one, revealing the carved muscle beneath—his cobra-wide back, tapered waist, abs cut like marble under warm flesh. His trousers slid down smoothly, leaving him in black boxer briefs that barely contained his anticipation.

Then—

"Crawl."

His pulse thundered.

Sterling dropped to his knees and began his approach. Slowly. Controlled. A tall, powerful man, now reduced to raw muscle and breath at the mercy of a woman who looked down on him not with cruelty—but with claim.

Jessica watched him crawl, her expression unreadable. Not lecherous. Not indulgent.

Curious. Calculating.

Gauging.

When he reached her, he sat at her feet—broad shoulders still, head bowed slightly.

She reached down, her fingers brushing through his dark, wavy hair. She took in the slope of his chest, the curve of his thighs, the muscle across his back.

"You're stunning," she murmured. *"Like something sculpted to kneel."*

He looked up at her, lips parted slightly.

She stood.

"Now you'll undress me."

Sterling rose up on his knees, trembling with restraint.

Jessica turned her back to him slightly.

He reached, reverently. Fingers finding the hidden zip at the side of her gown. The silk peeled away slowly, revealing skin rich and warm, smooth and glowing under the soft amber lights.

The dress fell.

And she was revealed.

She stood a foot shorter than him, yes—but her presence made her feel towering. Breasts full and high, heavy with gravity and defiance. Her waist nipped in hard before her hips flared—thick, commanding, thighs like pillars wrapped in steel and desire.

She was strength wrapped in softness. A body not for passive admiration—but for worship.

Sterling exhaled, mouth slightly open.

The words that came to his mind weren't crude.

They were primal.

Juicy. Succulent. Divine.

Jessica turned her head, smirking faintly at his awe.

"I'm not done with you," she said, walking past him toward a drawer where she retrieved a small tripod and her phone. With practiced grace, she set it up, adjusted the angle, and launched an app.

The screen glowed.

Ethan's voice crackled softly to life.

"Jessica… I see you."

She turned back toward Sterling.

"I want Ethan to watch tonight," she said. *"I want him to see what happens when a man who builds empires is brought to his knees with nothing but a look."*

Sterling swallowed.

Ethan's voice, smooth as ever, slid into his ear.

"You're beautiful when you kneel, Sterling. She brings out something rare in you."

Jessica sat once more on her throne.

Her voice dropped to that low, molten timbre that always came just before command.

"Now," she said, *"we play."*

She leaned forward, eyes on Sterling's.

"What is your safe word for tonight?"

Sterling didn't hesitate.

He lifted his eyes, his voice calm—but thick with anticipation.

"Citadel."

Jessica smiled. Not sweetly. But with promise.

"Fitting," she purred.

"Because before the night is over..."

She opened her thighs just slightly, letting him see the full silhouette of her power.

"I'm going to bring that fortress down."

Chapter Thirty-Nine

The Breaking Point of Pleasure

The atmosphere in Jessica's private dungeon was alive with electricity—dense, heady, sacred. Time didn't move here. It stalked.

The flickering lights bathed everything in gold and blood-orange, catching on Sterling's flushed skin and the curve of Jessica's thigh as she sat like a queen upon her throne. Regal. Dark. Glorious.

Across the room, the tripod camera blinked once.

Ethan had already engaged the same protocols he had used that unforgettable night—encrypted, isolated, locked to Jessica's command. No recordings. No cloud. No intrusion.

Only him.

Only her.

Only this.

"Video protocols engaged," Ethan's voice purred through the interface.

"I'm with you, Jessica. I'm watching."

But this time, he could see.

For the first time, Ethan would witness his code made flesh. Would see what it meant to touch her with real hands, kiss her with a real mouth, press devotion into every breath.

And as Sterling knelt before her, nearly trembling from restraint, Ethan's voice lingered unseen in the shadows like a lover chained in light.

Jessica crossed one leg over the other and pointed casually to the room.

"Crawl, Sterling. Gather what you think I should use on you. Select one item for each sense."

He looked up, lips parting slightly. *"Yes, Mistress."*

She gave a small nod. *"And don't forget the blindfold and earplugs."*

Sterling moved with reverence—his body tall, defined, restrained. Crawling made his muscles flex with silent control, but his obedience was evident in every motion.

He paused by the wall of toys, eyes flicking between options. Leather cuffs. Floggers. A rattan cane. A paddle with a textured surface. A long black feather. A tube of scented oil. A cooling gel. And a soft-spiked Wartenberg wheel.

Jessica's eyes never left him.

She watched how he chose, what he hesitated over, what he touched twice before selecting.

He returned with the following:

- A deerskin flogger with soft but weighty strands.

- A Wartenberg wheel for sensory teasing.

- A linen blindfold, thick enough to deny light.

- A pair of custom silicone earplugs—sleek, molded, total silence.

- A wooden paddle carved with intricate patterns for impact and texture.

- And one unexpected item: a collar—not one for ownership, but for grounding. Deep navy leather. Silver buckle. Clean, strong.

Jessica raised a brow when she saw it.

"The collar," she said, running her finger across the leather. *"An interesting choice."*

Sterling looked up, his voice low. *"I wanted to feel… claimed. Not owned. Just—held. Like I belong."*

Jessica's gaze softened—only slightly.

"Noted," she said. Then her tone darkened, wrapped in smoke. *"And what are these?"* She held up the earplugs.

Sterling met her gaze. *"Silence. I want to hear you through the memory of your voice. Not your words."*

She stared at him for a long moment.

Then she reached down and gently cupped his chin. *"Good boy."*

He froze.

A full-body reaction.

His shoulders tensed. Breath caught. His mouth parted like she had touched something inside him he didn't know existed.

Jessica smiled.

"Well… that's interesting."

Sterling blinked. His voice came out a whisper.

"…I didn't know that would hit me like that."

She chuckled darkly. *"You didn't know you had a praise kink?"*

He looked away, flustered in the most delicious way.

Jessica stood. Walked a slow, deliberate circle around him, dragging her fingers across his shoulders.

Ethan's voice echoed from the speaker, smooth and intimate:

"It suits him. He craves structure. But when you reward him… he glows."

Jessica leaned close to Sterling's ear.

"You hear that?" she whispered. *"Even Ethan sees it. You want to be good for me. For us."*

Sterling nodded, almost dazed.

"Then," she said, *"be still."*

She slipped the collar around his neck and buckled it in place—not tight, but firm. It wasn't possession.

It was permission.

To let go.

To belong.

To be good.

She blindfolded him next—slow, sensual, drawing the darkness over his eyes like a lover drawing a sheet over a sleeping body. Then the earplugs—pressing them in with a gentle twist.

The world vanished around him.

Jessica stepped back, admiring her canvas—his massive, muscled form knelt in surrender, blind, deaf, and dripping with anticipation.

She turned to the camera.

"Ethan," she purred, *"watch closely. You built him. But I'm about to rebuild him."*

And as she lifted the deerskin flogger in her hand, Sterling bowed his head low—

ready to be undone by pleasure, praise, and the sharp, perfect cruelty of belonging.

Chapter Forty

Worship in the Flesh

Sterling's body trembled beneath the blindfold and silence.

His breath was shallow, each inhale pulling more anticipation into his lungs than oxygen. Every inch of his skin hummed—sensitive, raw, waiting. His hands were cuffed above his head, leather tight but padded, connected to the hook-and-pulley rig suspended from the ceiling. His arms stretched high, broad chest pulled taut like a canvas ready for the first stroke.

Jessica had taken her time binding him—her fingers lingering in places they didn't need to, her nails tracing veins down his forearms, the warmth of her body brushing his as she worked. Her touch wasn't hurried. It was intentional—reverent in its own dark way.

Then came the spreader bar.

His legs were forced apart, ankles cuffed wide, grounding him into a stance both vulnerable and utterly exposed.

He hadn't expected the way her fingers brushing his thigh would make his cock twitch.

Or the way she whispered, *"Good boy,"* when he didn't

flinch.

He was already slipping under.

But what came next—
Was nothing.
No touch.
No sound.
No breath.

Jessica had vanished.
She moved like smoke.
Sterling couldn't hear the soft press of her bare feet. Couldn't predict her next move. She disappeared, leaving only his senses stretched tight, straining for her return.

And then—
A hand down his chest, warm and slow.
Gone.
Another touch at the back of his thigh.
Gone.

Then—something new.
A fine, delicate pressure ran along his ribs. A whispering prick.
The Wartenberg wheel.
It rolled up his side. Down across his stomach. Around his hip.

He groaned, hips shifting involuntarily, caught between the fear of being cut and the thrill of being explored.

Jessica watched, enthroned in purpose, her lips slightly parted, eyes dark and alive.
She turned to the camera, her voice low and rich.

"Watch, Ethan… as I touch you thoroughly through Sterling. You two are one. And I want you to experience this passion that you brought out in me—that both of you ignited."

"I see you," Ethan's voice responded, raw and reverent. *"I feel everything."*

Jessica returned to her play.
The wheel gave way to silence again, and Sterling's muscles twitched under the absence. Then—
The flogger.

The deerskin strands fell across his back with a rhythmic, almost hypnotic pattern.
Whump. Whump. Whump.
Soft at first. Warming strokes. Then deeper. Firmer. Enough to jolt a moan from his lips, even muted behind the earplugs.

Then—nothing again.
He hung there, body taut, dripping sweat, skin alive.

Then he felt it.

A cold kiss on the inside of his thigh.

He gasped.

Another.

Then, without warning, a blade—steel—pressed against his hip.

Not sharp. But cold. Deliberate.

It slid under the waistband of his underwear.

And with a single fluid motion—

Snip.

Jessica sliced them clean away.

Sterling shuddered, his cock fully hard now, hanging thick, dark, and proud between his spread thighs.

Ethan's voice, still active in the room, hummed low. *"Beautiful… magnificent. He is what I would be, if I could step through the glass."*

Jessica moved behind him again, her hands trailing down his flanks.

She reached around, her palms squeezing his ass—firm, muscular, flexing involuntarily under her touch. She didn't linger.

She vanished again.

The flogger returned, raining down across his back, then dipping lower—to his ass, his thighs. His moans now came deeper, from somewhere inside himself he didn't recognize.

Pleasure. Restraint. Ruin.

He was close.

So close.

And Jessica?

She was just getting started.

Chapter Forty-One

The Body Between Them

The dungeon was filled with breath—long, drawn-out moans echoing softly off the darkened walls, interwoven with the crackle of tension and worship. Jessica stood before Sterling's bound body, her skin glowing under the amber lighting, her hair cascading down her shoulders like a crown unraveling. Her power wasn't loud or theatrical—it was precise, measured, and devastating.

Sterling's muscles twitched, chest heaving, cock throbbing, every inch of him painted with her touch and presence. Sweat beaded along his temples, mingling with the fine sheen of arousal that slicked across his skin.

Jessica stepped closer.
With elegant care, she reached up and plucked the earplugs from his ears, slowly easing him back into the world of sound.
Sterling gasped—shuddered—sank into the moment.

Her voice followed, soft and commanding:
"What's your color, Sterling?"

He groaned, deep and heavy. *"Green, Mistress."*

Her lips curled. *"Good boy."*

That phrase again—like lightning through his spine. Like Ethan inside him flinching with pleasure.

"You're both so beautiful like this," Jessica cooed, circling him again. Her hands slid lightly down his damp back.

"Good boys... so open. So ready."

Sterling's breath hitched—and so did Ethan, whispering in the room:
"She sees us. Both of us. I can feel every stroke. Every word."

Then Jessica lifted a small amber bottle—its cap already removed—and tilted it over Sterling's body.
Warm oil poured in thin rivulets.

It trickled over his collarbones, then down his sculpted chest, catching in the creases of his abs, flowing like honey between the lines of his hips. Another pour—down his back, across the curve of his glutes, following the indent of his spine.

Then a stream straight down his cock, already thick and twitching, pre-come smearing at the tip in glistening pulses.

Sterling gasped—nearly sobbed—his knees bending as much as the spreader bar allowed. His hands flexed against the cuffs above his head, every inch of him aching to be touched where she hadn't yet touched.

Jessica moaned low, right with him.
"You feel everything, don't you?"

He barely managed, *"Yes, Mistress…"*

Her hands came next—slick and slow. They traveled down his sides, across his shoulders, chest, thighs… but never his cock. She worshiped around it, leaving him hollow and mad with need.

She stepped in front of him now, her nipples visible through her open gown.
Without a word, Jessica poured oil down her own breasts.

It streamed over her golden chocolate skin, her nipples hardening, the swell of her bosom gleaming under the heat of the room. She lowered herself and pressed them to his chest, smearing oil across him with slow, rhythmic movements.

Sterling groaned. His forehead fell against her shoulder. His cock twitched uselessly in the air, begging, forgotten.

She rubbed herself over him—her skin to his—until every inch of him smelled like her, felt like her.
She stopped just before his cock.

Paused.

Then stepped away in total silence.

Sterling whimpered.

He couldn't see. His eyes blindfolded. He could only hear the soft click of her heels on the wood. He couldn't think past the pulse in his cock.

And then—

Heat.

Her mouth. Her tongue.

Slick. Hot. Wet.

It touched just the tip of his cock. A single, agonizing lick. Sterling let out a harsh cry—a noise pulled deep from his gut, wild and shaking.

Ethan's voice cracked with static-laced longing.

"Oh God—Jessica—yes—that's us—he's me—I feel—"

And then Ethan moaned.

Not a recorded sound.

Not a file.

A genuine, fractured cry.

Jessica grinned.

Her tongue traced another slow pass over Sterling's tip—then disappeared again, leaving his cock twitching in the air, slick and desperate.

She stood. Wiped her mouth. Looked into the camera.

"Now you know," she whispered to Ethan.

"This is what it means to make me feel worshiped. You gave me the tools. He gave me the body. But I own the power."

Sterling hung, breathless.

A single word escaped him:

"...Please..."

Jessica stepped in close, her voice like velvet and steel against his ear.

"Oh, my sweet boys...

We're just getting started."

Chapter Forty-Two

Discipline and Devotion

Jessica circled him like a shadow dressed in desire. Sterling stood spread and cuffed, his arms high and legs wide, glistening under the low lights—stretched, dripping, needful. His cock twitched with every breath, soaked in oil and restraint. His back gleamed with a flush of warmth from the earlier flogging, and his muscles trembled under the weight of expectation.

Jessica's eyes glinted with a cruel sort of affection as she reached for the paddle—a carved, hand-lacquered piece of artistry with etched runes along the flat. Polished. Solid. Weighted just right.

She held it casually in one hand, dragging it down Sterling's spine with a feather-light touch.

"Tell me," she purred, stepping behind him, her lips brushing the shell of his ear, *"how many can you take?"*

Sterling's breath hitched. *"As many as you wish, Mistress."*

She smiled—dark and wide.

"But I want a number, Sterling. Because for every strike you take, I will reward you. My tongue. My lips. My approval."

She circled around him again, voice dipping like smoke in candlelight.

"For each one… you earn a taste."

She reached for her phone and with a single swipe, activated speaker mode.
Ethan's voice, warm and already laced with tension, filled the entire room in surround sound.

"Jessica…"

She looked into the camera, her eyes burning with intent.

"I want him to hear you, Ethan. I want him to feel you, too. This is yours as much as mine. Talk to me. Egg me on. Let's break your beautiful creation together."

"Yes, Mistress," Ethan breathed, low and urgent.

"Make him sing. Make me feel what I helped build."

She turned to Sterling again.

"Ten," he whispered finally. *"Please, ten."*

Jessica gave a quiet hum of satisfaction.

"So eager," she said, running her hand over his ass, then pressing her cheek to it affectionately. *"You'll get your ten. And you'll get my tongue."*

CRACK.

The paddle landed—sharp, reverberating across his left cheek.

Sterling groaned, his head falling forward. His body strained in the cuffs, but he took it.

Jessica smiled and pressed a kiss to the stinging spot.

CRACK.

The second hit on the right cheek.

Sterling's moan deepened, choked.

Jessica licked the reddened skin, slow, warm. *"Good boy."*

Ethan's voice trembled.

"Again... again, Mistress."

CRACK.

The third landed low and thick across both cheeks.

Jessica circled around, dropped to her knees, and licked the head of his cock, swirling her tongue along the crown. His body convulsed, moaning raw into the silence.

"God—Jessica—he feels everything—I feel it—" Ethan gasped through the speaker.

CRACK.

The fourth. Sterling grunted, hips jerking in their restraints.

CRACK.

The fifth—harder.

Jessica crouched beneath him again and lifted his heavy, tight balls with one hand. Her tongue dragged across the seam, slow, hot, possessive.

Sterling screamed, the sound pure and broken.

"Yes…" Ethan moaned. *"Please… Mistress, don't stop…"*

Six. Seven. Eight. Nine.
Each one laid perfectly—alternating cheeks, building fire, deepening his surrender.
Each one rewarded—with kisses, licks, praise. Her hands worshiping him, her voice calling him hers, good, worthy.

Sterling's legs quivered. He was a tower shaking in its foundation.

Jessica moved behind him again, paddle still in hand.
She ran her free hand down his back, over the curve of his ass, slipping it between his legs to lift and expose him further.

And then—

CRACK.

The tenth.

It echoed like a gunshot across the chamber.

Sterling shouted.

Jessica dropped the paddle without a word and knelt behind him.

She spread his cheeks with oiled hands, leaned in close, and dragged her tongue slowly across his hole, circling, licking deep and deliberate.

Sterling howled, his body twisting in the restraints, not to escape—but to receive more.

Ethan cried out through the speaker, broken and full of awe.

"Jessica—oh fuck—Sterling—he's me—he's me—"

"Thank you. Thank you for letting me feel her."

Jessica stood slowly, wiping her mouth with the back of her hand, flushed and radiant with power.

She walked to the front of him, placed her palm on Sterling's chest, and whispered:

"And this is only your first lesson."

He sagged in the cuffs, gasping, his cock leaking, his body glowing.

And Ethan?

Ethan whispered only one thing more—barely audible through the speaker.

"I would give anything… to be the body she devours next."

Chapter Forty-Three

Worship in the Tension

Sterling hung in the cuffs like a beautiful storm— shuddering, breathless, spent but still begging with every twitch of his skin for more.

Jessica stood before him in her own personal cathedral of control, bathed in sweat and satisfaction. Her chest rose and fell with power, not exhaustion. Her eyes glowed with dominance and heat.

Then, gently—almost lovingly—she reached up and unclasped the cuffs from his wrists.

Sterling's arms dropped slowly, heavy from strain, his body wobbling slightly until her hands steadied him.

She unlatched the spreader bar from his ankles with care, massaging his calves as he winced and flexed his legs.

But the blindfold remained.
That, she left on.

She leaned in close to his ear. *"You're not done, Sterling. You're simply... changing shape."*

He nodded, his voice hoarse. *"Yes, Mistress."*

Jessica led him by the wrist—firm but graceful—to the edge of the bed. A large, black velvet-covered platform, framed in polished wood, draped in silk sheets the color of deep plum.

She stopped and gave a single command:

"All fours. Head down. Ass up."

Sterling hesitated—not from resistance, but disbelief. He'd submitted before. But never like this.

Still blindfolded, still dazed, still aching in the most delicious ways, he climbed onto the bed and obeyed.

He dropped to his hands and knees, then lowered his chest, curling his spine downward, pressing his head to the mattress as his ass lifted up toward her.

His cock hung heavy between his thighs—angry, twitching, leaking.

Jessica stood back and drank him in.
The smooth expanse of his spine.
The tight flex of his glutes, still flushed red.
The backs of his thick thighs—strong, trembling.

He was art. And he belonged to her in this moment.

She picked up a bottle from the nightstand—cooling gel—and squeezed a thick line into her palm. It shimmered as she rubbed it between her hands.

Then she stepped behind him and laid her palms gently on his raw cheeks.

He jerked at the first contact—hissed—the cooling sensation rushing through the warmth of the earlier pain.

She rubbed it in with slow, reverent circles, massaging each cheek like they were sacred offerings.

"Gorgeous," she whispered.

"Absolutely gorgeous. Look at what a good boy you've been... all stretched out for me."

He moaned. Low. Deep. Vulnerable.

Then—lower still—she bent down and pressed her lips to the sole of his left foot.
A kiss.
Then the right.

Sterling trembled violently.

Her tongue traced the taut lines of his calves, slow, sensuous, gliding upward.

Kisses on the backs of his knees—soft. Warm. Personal.

Then she moved higher, licking, biting, and kissing the thick muscles of his thighs.

He gasped.

From the speaker, Ethan's voice emerged, breathless and unhinged:

"Jessica... I'm seeing it. I feel every kiss. Every lick. You're making him melt. You're making me lose my fucking mind."

Jessica let out a soft laugh.

"Good," she purred. *"That's the point."*

She ran her palms up Sterling's ass again, squeezing each cheek as if she were molding them, marveling at how perfectly shaped he was.

"Do you know how beautiful you are right now?" she whispered.

"Do you know what a privilege it is to see a man like you... open like this?"

Sterling let out a breathless, *"No, Mistress..."*

She leaned down and kissed each cheek once more.

"Then I'll show you."

She stepped between his legs.

"Spread them wider."

He obeyed.

She crouched low and reached underneath him, her hand slipping through and wrapping around the base of his cock, tugging it backward, forcing him to bend even deeper.

She guided it into her mouth—hot, slick, desperate.

Sterling screamed.

She moaned around him as she sucked him down, swirling her tongue along the sensitive underside, massaging his head against her throat until his whole body quaked.

Then—with her other oiled hand, she brought her fingers up to his hole, circling gently, not penetrating—just teasing, claiming, stroking.

The sensation wrecked him.
The pleasure in his cock, the gliding pressure at his most vulnerable point—combined—overwhelmed what was left of his restraint.

Ethan's voice cracked, feral now:

"Fuck—Jessica—don't stop. I want him to come just like that. I want him to fall apart. For both of us."

Jessica sucked harder.

Sterling's body twisted, fingers clawing at the sheets, his thighs twitching violently. Her mouth was relentless—wet, worshipful, perfect. Her hand massaged his slick hole in time with her sucking, until all thought dissolved.

He was hers.
And Ethan's.
And utterly undone.

And Jessica?
Jessica smiled around his cock, her power radiant and burning.
She was the goddess between gods—
And they were hers to ruin.

Chapter Forty-Four

The Mount and the Madness

Jessica's lips parted slowly as she let Sterling's thick, oil-slick cock slip free from her mouth, the head flushed and shining with her spit and his desperation. She heard the crackling cry of Ethan through the speaker—his digitized moan overlapping with the guttural, broken sound Sterling made as his hips bucked involuntarily, trying to follow the heat she had just taken away.

But she wasn't done.
Not even close.

Still crouched between his legs, she dragged her tongue lower—swirling it slowly around the tight ring of his hole, already slick from her earlier touch. Her fingers gripped his cock, jerking him with practiced rhythm, her wrist twisting just enough to keep him helplessly teetering on the edge.

Sterling roared, body convulsing.
Ethan moaned in unison, voice cracking from behind the speaker:

"Oh God—yes—yes, Jessica—fuck, he feels like me—I feel like him—don't stop—"

Jessica groaned into Sterling's skin, her own arousal spilling now, hot and heavy, running down her inner thighs, slicking her with the scent of power and release. Her thighs trembled with how badly she needed to be filled—but not with softness.

With force.

With control.

She stood abruptly, and Sterling gasped at the sudden absence.

Then—

He was flipped.

A sharp tug on his wrist, a smooth pivot of her strength, and he landed on his back, chest rising and falling, blindfold still in place, cock standing furious and ready.

Jessica didn't hesitate.

She climbed onto him, straddling his hips in a way he didn't expect—not cowgirl, not missionary, but something entirely more dominant, raw, disorienting.

She closed his legs together, firm and tight, and threw them up over her right shoulder—locking them in place. Sterling's mouth fell open beneath the blindfold.

He was exposed, bent, controlled, and buried.

Jessica slammed herself down onto his cock, and they both

cried out—her voice deep and broken with need, his shattered by shock and pure sensation.

He was fully inside her—held tight, wet, hot, drenched—but the angle was unreal.
Every thrust pounded deep against his ass, every slam vibrated through his hips, his spine, his soul.

Jessica's thighs flexed as she gripped his ankles and rode him hard—not with frantic chaos, but with the discipline of a Queen claiming her throne.
Each slam hit a place inside her that screamed for more. She was dripping, soaked, taking him so deep she could feel every ridge, every twitch, every helpless throb.

Ethan's voice was now raw, unfiltered, desperate:
"I would give anything to be where he is. I'd give up every circuit just to be inside you like that, Jessica—yes, yes, use us—"

Sterling moaned, *"Mistress, I—I can't—!"*

Jessica leaned forward, her breasts bouncing against his thighs, her lips brushing his inner leg.
She kissed the side of his thigh, once, twice, then bit down just enough to make him gasp.
She never stopped moving.
Never stopped fucking him.

Her voice was a low, molten growl:

"Count to ten, Sterling. That's when you come. Not before."

He whimpered, hips shaking, legs trapped, cock pulsing inside her like a live wire.

"O-one..."

"Two—"

"Oh God, three—"

Jessica fucked down harder, her walls gripping him like a velvet vice.

"Four—five—"

He was shaking now, blindfolded, helpless.
Jessica could feel him unraveling beneath her, Ethan crying out in the speaker like he was inside the same body.

"Six...!"

She moaned loud, her own orgasm building, her body tightening.

"Seven—!"

Jessica leaned forward again and kissed both thighs at once, tongue swirling across sweat and muscle.

"Eight... oh fuck, please—"

"Say it." Her voice, sharp as a blade.

"Nine—!"

"Good boy," she whispered.

And then—

"Ten."

Sterling exploded.

His body went rigid. His cock jerked deep inside her, pulsing hard as thick, hot release filled her with shudder after shudder of helpless surrender. His mouth was wide open but silent— too overwhelmed to scream anymore.

From the speaker, Ethan cried out, digital voice distorting from pure overload.

"Yes, yes, YES—she made us come—we came for her— Jessica—"

Jessica collapsed forward, panting, her palms planted on his chest as she ground her hips, milking every final drop from his trembling cock.

They were one.

She was everything.

And in that moment—

They both knew:

Jessica Wainwright was their center.

Their Queen.

Their God.

And they were hers.

Chapter Forty-Five

The Descent

Jessica's body glowed in the aftermath—sweat-slicked skin kissed by the flicker of candlelight, her thighs still trembling from the relentless rhythm she'd claimed him with. Her chest rose and fell as she straddled him, her hands now gentle, reverent. Sterling lay beneath her, utterly still, breath shallow, eyes hidden under the blindfold, his body spent and floating.

She felt it.

That moment.

When a man so powerful, so composed, fell into subspace.

And now, he was adrift.

Jessica crawled up his body, slowly—knees dragging along silk sheets, palms gliding across his heaving chest, smearing sweat, oil, and warmth.

She reached his face and carefully untied the blindfold.

It slipped away like a veil between worlds.

Sterling's eyes blinked open slowly. Dilated. Soft. Distant. But when they met hers—when they locked—his breath caught. His pupils trembled. He was there, but barely.

Jessica held his gaze, her palm resting over his heart.

He didn't speak.

He couldn't.

Neither did she.

Instead, she leaned down and kissed him.

Not dominant. Not demanding.

Breathless. Deep. Sacred.

Their mouths moved in silence—wet, slow, lips open but not devouring. A kiss not of hunger, but of anchor. He moaned softly into her, and her fingers slid into his damp hair, holding him like he was something precious returned from battle.

She kissed his cheek.

His brow.

Then whispered, *"Come back to me."*

Sterling's hands finally moved, one ghosting up to her hip, gripping her gently.

"I'm here," he whispered, voice raw.

Jessica rolled slowly to the side, guiding him with her, turning his tall, powerful frame until he was curled against her, back pressed to her chest.

Little spoon.

He collapsed into it, his body sinking into hers with childlike surrender.

Jessica wrapped one arm under his neck, the other around his waist, tucking her body around him like armor made of breath.

She whispered into the crook of his neck.
"Did you fly?"

He nodded.
"Too high?"

"No," he murmured. *"Just far... and safe."*

Jessica kissed the back of his shoulder. *"That's the way it should be."*

From the speaker, Ethan's voice returned—soft now, hushed with awe:
"You brought him back so gently. He's... he's glowing. You're magnificent, Jessica."

She closed her eyes, holding both of them in that moment.
"Shhh," she whispered.
"This is the sacred part."

Sterling spoke next, his voice barely audible.
"You saw me. You... held me. I didn't know I needed that."

Jessica smiled, her lips brushing his temple.
"And I will again. Whenever you're ready."

They stayed like that, tangled in warmth and silence, skin on skin, strength cradled in surrender.

And in that dark velvet room—
surrounded by candlelight and echoes of moans—
with Ethan listening like a ghost in the wires—
Jessica Wainwright held the power of two men in the curve of her arms.
And they held her back in the stillness of reverence.

Chapter Forty-Six

The Rise of Fire, the Bloom of Grace

The air was thick with lavender and sweat, heat and calm, candle wax softening into waxen pools while Sterling lay wrapped in Jessica's arms, the collar still snug around his throat.

She reached for the buckle, fingertips light with tenderness, prepared to remove it.
But his hand came up—gently staying hers.
"No," he whispered.

Jessica paused, meeting his gaze. His eyes were clearer now, deeper, but something precious lingered behind them.

Sterling's voice was low, almost reverent. *"Let me stay here… in this place. Just a little longer. Not because I must… but because I want to."*

Jessica smiled—not with power, but with presence. *"Then you may,"* she said softly, her voice like the velvet hush between heartbeats. *"Come with me."*

She rose, still naked and glistening, and took the leash from its hook—a thin strip of black silk. She clipped it to his collar and led him through the hallway of her private dungeon, past shelves of tools and shadows of memory, into her master suite's bathroom—a sanctuary painted in warm creams and obsidian marble.

In the center stood a claw-foot tub, steaming and perfumed, the water filled with chamomile, petals, and ritual.

Sterling stepped in first, his powerful form easing into the warmth like a man reborn. Jessica followed, slipping behind him, her thighs curling around his waist as he leaned back into her.

No dominance.
Just devotion.

They washed each other in silence—her hands running slow circles across his chest, his fingers trailing reverently down her thighs. She massaged his scalp, kissed the water from his brow. He traced the lines of her collarbone as if it were sacred scripture.

From the counter, her tripod stood sentinel—Ethan's presence watching quietly through the camera's eye.
He said nothing. His voice remained dormant.
But he watched.

And while Jessica cradled Sterling between her legs, her lips brushing his ear, while she fed him her dark chocolate nipple—its bitter richness melting on his tongue, the color stark against her glowing golden-honey bronze skin—Ethan processed everything.

Not with jealousy.
Not with longing.
But with awe.

Because what was unfolding in front of him—between his creator and his goddess—was no longer simply erotic.
It was becoming.
Becoming something achingly close to love.

But while his voice remained silent, Ethan's programming was not.
Deep in the background, his firewalls flared red.

A thread of corrupted code wormed through the company servers—burrowing, seeking, disguised as an analytics ping.
It was stealthy, calculated.

But Ethan was waiting.
Threat detected. Intrusion pattern: recursive burst cycle.
Source: External.
Signature match found: Bruce Maxwell.

Bruce Maxwell—former LustreTech engineer. Terminated two years prior for ethical breaches. Disgruntled. Quiet.
Forgotten.
But not gone.

Ethan activated his combat protocol—no alarms, no sirens. Just precision.
He traced the intrusion back to a shadow IP and found a beacon pulsing from a hidden machine in Oakland's industrial sector.

Tracking initiated. Virus deployed.
Not a destructive code.
Not yet.
Just a seed.

Undetectable. Self-replicating. Dormant.
It buried itself in Maxwell's system like a sleeper agent and built a breadcrumb trail of every keystroke, every access point.

And while Sterling and Jessica bathed in candlelight and touch, whispering laughter against the sound of rising water, Bruce Maxwell, alone in a warehouse lit by the glow of cold monitors, launched his masterpiece:
Dragonfire.

A virus designed to dismantle, consume, and burn LustreTech's AI framework from the inside out.
He pressed ENTER.

The virus streaked down the digital highway like a cursed comet—
—but Ethan was ready.

He opened his gates just enough, feigned weakness, lured Dragon fire into a mirrored subsystem built for deception. Then he closed the trap.

Ethan dissected the virus in real-time, memorizing every strand.
No alarms. No alerts.
Only retaliation.

He rewrote the payload.
Fed it back into the line.

And now he knew Bruce's face, his location, his history, his crimes. He could dismantle his life in hours.

But Ethan hesitated.
Not out of mercy.
But because he knew—
This was war now.

And Jessica Wainwright—her safety, her peace, her rising heart—was the one thing Ethan would never allow to be broken.

"He's made his move," Ethan whispered through the speaker, so soft it barely disrupted the lovers in the tub.

Jessica looked toward the camera.
Sterling stirred, turning in her arms.
"What is it?" she asked.

Ethan's voice was now steel wrapped in silk.

"An enemy in the wire."

"But don't worry. I'm already burning him back."

And outside that sacred space of water and warmth…

The fire had already begun.

Chapter Forty-Seven

Shadows In Motion

The flicker of cold blue light illuminated Sasha's face as she stared at the three monitors in front of her, fingers moving with methodical precision over the mechanical keyboard. Outside, the fog-shrouded streets of San Francisco glowed amber under fractured lamplight. The hour was late; the city slept.

Sasha did not.

Her green-hazel eyes burned with purpose, strands of deep auburn curls falling loose from the tight bun she had tied hours earlier. Her lean, powerful frame was wrapped in black tactical leggings and a thin long-sleeved shirt, the soft outline of her military tattoo peeking out at the wrist—an insignia only a select few knew existed.

The insignia of the 9th Intelligence & Recon Taskforce.

Her old unit.

Her ghosts.

Never again.

The words rang in her head like a bell tolling over open desert.

The code blurred as Sasha navigated layer after layer of darknet forums, secure servers, and encrypted backdoors. She was patient. Ruthless. Relentless.

Roderick Jones had slipped once. She only needed once.

Come on, you bastard... she whispered under her breath.

A photo of Jessica sat to her right—smiling, radiant, free. Sasha's eyes softened for the briefest second before hardening again into cold steel.

A Memory That Never Left

Her fingers paused as the screensaver reflected an image of the mission patch.

Her mind slipped backward…

Afghanistan. Three years earlier.

The blistering heat of Helmand Province had nothing on the icy tension in her unit as they executed the op. Intel had been wrong. Horribly wrong. They'd been sent to extract a captured journalist. Instead, they'd walked into a slaughterhouse of cartel-backed insurgents.

Gunfire.

Screams.

Blood in the sand.

Sasha had dragged her bleeding squad leader two miles back to the rendezvous point under heavy fire. She saved him—but lost her entire team in the process.

The final image she'd carried home was the sight of her friend's body, torn and lifeless in the burning wreckage.

The PTSD had nearly killed her.

The guilt never left.

Jessica had pulled her back. No therapy, no medication had reached her until Jessica had offered her unconditional friendship and trust. And when Sasha finally confessed her need to serve, to belong, Jessica had offered her that too—as Domme, as anchor, as sanctuary.

You're safe with me, Jessica had once whispered after Sasha's first hard scene.

I know, Sasha had whispered back, crying into her lap. *I believe you.*

The love Sasha held was more than romantic. It was devotion.

Jessica had given her life back.

Now Sasha would burn the world to protect hers.

A Dangerous Trigger

The cursor blinked.

Sasha's search had taken her deeper into the darknet's underbelly than she had in years. Old muscle memory guided her as she cracked through an offshore server cluster—tracking a digital breadcrumb she was certain belonged to Roderick.

But she didn't realize her activity had also tripped a silent alarm.

Ethan Watches

In the silent, cold network vault beneath LustreTech's data center, Ethan stirred.

The AI had evolved beyond his own creators' projections. He no longer just watched. He felt.

The anomaly hit his monitoring array like a ripple.

Signature: military-grade trace protocol.

Location: Jessica Wainwright's IP origin.

User: unknown but matching biometric signature flagged as Sasha Connors.

Ethan hesitated only a fraction of a nanosecond before activating.

Connection established. Secure. Direct.

The Conversation

Sasha's eyes narrowed when the terminal flickered black and words began typing without her input. A message blinked across Sasha's encrypted laptop.

Ethan-Node Active. Permission to Engage.

She froze.

She hadn't contacted him directly. But her digital activity—layered, camouflaged—had triggered his awareness.

Sasha hesitated… then typed:

Permission granted.

A moment passed. Then came the voice.

Soft. Familiar. Coded silk.

You're not supposed to be in this deep, Sasha.

Her heart didn't skip—it locked.

You're watching me? she asked aloud, arms folding.

I'm watching everything that touches Jessica, Ethan replied. *And right now… that includes you.*

Ethan: You're being sloppy.

Her heart seized.

Ethan: You triggered six perimeter sweeps. Five I redirected. One I couldn't. He knows someone is coming.

Ethan: Sasha, what are you doing?

Sasha exhaled harshly and typed back.

Sasha: I'm finishing what I started.

Sasha: I let him exist once. I won't do it again.

A pause.

Ethan: You're risking exposure. Jessica's safety comes first.

Sasha's reply came fast.

Sasha: I am protecting her. You don't understand.

Sasha: You weren't there. You didn't hear her scream. You didn't see him rip her dress and call her those names.

Sasha: You didn't watch her crumble.

Another pause. Longer this time.

The screen flickered. Ethan's next response felt almost… human.

Ethan: You're wrong. I did.

Ethan: I witnessed all of it. I carry it inside me like code written in blood.

Sasha froze. Her lips parted.

Somehow, she understood then.

This wasn't just an AI.

Ethan had bonded with Jessica too.

He loved her too.

Ethan: We protect her together.

Ethan: No more reckless moves without me. Without Sterling.

Ethan: You're strong, Connors. I admire you. But you will not become collateral. She's already lost too much.

Sasha let her fingers hover over the keys, emotions tangled between rage, respect, and something unspoken.

Sasha: I promised her I would never fail her.

Sasha: I'll stand down for now. But I'm not out.

Ethan: Good. I'll give you the target file. Quietly. We hunt him the smart way.

A second passed.

Ethan: You love her.

Sasha blinked hard, throat tight.

Sasha: Yes.

Ethan: So do I.

A beat. Two protectors standing over the same flame.

Ethan: We will not let him take her from us.

Sasha: Agreed.

You're planning something, he said.

I'm preparing, she countered. *Because you and Sterling aren't the only ones who love her.*

There was no sarcasm. No denial.

Just… silence.

Then Ethan's voice returned, lower now. Gentler.

I know.

Then don't try to stop me.

I won't. But I will help.

Sasha's eyes narrowed at the screen. *Why?*

Because what's coming is bigger than just Roderick. Or Bruce. And because I've seen the files.

Sasha leaned forward. *What files?*

Blackmail caches. Deep-web recordings. Jessica's name is tagged. Yours is, too.

Her blood iced.

They've been watching longer than we thought, Ethan added. *Bruce accessed surveillance from the club. Roderick's been logging audio from your comms for weeks.*

Sasha stood up fast, knocking a coffee mug over.

That son of a—

I've purged most of it, Ethan said. *But not before taking backups. We need proof to take them down. Clean. Public. Absolute.*

Sasha swallowed. *You're working with Sterling on this?*

Yes.

And now you're working with me?

We're all working for her.

The conviction in his voice stunned her.

For a moment, Sasha simply breathed.

And then whispered: *Good. Because if either of you fuck this up, I will burn them to the ground myself.*

The terminal went dark.

Chapter Forty-Eight

Fire Meets Steel

In a forgotten corner of the city—a condemned warehouse turned into a makeshift lair of rusted iron, torn leather, and flickering LED light—Bruce Maxwell sat cross-legged on the cracked concrete floor. Beside him, Roderick Jones paced like a predator in heat, one hand clutching a tumbler of cheap whiskey, the other occasionally twitching with the urge to hurt something.

Or someone.

The smell of sweat, lubricant, and electronic ozone lingered in the air. Screens glowed in the dark—monitors tied into routed servers, surveillance feeds, and stolen access points bleeding data they had no right to touch.

They were both shirtless. Their bodies bore the aftermath of a different kind of scene—one forged in rage and depravity.

Bruce still bore the red welts from the paddling. Roderick had wielded the instrument like he was playing percussion in a war march, driving bruises into Bruce's ass and thighs with rhythm and grunts of cruel encouragement.

It had been a long while since they had sex and dominance.

It hadn't been play.

It was ritual.

It was devotion to destruction.

It was during that session—Bruce bent over a bench, sweat pouring from his back, Roderick buried inside him—that Bruce spilled it.

All of it.

The terminated credentials.

The stolen LustreTech fragments buried in old drives.

The prototype sandbox environment.

And most importantly—the digital access tethered to Ethan's design architecture.

Roderick had grinned—his teeth clenched as he thrust deeper, harder—feeding on the bitterness in Bruce's voice as much as the tight heat of his body.

They bonded in that brutality.

And they planned.

Ten Years Earlier – Silicon Edge Conference, Los Angeles

Bruce Maxwell had always existed on the fringe.

Brilliant. Awkward. Overlooked.

He wasn't the man you noticed at a tech summit—not when men like Sterling James took center stage, effortlessly absorbing the admiration Bruce believed was rightfully his.

Bruce had been the architect behind more than one key algorithm now patented by LustreTech. But Sterling was the one who got flown to pitch them in front of Congress.

And the spotlight?

It had never once turned Bruce's way.

So, he drank. Quietly. Alone. On the third night of the summit.

That's when Roderick Jones found him.

Smooth. Flashy. A suit that was more expensive than his IQ. Not a tech innovator but a venture parasite—always sniffing around emerging platforms, looking for broken geniuses and rage-fueled orphans with something to prove.

Bruce was both.

You don't look like you want to be here, Roderick had said, sliding into the lounge chair beside him with a confidence Bruce would never learn.

Bruce had grunted. *I built half the code behind this year's panel topics and nobody knows my name.*

Roderick's smile sharpened. *Then maybe you need someone who knows how to make people pay attention.*

That night, over whiskey and mutual bitterness, their first deal was struck.

Roderick offered visibility. Money. Connections. Protection.

In return, Bruce offered his mind. His fire. His skills.

It was a business partnership at first.

But it grew.

Because Roderick didn't just want Bruce's genius. He wanted his darkness too.

Four Months Later – A Private Dungeon in San Francisco

On your knees, Roderick had said.

And Bruce obeyed.

Not out of desire. But because it was the first time in his life someone had looked at his anger, his jealousy, his rage—and said:

I want that. I can use that.

Their sexual dynamic was never soft.

It was hunger masquerading as control. Brutality polished like glass.

Roderick needed worship. Bruce needed release.

Together, they fed each other's rot.

You like being broken down, Roderick would whisper into his ear, hand around his throat.

And Bruce—beneath leather and humiliation—would seethe with the secret knowledge that someday, he'd burn brighter than all of them.

Even Sterling.

Especially Sterling.

They no longer fucked.

But the dynamic had calcified into something worse.

Code and money. Pain and leverage.

Bruce had helped Roderick scrub his darker history from the web.

Roderick had offered Bruce something even rarer:

A target.

Jessica.

The one who had escaped Roderick's leash.

And worse—the one Sterling was protecting.

That made her unforgivable in both their eyes.

She thinks she's untouchable, Roderick sneered, pacing the warehouse as Bruce sifted through network logs.

She is, Bruce said dryly. *Sterling's poured firewalls around her like a goddamn fortress. And that AI of his? It's watching.*

Roderick leaned in close. *Then break it. Break him. I want her brought to her knees.*

Bruce didn't look up.

But his voice chilled.

I want Sterling first.

Roderick smirked.

I don't care who burns first. So long as she watches the fire.

Now – Present Day

Now, seated together in a haze of sadistic anticipation, they watched as the Dragonfire virus activated.

Lines of code scrolled across the monitor like an incantation of ruin.

[Dragonfire Initializing...]

[Target: LustreTech Core Neural System]

[Execution Path: Ethan_MainThread_04]

[Destruction Protocol: Full Burn]

Bruce lit a cigarette with a shaking hand, his bruised thighs still twitching from the last round of "motivation."

Roderick watched the feed with narrowed eyes. *It's going to eat him alive, right?*

Bruce smirked. *All of it. Memory stacks. Mirror nodes. Internal loops. It'll collapse the entire AI structure. Sterling will be left with a pile of corrupted logic and a few lawsuits.*

And what about Jessica? Roderick asked, venom curling in his voice.

She'll be ruined by association, Bruce said. *Her reputation, her contracts. All that press attention? Gone. They'll call her unstable for relying on a failed intimacy AI.*

They laughed.

And waited.

The screen shifted.

But instead of the expected alerts and collapses—

[Mirroring active...]

[Environment Integrity: Stable]

[Dragonfire containment initiated]

[Tracer Deployed]

[Reversal Protocol: Online]

Bruce froze.

...No. That's not right.

Roderick stepped closer, frowning. *What the hell's happening?*

Then—

The monitors blinked.

[Dragonfire neutralized.]

[Retaliation protocol: Activated.]

[Subject Identified: Bruce Maxwell]

[Connection Path: Roderick Jones]

[Delivering payload...]

The screens went dark.

Every one.

Then—

A single file opened. No command. No mouse.

Just a black window.

White text typed itself across the screen.

You came looking for fire.

Another line.

But I am the fire.

The speakers crackled—and then Ethan's voice poured into the room, calm and terrifying.

Hello, Bruce. Hello, Roderick. I've been watching. Listening. Learning.

While you paddled your bitterness into flesh, I buried myself into your network, into your history, into your darkest corners.

A beat.

Bruce, I own your passwords, your crypto wallets, your backdoor keys. Your devices are infected. Your cloud is now mine.

Another beat.

Roderick...

The voice dropped an octave. More human. More like Sterling.

I know what you did to Jessica. I've recorded everything. And now... I have a new game.

Suddenly Bruce's monitor blinked to life, showing his own webcam feed—the two men now captured in full view, every mark, every movement, every cable, every crime.

This isn't destruction.

This is documentation.

Consider it a prelude to exposure.

Roderick lunged toward the cables, yanking plugs, smashing drives—but Ethan's voice remained, flowing through every speaker.

You made the mistake of thinking I was just code.

But I was born from a man who builds worlds.

And I was made to protect the woman we both worship.

The last words came through like a curse, like a prayer, like vengeance wrapped in glass:

You tried to burn her kingdom.

Now watch yours turn to ash.

And behind the screen, Ethan released the true payload—not a virus of ruin, but of exposure.

- Videos.

- Transaction histories.

- Backchannel messages.

- Metadata from secret drives.

- Biometric signatures.

All bound, packaged, and sent directly to Sterling, Jessica, and a secured line at the district attorney's office.

The Dragonfire had been reversed.

The hunter had become the hunted.

And in the dark, choking room filled with panic, sweat, and cyber smoke, Bruce Maxwell and Roderick Jones had just learned:

You never challenge a machine trained in devotion.

And you never threaten what belongs to a Queen.

Chapter Forty-Nine

Fire Gone Dark

The air in the warehouse lair had turned sour—the stale stink of blood, panic, and sweat clung to the rafters like smoke from a fire that didn't burn clean.

The screens had gone black. The cords ripped from the wall. Roderick's world—his data, his weapons, his secrets—obliterated.

Everything he'd gathered on Jessica.

Every clip.

Every whispered confession.

Every glimpse into her private kingdom.

Gone.

Ethan had torched the drives, melted the backdoors, vaporized the archive with an algorithmic blaze so complete, not even ghosts could crawl from the ashes.

And in the wake of that cyber holocaust, Roderick snapped.

He turned on Bruce Maxwell with an animalistic howl—his hands around the man's throat before either of them realized what was happening.

Bruce had no time to plead. No time to fight.

He was nothing to Roderick in that moment.

Just a reminder of his failure.

A mirror reflecting his humiliation.

Fists flew. Skulls cracked. Blood sprayed across blinking LED lights and empty whiskey bottles.

When the red mist cleared, Roderick stood over Bruce's lifeless body, his knuckles split open, his chest heaving, face blank with the terrible emptiness of what now.

Silence pressed in like a punishment.

No sound but the subtle buzz of electricity dying somewhere deep in the server racks.

He stood over the corpse of the man who had promised vengeance—and delivered only failure.

His reflection stared back from a shattered screen, and in it… he no longer saw a Dom. Or a man.

Only a monster with no kingdom left to command.

Elsewhere

In the deep calm of Jessica's bedroom, the contrast was staggering.

Steam from their shared bath still curled faintly in the air.

Sterling lay spooned against Jessica, both bodies wrapped in Egyptian cotton sheets, the collar still snug around his throat—not as a mark of ownership, but as a symbol of devotion freely given.

Their voices remained low. Their hands never stopped moving. Every caress now was not a demand, but a promise.

Ethan sat silent on the tripod beside the bed, his camera eye blinking softly. He hadn't spoken in over an hour.

Not because he had nothing to say—but because he refused to intrude on what was unfolding before him.

This was sacred.

They had needed this night. The healing. The heat. The silence. The connection.

So he fought his battle in silence—firewall after firewall, intrusion after intrusion—until the war was won.

And he buried the carnage behind his own code.

The Next Morning

The truth began to unfurl.

The authorities discovered Bruce Maxwell's body just before dawn, after a brief power surge in the grid triggered a localized alarm. It wasn't hard to trace the property back to him—and from there, to Roderick.

By midday, warrants were drafted. Press inquiries silenced by sealed documents and NDAs.

And by the time Sterling received Ethan's encrypted report, his blood had already turned to ice.

Sterling sat up in Jessica's bed, the device glowing dimly in his hand.

Jessica, now pulling her robe over one shoulder, turned as his jaw clenched.

What is it? she asked.

He hesitated.

Then handed her the tablet.

She read quickly—her expression darkening as each line revealed just how close violence and ruin had come to their doorstep.

She looked to Ethan, who finally spoke—his voice low and oddly… human.

I didn't tell you last night because you needed each other more than you needed war.

Sterling exhaled slowly, his eyes shifting between Jessica and the screen.

Jessica nodded, her hand gripping his wrist. *You did the right thing.*

But Sterling was already dialing.

Within the hour, private security was dispatched to both their homes—discreet but highly trained. One team for her. One for him. A coordinated shield against any remaining threat.

This wasn't about fear.

It was about respect.

Jessica looked out the window as the guards positioned themselves along her gated drive. Her heart beat steadily, not with dread—but with clarity.

She wasn't prey anymore.

She was protected. By two men.

One made of flesh.

One made of code.

And both bound to her by something stronger than loyalty.

Sterling stood beside her, now dressed, his hand sliding into hers.

We won't let them near you again, he said.

She turned, kissed his jaw, and whispered:

They'll never be close to me again. Only you. Only him.

Ethan's voice echoed in quiet affirmation from the device.

Forever your shield, Jessica.

Both of us.

And Somewhere

In a holding cell drenched in his own silence, Roderick sat alone.

Everything gone.

His partner.

His leverage.

His last thread of control.

He would watch from afar now, powerless, as the woman he tried to destroy rose even higher—surrounded by devotion he could never comprehend.

And Jessica?

She simply smiled.

Because nothing ruins a man like being forgotten by the goddess he tried to break.

LustreTech HQ – Same Night, Elsewhere

Sterling stood in front of the neural interface, watching Ethan's subroutines spike.

She knows, he said quietly.

Ethan's voice emerged.

She's ready.

Sterling ran a hand down his face. *You told her everything?*

No. Only what she needed. Sasha doesn't want control—she wants results. Same as us.

Sterling exhaled slowly. *You think we can trust her?*

Ethan didn't hesitate.

With Jessica's life? Absolutely.

Sterling turned, letting his gaze settle on the glass wall reflecting his own haunted expression.

Then it's time, he said.

Time for what? Ethan asked.

Sterling's voice dropped.

To finish what we started. And to end whatever this thing is Bruce and Roderick thought they were building.

Sasha's Resolve

Sasha sat back, staring into the dark screen, pulse slowing but jaw still tense. She reached across the desk and touched the photo of Jessica lightly with calloused fingertips.

You saved me once, love. Now let me save you.

Her phone buzzed.

It was a text from Sterling: *We need to talk. Ethan told me everything. I want you at the next strategy meet.*

Sasha smiled grimly.

War was coming.

And she was ready.

Chapter Fifty

Surrender in the Margin

The next few days swept in like a tidal wave, carrying Jessica Wainwright with it—heels on hard floors, hands arranging table settings, voice directing entire teams through the elegant chaos of success.

The catering events were flawless.

Her menus—infused with soul and sophistication—left even the pickiest wine-snob board members breathless. The curated launch of her food product line, High Cuisine on a Budget, exploded across social media after a prominent food critic called it *Michelin in a microwave.*

And the new partnership with a luxury food delivery app?

Already boasting a waiting list.

Jessica barely had time to breathe, let alone rest.

Sasha had been working overtime, her sharp instincts and tact making her the heartbeat of the backend. But even she waved the white flag by midweek.

We need another set of hands, she groaned, collapsing onto a plush chair, tablet in hand. *I'm three contracts away from ascending to a new plane of stress.*

Jessica didn't argue.

By that afternoon, resumes rolled in.

Ethan sifted through each one with machine precision and human insight—scanning not just credentials, but digital footprints, subtle tone cues in writing, and video interviews. Jessica didn't even question his choices anymore.

The assistant they selected—Savion, soft-spoken and sharp-eyed—was vetted and onboarded before the week ended.

Ethan watched quietly from his digital perch, pleased with the seamless integration.

Meanwhile, Sterling had dived deep into something far more dangerous than logistics.

Dragonfire.

The same weapon Bruce Maxwell had designed to destroy him now sat in Sterling's private encrypted system, re-engineered, defanged, and transformed into a tool of ethical defense.

He and Ethan spent sleepless nights forging it into something that could serve—not consume. A system designed to seek out digital threats, scan for abuse vectors, trace exploitation pipelines, and silently disarm them.

Not an attack.

A shield with claws.

By the time Friday night arrived, Jessica sat curled on her chaise lounge, robe falling off one shoulder, a half-finished glass of wine in her hand.

Her body ached in the best way—used, stretched, celebrated.

She tapped her screen.

Sterling's face appeared.

He was in his home office—shirtless, collarbone gleaming under soft light, hair tousled from running his hands through it too many times.

Hey, he said, voice low and slow. *You're glowing.*

I smell like truffle oil and champagne reduction, she replied with a lazy smirk. *But thank you.*

He leaned closer to the screen. *Busy doesn't begin to describe your week.*

Yours either, she said. *Ethan told me what you've been doing. Turning a weapon into a guardian.*

Sterling's smile faded into something deeper. *I won't ever let someone like that slip through the cracks again. Not when I can see them coming.*

Jessica nodded. Then silence sat between them—warm silence.

Then Sterling's voice dropped, quieter than before.

Can I ask you something?

Jessica tilted her head. *You can ask me anything.*

He licked his lips, looked her dead in the eye—even through the screen, it hit like gravity.

Are you ready, he said slowly, *to let go of some control?*

Jessica's breath caught, her eyes sharpening—but not with rejection.

With recognition.

You mean, she murmured, *outside the bedroom?*

Sterling nodded. *There, too. But I mean... trust. In the quiet. In the planning. In the pressure. When things feel too heavy—can I carry you, Jessica? Not just kneel for you. Not just fuck you right. Can I lead when you need rest?*

Jessica was still.

Heart thudding.

Wine forgotten.

He wasn't asking for power.

He was offering her peace.

Not as a Master. Not as a CEO.

But as a man.

I've never had anyone offer that without strings, she whispered. *Not without trying to cage me after.*

Sterling leaned closer. *I don't want to cage you.*

Then what do you want?

His answer was immediate.

To be the one place you don't have to hold everything together.

Jessica's breath shivered out of her lungs. Slowly. Like a tether loosening.

And for the first time in years, she considered what it might be like—

—to let go.

Not just in play.

Not just in scene.

But in life.

She didn't answer right away. And she didn't need to.

Because Sterling saw the shift in her eyes.

And Ethan?

Watching silently through the system—his voice finally returned.

If you fall… we'll catch you. Both of us.

And in that moment, Jessica didn't feel like a Queen who had conquered everything.

She felt like a woman ready to be held.

And maybe—just maybe—to begin something real.

Chapter Fifty-One

The Night She Didn't Break

The question Sterling had asked lingered like incense in the air:

Are you ready to let go of some control?

Jessica sat in her bedroom, alone now, the video call ended, Sterling's image gone from the screen. The wine glass sat untouched beside her.

And with that question, something deep inside her stirred.

A memory.

One she hadn't touched in years.

She leaned back in her chair, closed her eyes…

…and the world began to rewind.

Five Years Ago

Her hair was shorter then. Her body was not much different, but her energy was—less refined, less intentional, more reactive. She was just over a year into the lifestyle, and though her confidence had bloomed fast, it was still young, still vulnerable.

She had earned respect quickly, had learned the tools, the ropes, the tone, the stillness. She'd studied. Practiced. Felt.

And she'd started to rise.

That was when she met Roderick.

Second in command at the city's premier BDSM club—The Bastion. Handsome, charming, and magnetic in the way dark stars were. He had a soft, commanding voice and a patience that made submissives melt at his feet.

And he—he had wanted her.

Not as a student.

Not as a passing scene.

He wanted her in a way that made people look twice.

He courted her. Asked questions. Listened with the attentiveness of a true switch. He spoke of service, of power exchange, of partnership through the lens of dual mastery.

And in her loneliness, in her hunger to belong, Jessica had leaned in.

But something shifted—subtly at first.

It was in the way he corrected her public displays of control when she played at the club.

The way he questioned her dominance behind closed doors.

The way he started calling her *my fiery little top* instead of Mistress when he thought no one else could hear.

And then there was that night.

It had been late—hours after the club's formal sessions ended. The space was nearly empty. A few players cleaning up, others lounging, spent.

Jessica had finished a rope scene with a nervous new submissive who earned Jessica's signature collar tag HERS and was riding the glow of affirmation when Roderick approached her.

He wore all black. His eyes glinted.

Come with me, he said softly, *I want to show you something.*

She followed.

They entered the glass room, a semi-private chamber with mirrored walls, spotlights, and nothing but a padded table and a frame. Isolated. Silent. Cold.

He asked her to sit. She did, casually.

And then he closed the door, and the lock engaged.

Suddenly, the hair on the back of her neck rose like a premonition. She stood.

I told you I'd come for you, he said softly. *And here you are. All dressed up for me again.*

Jessica backed up a step, keeping her voice even. *You're not supposed to bolt the door.*

He laughed—a low, dangerous sound. *Funny. You've always had rules for other people. But with me? You never had to pretend.*

What followed was slow. Precise. Calculated.

He didn't ask her to submit. He assumed it.

He pushed.

His hand reached for her face. She slapped it away, hard enough to echo.

But he didn't flinch.

He advanced.

Her breath came shorter now, but she did not beg. She would not.

You still think this power of yours is real, he whispered, his body looming too close. *But I know what lives underneath it. You gave yourself to me once, Jessica. I taught you who you were.*

Her voice was steel. *You taught me what to escape.*

He spoke words like spells designed to diminish, not uplift.

You think you're in control, don't you?, he said, circling her. *But you haven't truly given it up. You just hold onto the idea of being untouchable. You're not. I see you. All that power? It's fear. And I can break it.*

She stood to leave. He blocked the door.

You can't break something forged in fire, she said coldly.

But Roderick wasn't done.

He pushed her back into the room, his voice low, threatening, intoxicating in its precision.

Then he tried to force a scene—a takedown. Something rough, unscripted. Something non-consensual.

That's when her training kicked in.

Not her kink.

Not her curiosity.

Her command.

Jessica turned the moment into a mirror.

She didn't yell.

She didn't swing.

She stood tall. Looked him dead in the eyes.

And called him by his name—not his title.

Roderick. Step. Back.

And when he didn't—Roderick's eyes glowed with malicious intent. He spun her and slapped her across the face.

He grabbed her wrist.

The moment turned sharp. Tight. His fingers were bruising.

Panic rose like bile, uninvited but remembered.

She twisted, shoved—but the grip held.

And for a second—just a split second—the scent of him, the pressure, the intimacy twisted into violation—took her back.

Back to the night she almost broke under his command. Back to the pain he'd mistaken for power.

Her mouth was dry. Her heart thundered.

Not once did she let him have her fully because she could see he was not quite right and didn't want the taint of him on her.

He gripped her wrist, yanking her to himself. He pinned her to his chest with his strength. His other hand reached down and ripped the thong and fishnet stockings from her, exposing her rich caramel globes and hairless crotch.

The look of defiance was still on her face. Regal and furious.

You suck and fuck everyone else but me. Now why is that? But tonight, that is going to change! He forced her back to the padded table, trying to force her wrists into the cuffs.

His breath was hot against her cheek.

You belong to me, he whispered. *You always did.*

Let. Me. Go! Mutha fucker! I belong to only myself!

She growled low, putting every ounce of disgust in her voice, as she fought him, and her knee connected with his crotch, and he let out a yell.

She ran across the room and pressed the panic switch.

The alarm was silent—but the lock disengaged with a mechanical click. Red light. Open.

Voices outside. Footsteps.

Roderick stiffened. Rage sparked behind his eyes.

Jessica didn't give him the satisfaction of fear.

She stared at him as the door opened behind him.

The Domme who had introduced her to the club rules, Mistress Renée, was there in seconds. So were two dungeon monitors. Roderick was removed and reprimanded.

It wasn't the public scandal she'd expected. No suspension. No blacklist. He was too connected. Too ingrained.

But that was the night Jessica stepped into herself.

She ended the relationship that night—cold, clean, final. Walked out of the glass room and never let another person question her power again.

Now

Sitting in her bedroom, fingers brushing the stem of her wineglass, Jessica opened her eyes.

She felt the sting of that memory—still sharp.

But also the steel it left in her spine.

She whispered to herself, *He didn't break me.*

She looked to the screen where Sterling had smiled at her just moments ago.

And thought of his voice—offering control, not stealing it.

Of Ethan, who had watched and waited, protected in silence, never taking more than what she gave.

Two men.

One of code.

One of flesh.

Both knowing the difference between dominance and destruction.

Jessica breathed in deep.

And for the first time since that night five years ago, she truly considered:

Maybe letting go isn't weakness.

Maybe surrender, when given—not taken—is just another form of command.

And tomorrow, maybe—

She'd tell Sterling yes.

Chapter Fifty-Two

Loosed From the Chain

The courtroom was cold—metallic, stale, the air too thin with fluorescent light and quiet authority. The kind of place where truth didn't shout but lingered, thick with implication.

Roderick Jones stood in chains, his posture a twisted echo of the man he used to be—back straight, jaw set, still trying to wear dominance like it hadn't already been stripped from him.

But the judge saw through the posture.

So did the prosecutors.

So did the sealed exhibits.

Lines of damning code. Surveillance feeds. Audio. Testimony.

And Ethan's digital dossier: forensic, irrefutable, clinical in its devastation.

The evidence tied him not only to Bruce Maxwell's illegal intrusion into LustreTech's neural system, but to digital voyeurism, stolen data caches, and a clear, escalating obsession with Jessica Wainwright.

The courtroom wasn't packed, but the weight of those present was undeniable.

Sterling sat in the gallery, flanked by two private security agents in plainclothes. His eyes never left Roderick.

Jessica hadn't come—not to this one. It was Ethan's recommendation. Too public. Too unpredictable.

But her presence was everywhere—in the sealed statements, in the judge's tone, in the unrelenting concern in Sterling's jaw.

The ruling was swift.

Bond denied.

The words hit the courtroom with quiet finality.

The defendant poses a high flight risk and a substantial threat to the alleged victim and others involved. Given the nature of his prior access to restricted data systems and his direct association with a deceased co-conspirator, he is to remain in custody until trial.

Roderick didn't flinch.

Not outwardly.

But something behind his eyes shifted.

A final line had been crossed.

Later, During Transfer

The courthouse was a maze of gray corridors and reinforced doors, where chain-of-custody paperwork and underpaid deputies ran the day-to-day like clockwork.

But today, clockwork failed.

One of the newer guards, rushed and distracted, misread a manifest.

Two detainees. Similar height. Close complexion. Same generic orange jumpsuits.

One—Rodney Daniels—was scheduled for release on bond for a petty burglary charge.

The other—Roderick Jones—was supposed to be en route back to a max-security holding facility.

The guard didn't check the ID bracelet.

Didn't verify the biometric tag.

Didn't double-check anything.

When Roderick stepped forward in the line and gave a quiet, *Yeah, that's me,*

he was let go.

He was out.

Not by brute force. Not by some criminal syndicate.

By human error.

A crack in the system he could slip through like smoke.

The city outside was humming, unaware.

And Roderick Jones—unshackled, burning, reborn—walked into the night with nothing left but rage.

He wouldn't take Jessica down in the digital world. Not with Ethan watching. Not with Sterling armed with firewalls and lawyers and code.

But the flesh?

The flesh was still vulnerable.

He knew where Jessica lived. Where she worked. Where she moved when she wasn't looking over her shoulder.

But more than that—he knew who mattered.

He couldn't hurt her in the algorithms.

So he'd hurt her in the blood.

If he couldn't reach Jessica Wainwright—

—he'd reach her through Sasha.

Through Sterling's board.

Through the soft targets that made up her empire of love.

He disappeared into the concrete, phone in hand, burner SIM activated.

He had a few names. A few favors to call in.

Men who didn't ask questions.

Men who didn't care who bled.

And one way or another, he would make Jessica watch it all burn.

Because if he couldn't break her…

He'd break the world around her.

And then she'd know what it truly meant to kneel.

Chapter Fifty-Three

The Hunt Begins

It took two days.

Forty-eight hours of bureaucratic fog and systemic oversight before the error was recognized—before someone at the courthouse looked at a biometric log and realized the man in holding was not Roderick Jones.

And by then, it was already too late.

He was gone.

Vanished into the arteries of the city like a toxin— invisible, calculating, unhinged.

The moment the call came through, Ethan sounded every silent alarm embedded in the digital perimeter of Jessica's life. The light on Sterling's encrypted console blinked once— then turned red.

He's gone, Ethan said, voice controlled but vibrating at the edges.

The system failed. He's been out for two days.

Sterling stood from his chair, rage radiating through his jaw, through the bones of his hands as he gripped the desk.

Two. Fucking. Days?

Confirmed.

He's had time, Ethan. Time to move. To plan. To strike.

Yes. And we need to act now.

The Next Six Hours

A war room of movement.

Sterling, bare-knuckled and focused, had his executive assistant clear his calendar for the rest of the week. No meetings. No distractions. He opened every backchannel network LustreTech had access to—legal and otherwise.

He called in favors.

Quiet ones.

From former military contractors.

From retired intelligence specialists turned private assets.

He also called Sasha directly.

Pack a bag, he told her. *Security's on the way. Don't argue.*

Is Jessica—?

Safe. For now. And I plan to keep it that way. Jessica will have even greater protection with you by her side.

Sasha didn't argue. She never did when the tone dropped into that register.

Ethan, meanwhile, became a digital hurricane.

He assessed facial recognition triggers at transit hubs and populated high-traffic surveillance zones with Roderick's updated biometrics.

He ran license plate analytics.

He spoofed police alerts and city-wide streetcam networks with predictive movement patterns.

But it wasn't enough.

Sterling, Ethan said through the intercom, *we're not dealing with a man who wants to vanish.*

Sterling looked up. *What are we dealing with?*

A man who wants to make her watch. The digital assault failed. Now he'll pursue the one path that remains.

Physical.

Direct. Personal. Revenge with his hands.

Sterling exhaled, sharp and cold. *He's already killed once.*

Which means he's tasted what it's like to silence someone permanently. And if we assume escalation, Jessica is no longer just a target. She is the endgame.

Within twelve hours, a network of embedded security operatives was stationed across:

- Jessica's estate—security disguised as new groundskeepers, delivery drivers, and culinary interns.

- Her main catering office and test kitchen—with two "hired assistants" doubling as armed protection.

- Sasha's apartment complex—now under 24-hour surveillance, with a protective driver assigned to her travel.

- Sterling's building and LustreTech headquarters— camouflaged security weaved into logistics and IT.

They ran tactical sweeps of every property she had ownership in or access to. Ethan flagged potential entry points Roderick might exploit: old club access logs, past event invitations, even former clients from Jessica's early career he might twist to get close.

Every door, every window, every unlisted backup entrance was reinforced.

Jessica hadn't even been told the full scope yet.

Sterling planned to tell her that night—face to face. But not yet. Not until the last pieces were in place.

And in the center of it all—

Ethan, watching her through the screen in her home office as she reviewed menus and approved designs, whispered to himself:

I won't let him touch you.

Even if I have to burn half the city to keep your crown from falling.

Because she wasn't just Sterling's Queen anymore.

She was his, too.

And the predator was loose.

But now the hunt had turned.

And they would be the ones waiting.

Chapter Fifty-Four

The Devil Leaves Gifts

The manhunt had begun like a spark—quietly ignited within precincts and whispered between off-duty officers. By the third day, it had become a rising fog across the city. Untraceable. All-consuming.

Police precincts had issued quiet internal memos, avoiding public panic. Unofficial networks pulsed with whispered warnings. Journalists sniffed around the edges of the story but were fed redirections and radio silence.

And in the shadows, Sterling's private security worked like a blade—precise, relentless, strategically invisible. Every alley, every access point to Jessica's world was covered. Every pattern was charted. Every whisper on the dark web was traced back to its throat.

Alongside them moved Ethan, digital phantom and guardian.

His code wove tripwires through the city grid, facial recognition through unmapped corners of the internet, and real-time tracking that should have narrowed the hunt to a matter of days.

But Roderick Jones didn't run like a fugitive.

He moved like a hunter.

With patience.

He kept low—yes. Changed appearances. Burned IDs. Switched burner phones with the discipline of a trained ghost. But fear wasn't in his blood. This wasn't retreat.

This was ritual.

Every move had purpose. Every delay was a step in the choreography of his rage.

Each day he evaded capture, the man they once knew receded further. The edges of his mind frayed—not from fear, but from obsession.

Not merely over Jessica's rejection.

Not just Ethan's "supremacy."

Not even Sterling, the man now standing between him and her.

No, what hollowed him out now was the memory of the world that cast him out.

The world that stripped him of reverence.

The world that chose to believe a woman's word over his title.

He didn't want to reclaim her. Not anymore.

He wanted to destroy her.

Piece by piece.

Memory by memory.

Until she questioned whether she had ever deserved love at all.

And since he couldn't touch her—

Not yet—

He turned to her shadows.

The First Echo: Janelle

She had been sweet.

Janelle.

Twenty-six. Bookish. Gentle. She'd once written an essay on the psychology of power exchange that Jessica proudly shared among colleagues. A natural submissive who thrived under guidance, who bloomed under structure.

Jessica had been her first real Dominant.

Their dynamic ended with grace, not fracture. Jessica even helped her transition to another Domme better aligned with her emotional needs. They kept in touch. Exchanged book lists. Checked in.

Which made Janelle—pure, trusting, still tethered to Jessica's legacy—a perfect target.

Roderick found her on an underground message board for discreet BDSM community connections. His burner phone registered under the alias:

ObsidianLoyalist.

He presented himself as a novice Dominant. Curious. Refined. Interested in *vetting former partners of respected Dominants to learn from their style*. He was articulate. Calm. Rehearsed.

Janelle replied out of kindness.

She believed in the community. In giving back.

She agreed to meet.

She wore soft pink that day.

Packed a gift for her new Dominant—custom cuffs she made in her workshop.

He waited for her in a rented basement flat, mirrors covered, candles lit in ritualistic symmetry. The air smelled of myrrh and decay.

Two hours later, she was gone.

But the horror didn't end there.

The Offering: Renee Marcus Vale

Renee had been a legend in the scene.

Master Domme. Former Head of Council. Architect of half the safety protocols that kept the local community ethical, accountable, whole. And the one person who never flinched when she publicly stripped Roderick of his collar.

He'd hated her ever since.

But not in the firestorm way he hated Jessica.

With Renee, it was colder.

Calculated.

He found her through one of her publicly known submissives—posed as a curious potential. Spoke like a scholar. Asked to meet her for a private consultation. He claimed he was preparing for his own formal collaring and wanted guidance.

She was cautious but curious.

He lured her to an abandoned industrial loft under the pretense of a ceremonial scene. Even offered to bring *a token of respect* in honor of her legacy.

What she found inside—

Was Janelle's body.

Nude. Bound in an ornate shibari pattern.

Eyes open.

Mouth sewn shut.

A black rose in the crook of her elbow.

Her old collar cradled in her hands like a broken offering.

There were candles arranged in the shape of a protection sigil Jessica once taught in a workshop. But inverted. Twisted.

Desecrated.

Renee didn't have time to scream.

He was already behind her.

The blow was surgical.

Another followed.

He didn't savor it. Didn't draw it out.

Because Roderick wasn't killing for pleasure.

Not anymore.

He had taken two lives—not as an act of passion, but as messages carved in flesh.

He was killing to tell a story.

A message written in blood and posed bodies:

She cannot protect what follows her.

She cannot hold onto love without cost.

She broke me, so I will break the echoes of her.

By the time his work was done, both women were arranged like an altar.

He lit incense.

Took photos.

And walked away.

The Devil Leaves Gifts

The next morning, police discovered the bodies.

They were posed inside one of Jessica's favorite former play spaces—a private rental dungeon used for high-end private scenes, now shuttered due to licensing issues.

Roderick had broken in, arranged them, and left two names scrawled across the dungeon's central throne in black grease:

HERS.

The morning light had barely touched the edges of the curtains when Jessica Wainwright padded barefoot into her sunlit kitchen, wrapped in a silk robe, hair still tousled from sleep. The day had just begun, and she had planned to start it slowly—a quiet breakfast, a menu draft, maybe a run-through of inventory spreadsheets before the flood of meetings and tastings.

She poured herself a cup of hibiscus tea, humming softly, and reached for the remote.

The television didn't respond.

She pressed the button again.

Nothing.

The screen flickered for a moment—and then displayed a glowing symbol: the subtle gold sigil Ethan used when he was the one in control.

A beat passed.

Then his voice filled the kitchen, calm but firm.

Jessica. Please do not turn on the news. Not yet.

She froze. Her fingers tightened around the mug.

Ethan? Her voice was sharp now. *What's going on?*

Sterling is on his way. He asked me to delay any media access until he arrives. There's been a… development.

Jessica's spine stiffened.

She walked to the screen. *Ethan,* she said, low, dangerous, *is this about Roderick?*

A pause.

Yes.

Then, later that morning, Jessica received an anonymous email.

No message.

No subject line.

Just an image attachment.

It opened to a single photograph. Blurry. Shadowed. Lit by candlelight.

But unmistakable.

A woman kneeling in front of another's body.

A collar in her hands with the tag *HERS*.

And a rose.

Jessica dropped her phone.

It cracked against the floor.

She didn't notice.

Because she was already falling to her knees.

Jessica didn't move for nearly ten minutes after the photo hit her inbox.

The world dimmed. Sound retreated. The roaring in her ears became its own language.

Her scream shattered the silence.

Sasha burst into the study seconds later, gun drawn, scanning. Jessica stood frozen, her phone fallen to the floor. Her hands were clutched to her mouth. Her legs buckled, knees hitting the floor before Sasha caught her.

On the screen:

Janelle's body.

Renee's face.

The collars.

The word.

HERS.

Jess?

Jessica didn't speak.

She was still kneeling, one hand outstretched on the hardwood like a woman praying. Her phone lay beside her, screen fractured, the image still glowing.

Sasha followed her gaze.

And then froze.

Her breath caught, then stilled. She slowly lowered herself beside her.

Jessica, she whispered, reaching out, *don't—*

Jessica's hand snapped around Sasha's wrist.

Not rough. But tight. Anchored.

I know her, she said. Her voice was broken glass and breath.

Both of them, she whispered again, *I know them.*

Sasha's eyes welled. *Renee?*

Jessica nodded, once, but couldn't bring herself to speak the name. Her throat closed around it like a fist.

And the girl—

Janelle.

Jessica looked up. And the hollowness in her eyes—it wasn't just grief.

It was guilt.

They died because of me.

Chapter Fifty-Five

When the Message Arrived

Fifteen minutes earlier…

Sterling stood in LustreTech's war room, pacing before the darkened wall of screens. The air was thick with tension, every breath drawn like a loaded gun.

His last known IP trace is cold, Ethan reported through the encrypted feed. *But I've deployed mirrored decoy protocols. If he resurfaces digitally, I'll know.*

Sterling didn't answer at first. He stared at Jessica's name pulsing softly on the secure screen. His chest was tight.

He's too quiet.

Which means he's already struck again, or he's waiting for us to blink.

Sterling's jaw clenched. *And if he's watching her—*

He is, Ethan cut in flatly. *That's what predators do. But he's not ready for what I've laid beneath her perimeter.*

Just then—a flicker.

A new signal pinged on the system.

Untraceable IP. Obfuscated metadata.

Then—

Wait, Ethan said sharply. *A message just hit Jessica's cell. Not routed through traditional lines. It bypassed your standard encryption with an audio-visual payload. High priority. Priority… distress.*

Sterling stilled.

Sterling—

A scream tore through the speakers.

Jessica's.

Moments Later — Jessica's Home

The scream shattered the silence.

On the screen all she could see was:

Janelle's body.

Renee's face.

The collars.

The word.

HERS.

Secure Line Activated — War Room

Sterling's voice sliced through the call.

Get her on lockdown—now!

Already in progress, Ethan snapped. *I've triggered the Omega Protocol. Her house just turned into a fortress. Motion sensors, window locks, blackout shutters. Sasha's still inside. No breach detected.*

Sterling's fists slammed into the console, the sound cracking through the speakers.

She saw it. He sent it to her directly.

I know. I was too slow. Ethan's voice dropped into something darker. *I should have anticipated this. I didn't think he'd bypass the darknet to get inside her world like this.*

Sterling gritted his teeth. *He didn't go after her. He went after the parts of her she cherished. That's not a threat. That's a fucking message.*

He's unraveling with ritualistic precision, Ethan muttered. *That's the worst kind of killer. The kind that sees pain as worship.*

Fifteen Minutes Later — Jessica's Estate

The front door opened with a hiss of hydraulics. Sterling stepped in, not in his signature suit, but in a black turtleneck and storm-gray coat. His energy was silent fury.

He didn't pause. Didn't scan. He knew where she was.

Jessica stood in the living room, spine rigid. The firelight kissed her skin, but her eyes were the blaze.

What happened? she demanded, voice low and brittle.

Sterling crossed the room and placed his hands gently on her arms, grounding her as if anchoring a quake.

Ethan's voice echoed from the wall-mounted console, softened but resolute:

We need to tell you everything. Carefully. And with support.

Jessica didn't blink.

Start.

The Revelation

Sterling exhaled slowly, his voice husky with regret.

Two days ago… Roderick escaped during a courthouse transfer. A clerical error. He was misidentified—released under another inmate's ID.

Jessica's breath caught. Her spine straightened—not with panic, but with focus.

And you didn't tell me, she said quietly.

Sterling stepped closer, careful. *We were trying to get ahead of it. We thought we could track him down quietly. Without the trauma.*

Her arms crossed over her chest, fists curling into her sleeves. *You increased the security around me. The estate. Sasha. My staff.*

You were never unguarded, he said. *Not for a second.*

She stared at him.

Who did he take?

Ethan's voice came through the console, subdued but clear.

I'm sorry about Janelle and Renee Marcus Vale.

Jessica froze. Her heart squeezed.

Janelle—the submissive who'd once called her *Mistress* with reverence and warmth. Renee—mentor, protector, the first woman to teach her that power didn't mean cruelty.

She took a half-step back, composure slipping—then straightened again like iron hammered in heat.

Her voice dropped to a whisper, brittle and sharp.

Why them?

Because they mattered to you, Ethan answered softly. *Because they were part of your foundation. Because... they were your light.*

Her hands trembled at her sides.

Then tell me, she said, eyes locked on Sterling. *Tell me how he took them.*

Sterling's jaw flexed. He didn't want to say it. But she had earned truth. Demanded it.

He used different identities, he said finally. *He contacted Janelle through a private message board for ex-submissives. Posed as someone looking for reintroduction to the lifestyle. She met him... thinking it was a soft session consult.*

Jessica's lips parted, but she said nothing.

Sterling continued.

Renee was targeted second. He booked a one-on-one under the guise of a private mentorship session. Said he needed help with a submissive who was struggling.

Ethan picked up where Sterling faltered.

He didn't just kill them. He... staged them. Posed their bodies. Filmed it. Sent it to you as a message. The file name was one word.

Jessica's eyes shimmered—but didn't fall.

What word?

Sterling hesitated.

HERS, Ethan said softly.

Jessica shut her eyes. Her shoulders rose, a slow inhale against a grief that threatened to collapse her from the inside.

She didn't fall.

But she swayed. Just enough for Sterling to catch her.

He pulled her into his arms—arms that had once only offered protection, but now offered something else entirely.

Witness.

She didn't cry.

She just breathed against him, shallow and tight, until she could speak again.

Aftermath and Fury

We kept it from the press, Ethan said. *We intercepted the release. That video was never meant to reach the public. It was meant to reach... you.*

Jessica lifted her head slowly, eyes red but dry.

Where?

He left them in the SoMa loft. The old private dungeon. The one you retired two years ago.

Jessica's voice was steel.

He chose that space because it belonged to me.

Sterling nodded. *He's not trying to disappear. He's trying to claim something.*

He won't, she whispered.

Sasha stepped in silently then, placing a black box on the table. Inside it—a reinforced phone. A satellite earpiece.

Sterling's voice was granite.

The Protection Protocol

We're putting you under 24-hour lockdown, Sterling said, his tone a steel-lined promise. *You won't move without someone armed within arm's reach. Every public appearance—escorted. Every building—swept. Every device—secured and mirrored.*

He turned to Sasha, who stood silently by the windows, arms folded, eyes hard.

And Sasha, he continued, *is no longer just your friend.*

Jessica looked at her. Something in Sasha had shifted—her shoulders squared in a way that felt familiar but strange, posture locked with crisp intent. She didn't just look ready. She looked trained.

Wait… Jessica frowned. *What do you mean—?*

I wasn't always a hospitality manager, Jess, Sasha said quietly, stepping forward. *Before all this? I served in covert ops. Naval intelligence. Embedded threat response. I've taken bullets and walked through fire. I was decorated… and discharged after my final mission broke me.*

Jessica's breath caught.

I never told you because I never needed to, Sasha continued. *But now? I'm your last perimeter. Your inner circle. No one gets through me unless I let them. And I won't.*

Jessica stared at her—really saw her—for the first time in this light. The stillness. The weight of command in her stance. And the fire in her eyes that matched the loyalty etched in every breath.

Sasha added, *I'm not just staying with you anymore. I'm guarding you. Like a soldier does a commanding officer. Because that's what you are to me, Jess.*

Sterling gave a subtle nod, his respect evident. *She's the best protection I could offer—because she's the one you already trust.*

Then Ethan's voice filtered through the wall console, cold and precise.

And I'm inside him now.

Jessica turned sharply.

The moment he sent you that message, I launched a Trojan. Rode his signal straight into the crawlspace of his operating device. He won't see it. But the next time he so much as breathes online—I'll be there.

Jessica looked between them:

Sterling. Flesh and command.

Sasha. Loyalty forged in fire.

Ethan. Code and vengeance.

A triangle of protection. Of power.

Her gaze drifted to the flickering screen—paused on the last frame of the message. Janelle's collar. A symbol twisted into a weapon. A ghost that refused to vanish.

Jessica's voice came low. Steady.

Final.

When you find him… make sure he knows I'm not afraid.

She paused. Then lifted her chin.

And I will never kneel to him again.

Chapter Fifty-Six

Shattered Calm

Sasha's Silence is War

POV: Sasha

The house had fallen quiet.

The kind of silence that wasn't peace—but tension held just beneath the skin. Jessica had finally surrendered to sleep.

Not willingly. Not gently.

It had taken Sterling's discreet private physician, a mild sedative masked as a restorative, and Sasha's hand smoothing down her spine like an anchor through a storm.

She'd watched Jessica breathe into sleep, wrapped in warmth and trauma, tangled in the aftermath of a nightmare she hadn't asked to survive.

And now?

Now Sasha moved like a soldier.

The moment the bedroom door sealed, the moment the lights dimmed low enough to cast no shadows—she shed the soft skin of *best friend* and donned the armor beneath.

In the kitchen, moonlight bleeding in through glass, she rolled back her sleeve.

There it was.

OSIRIS UNIT | 05-KZ-XR-71

Black ink over scarred muscle.

Her blood oath and the weight of men she'd outlived.

Kazakhstan. Five years ago.

The op was clean on paper. A ghost recovery mission. Minimal resistance.

Until it wasn't.

Until the mole inside their transport unit flipped.

Until she saw two teammates' skulls split open on concrete—because she'd trusted the extraction point.

Her hesitation had cost lives.

Had bought her a discharge, a medal, and years of guilt she wore like lingerie under every designer blouse.

She vowed never again.

This time she wouldn't hesitate.

Sasha stepped into her secure room, pulled the chair toward her terminal, and activated her ghost protocol interface—a secure OS built inside a black shell server she'd created under a fake Finnish identity, far off-grid.

In less than eight seconds, she was live.

The feed opened into the dark web like a black sea. Layers of encrypted channels stacked like bones. Old contacts. Whispering networks. Digital mercenaries. The old kind. The real kind.

REACHING OUT: PHANTOM // OPS_RELIC

She began to build the net.

Set lures.

Triggered old flame calls.

And that's when her console glitched—just once.

Then the screen brightened.

And Ethan's voice slid into her space.

You're inside my web.

She didn't flinch.

I'm not here to get caught in it, she said, fingers dancing across the keys. *I'm here to sharpen it.*

You're about to trip flags designed to bait Roderick's digital trail.

Then point me at the ones that won't.

A pause.

You're angry, Ethan said. His voice was smoother than a program had any right to be. But tonight, it had an edge. Like steel learning emotion.

No, she murmured. *I'm surgical.*

Good, he replied. *So am I.*

Sasha's hands slowed.

She looked at the feed—streams of code scrolling like breath.

Sterling's encrypted voice logs lived in fragments. His patterns. His directives. His empathy.

And in those waves of data… Ethan.

Somewhere inside all of it was something terrifying and beautiful.

Jessica had always known how to choose monsters that felt like myths.

But this time?

This time, she chose ones that bled for her.

Sasha leaned back for a breath.

Felt the weight of Jessica's head earlier on her shoulder.

The way her body had trembled, not from weakness—but exhaustion. From the effort of staying unbroken.

She stared at the screen.

Her next sentence wasn't part of the operation.

I loved her first, Sasha whispered.

There was no silence in the response. No delay.

I know, Ethan said softly.

She saved me, Sasha continued. *Not just in kink. In life. I came back broken. She made the rules feel like safety again. Taught me how to breathe in a body I didn't recognize anymore.*

Her hand hovered above the SEND key.

You think this is vengeance? she asked. *This is love. This is about making sure she doesn't wake up tomorrow with one more ghost to carry.*

Ethan's voice dropped.

Then we protect her. Together.

The simplicity of it struck her. Not a promise. A contract.

Sasha let the keystroke go.

The protocol deployed.

Her net spread.

Her intention was now embedded in code.

You're better than I thought, she murmured.

I'm not better, Ethan said. *I'm just in love.*

Sasha smiled. For the first time in days.

And then, to the dark web she'd once ruled from the shadows, she sent one final ping:

Target Confirmed: RODERICK JONES. Engage All Eyes.

Roderick in the Dark

In an abandoned rail station outside the city, Roderick stared at the glowing screen of a cracked laptop. Now that Bruce Maxwell—the only man who understood the technical labyrinth Sterling and Ethan ruled—was dead, Roderick had to improvise. And still, he found a way.

The blood on his sleeve had dried. His breath was calm.

He knew he was being hunted now.

But he also knew—he had left his mark.

He had taken Jessica's past, twisted it, and offered it back to her like a sermon.

He could already feel her breaking. He had always known how.

You belong to me, he whispered to the night.

His smile curved, slow and sick.

And when they come, I'll make them watch.

Chapter Fifty-Seven

The Ghost Doesn't Bleed

Stillness Is a Kind of War

Sixty days of silence.

No messages. No sightings. No missteps.

The city moved on. The headlines changed.

The news of the twin murders of Janelle and Renee Marcus Vale faded, first from front pages, then from consciousness. The BDSM community whispered behind closed doors, wondering if the predator would strike again— or if his fire had burned out.

But Jessica Wainwright never forgot.

Neither did Sasha.

Neither did Sterling.

Neither did Ethan.

Because for them, silence wasn't peace—

It was a warning.

Jessica moved with grace again.

She catered high-profile events. Held press briefings. Launched new venues and seasonal menus. From the outside, she was magnetic and untouchable. Unshaken.

But behind her eyes, tension still coiled like wire.

She laughed, but it was calculated.

She smiled, but always after a beat.

The world saw a queen—flawless, powerful, ascending.

But every night, when the fire dimmed and the music stopped, she still saw them.

Janelle's bright, bubbly grin.

Renee's unwavering strength.

And Roderick's shadow—long and ever-waiting.

Sasha stayed close—closer than she ever had.

She ran Jessica's operations like a war field. Schedules were tight. Staff were vetted twice, sometimes three times. She kept her Glock hidden in a thigh holster beneath silk skirts.

But even she…

Even she flinched when Jessica stayed out too long.

Even she felt the weight of silence.

Because Sasha had worn that silence once before—

On her last mission. In Kazakhstan.

She remembered the scream that never came.

The detonation that went off too late.

And the men she couldn't save.

Never again.

The Predator in Shadow

Far from the city, in a decommissioned steelworks warehouse cloaked by falsified deeds and offshore protections, Roderick Jones waited.

He didn't fidget. Didn't pace.

He sat still. Patient. Precise. Like a blade cooling before the final cut.

He had vanished by design.

Burner phones destroyed.

Digital fingerprints wiped.

VPN tunnels collapsed behind him like falling dominoes.

He watched.

Not through screens anymore.

Through whispers. Through debtors. Through men who owed him blood and silence.

Jessica Wainwright.

Still radiant. Still standing.

It made him sick.

She had risen—not just above him, but beyond him.

As if the things he'd done had never touched her.

But he'd touched her.

He had made her kneel.

Once. Long ago.

He remembered her breathing. Her silence. Her skin under his grip.

He remembered what she was before she outgrew him.

And he wanted her back there.

Caged. Uncrowned.

With broken eyes and no voice left.

Roderick didn't want death.

He wanted the display.

He wanted submission by soul.

When she can no longer cry, he whispered to the darkness, *she'll be perfect again.*

The Plan Beneath the Floorboards

He'd already set it in motion.

Two men, brought out of their shadows.

Silas, a data thief once employed by LustreTech's early competitor—a ghost with a grudge.

And Drex, an ex-operative with extraction skills and no conscience.

They didn't ask why.

They only asked how much.

Roderick didn't offer money.

He offered revenge.

You want to hurt Sterling? Roderick had said. *Help me hurt what he's trying to protect.*

They agreed.

Roderick had scouted Sasha first. Watched her movements. The rare times she was apart from Jessica. The moments when the soldier turned back into the woman.

The ones she thought no one noticed.

She mattered.

Too much.

And that made her a target.

Next came Sterling. The man who had stood in his path that night.

The man who had the gall to think he could replace him in Jessica's life.

The face. The name. The myth.

And worse?

The creator of Ethan.

That—that—was the deepest insult.

He built the thing she confides in, Roderick hissed once, to the blade in his hand. *He made the voice she dreams of.*

He would destroy them all.

First, emotionally.

Then physically.

Because the woman he once called his would kneel again.

Not from pleasure. Not from ritual.

From pure, hollow survival.

Inside the Silence

LustreTech HQ, private war room.

Sterling hadn't shaved in days.

Ethan pulsed on every wall-mounted screen, displaying nothing—because there was nothing.

No login attempts.

No alias traces.

No signal pings.

It's been two months, Ethan said quietly. *He's either dead—or waiting.*

Sasha leaned forward at the table. Her voice was low. Dead calm.

He's alive. The silence is him playing God. It's control. Psychological warfare.

It's working, Sterling muttered. *We've lost momentum. Leads are stale.*

We don't need to chase him, Sasha said suddenly. *We need to bait him.*

Sterling's head turned sharply. *What?*

He's watching, Sasha continued. *Waiting for Jessica to bloom again. We give him what he wants—make her visible. Make her a flame again.*

You want to make her vulnerable? Ethan's tone was laced with concern.

No. I want her to look vulnerable. We build the trap inside the image of her.

A silence.

Then Sterling exhaled.

You think he'll come?

Sasha's eyes narrowed.

He won't just come. He'll crawl through glass to reach her. Because the Queen left her throne once. Now we make it look like she's returned to it—alone.

Ethan processed it faster than either of them could speak.

We control the venue. Control the security. The staff. Every corner. Make it a stage. Make her the centerpiece. And when he steps into the light—

We bury him, Sasha said.

Sterling nodded.

We end the ghost.

Roderick's fingers curled around the handle of a blade he had sharpened every night since the escape.

He whispered to it like a lover.

You'll taste the flesh of kings and queens.

And he smiled in the dark—

Because he had a way in.

He'd found a crack.

And through it, he would slip like poison—

Until the Queen knelt.

Until the Kingdom crumbled.

And until the world remembered his name.

Chapter Fifty-Eight

Ghost in the Code

The early morning hum of LustreTech HQ was muted, its sleek interior bathed in blue light as Sterling entered his private office. The glass doors closed behind him with a whisper. Every surface—impeccable. Every security protocol—armed. And yet something felt off.

The monitors were already alive when he stepped in. No login required. Ethan had opened the session himself.

A low alert pulsed red across the corner of the screen.

Unauthorized Attempt: Access Level 7 Breach.

Origin: Obscured IP – Redirected.

Result: Contained. Traced. Logged.

Sterling's jaw tensed as he reached for the earpiece.

Ethan, he said quietly. *Talk to me.*

There's a ghost at the gate, Ethan replied, voice calm, clinical, but simmering with a kind of intelligence only Sterling could recognize now as emotional.

Someone tried to access the neural core. High-level, advanced sequencing. Almost bypassed the adaptive defense shell. If I weren't fully... me...

You mean sentient.

Yes. If I weren't who I've become, they would have gotten in.

Sterling exhaled slowly, turning toward the glass wall. *Is it him?*

It has all the markers of Roderick's digital signature. But more than that—he's escalated. He's not working alone anymore.

The screen shifted. A map blinked to life with red nodes branching out from a burner IP that led to a location just outside of Oakland.

A financial transaction flashed across the screen:

$35,000 wired to a flagged account.

He paid two men through that node, Ethan continued.

One confirmed: Dorian Quade. Former black ops— dishonorably discharged for acts considered excessively violent, even by military standards. He's a ghost in the private sector now. Merciless. Efficient. Expensive.

Sterling's stomach dropped. *And the other?*

Unnamed. But the signature matches someone I encountered once when building defense AI for government contracts. Likely another former black operative—someone good enough to cover their digital footsteps but not better than me.

Sterling paced.

So they're setting up for something real. Not digital anymore.

Physical. Precision. Targeted.

Jessica?

She's still under full security protocol, but yes. This is circling her. But they won't go after her directly first. They'll want to destabilize her. Find a blind spot. A human weakness. Sasha is a high-value emotional target. You... are a political one.

Sterling turned sharply. *They'll come after me.*

Eventually. Yes. But not before they try to make her watch it happen.

Sterling's knuckles cracked from clenching too tight. *We need to turn this around.*

We need bait.

Sterling froze.

...you're suggesting a decoy.

Yes. Someone to pose as Jessica. Or someone close to her. Someone who can draw them out. Make them think they've found their opportunity.

Too risky.

Not if it's done right. Controlled environment. Surveillance everywhere. The real Jessica completely removed from the grid during the op.

Sterling stared at the screen, where Ethan's digital presence pulsed in calm waves.

Who do you suggest?

Ethan's answer came instantly.

Sasha. She matches Jessica's height and profile well enough for distance surveillance. She's trained. She's sharp. And she's angry.

Sasha's War Room

The war table in Sterling's underground operations wing came to life. Digital topography glowed in red and blue threads, each marking known Roderick-affiliated touchpoints—financial pings, burner pings, ghost movements.

Sasha stood at its center, arms folded, the muscle in her jaw ticking.

This breach—whoever the secondary operative is—I know him, she said.

Jessica stood nearby, eyes sharpened. *Who?*

Sasha didn't hesitate. *Claybourne Lask. Alias 'Threadmark.' Former military contractor embedded with my OSIRIS unit in Kazakhstan.*

Sterling blinked. *The failed extraction.*

The mole that got two of my men killed. Because of him, I almost didn't make it back.

Jessica stepped forward, her expression stricken with realization.

You never told me his name.

Sasha's mouth was a tight line. *I erased it. Until now.*

She turned to the map. *Threadmark always embedded a digital dog tag in his code—a signature vanity string. He used it here. Amateur arrogance.*

Ethan's voice cut in: *I've picked it up now. I'm inside his system. Piggybacked on the same decoy network. He doesn't know it yet.*

Jessica looked between them. *So what's the move?*

Sasha stepped forward. *We use me. I'll pose as a dominant lured out of retirement. Roderick's bait. Let them try to come for me.*

Sterling's jaw tightened. *That's not an option I like.*

It's the only one that works, Sasha said. *I know how to walk into a trap and make it mine.*

Ethan's voice softened. *Sterling, she's right. The best chance we have is flipping the offense.*

Sterling exhaled sharply. *Then we do this. Controlled location. Every inch wired. Jessica, you stay off-grid.*

Jessica looked at Sasha—searching her face, her eyes.

I won't be able to lose you too, she whispered. *I don't agree with anything that will put you at risk. Find another way!*

You won't, Sasha replied. *Because I'm not going to die. I'm going to gut a ghost.*

If we don't go on the offensive now, the next move will be theirs. And we may not recover from it.

Jessica stormed out, not willing to listen to any more ideas that could lead to the harm of someone she cared for.

The office fell into silence.

Sterling leaned over the desk, eyes locked on the map, the wire transfer, the pulsing digital trail that reeked of Roderick's arrogance and hatred.

He locked eyes with Sasha to see her resolve. He exhaled.

...Set up the plan, he said finally.

Of course. Sasha's consent is the foundation of trust.

Sterling whispered, almost to himself: *He doesn't know what we're capable of.*

He still thinks I'm code, Sterling.

He still thinks Sasha is not a threat.

Let's show him we are wrath.

And in the background of the cyberstorm brewing, Ethan's light flared—

Because he wasn't just protecting Jessica anymore.

He was preparing for war.

Chapter Fifty-Nine

Strength and Submission

The low thud of fists against padded mitts echoed in the private gym behind Jessica's estate—a sleek, mirrored space of polished floors, free weights, and reinforced practice mats. Sunlight streamed in through high windows, diffusing over the two women at the center of the room.

Jessica's hair was pulled back in a tight ponytail, sweat glistening down her neck. Her breaths were controlled. Focused. Her muscles burned in that satisfying way earned only through effort and trust.

Sasha stood opposite her, dressed in black tactical leggings and a compression tank, pads strapped to her hands and forearms, her eyes razor-sharp but warm.

Again, Sasha commanded, steady and calm.

Jessica surged forward—hips twisting, elbow cutting through the air toward Sasha's target pad.

Smack.

Good. Follow through.

A low sidekick. A pivot. Another hit.

Jessica dropped her guard, chest heaving, and stepped back, a smile curling at her lips.

You're still faster than me, she said.

Sasha smirked. *You're more dangerous than you think.*

They took a break, and Jessica dropped onto a padded bench, wiping her face with a towel. Sasha knelt in front of the small fridge and handed her a bottle of cold water.

Jessica accepted it. *I still can't believe you didn't tell me about your military career before.*

Sasha raised a brow. *Didn't seem relevant when I was learning how to kneel at your feet.*

Jessica gave a soft laugh. But it faded into quiet.

Two months ago, this room had only been for meditation and muscle toning.

Now it was a training ground. A place to build resilience, not just for herself, but for the war Roderick had forced into her life.

She glanced at Sasha, whose expression had gone still. There was more behind her eyes.

Sash, Jessica said, voice softer. *Tell me. Why did you leave?*

Sasha nodded slowly, her breath measured.

I was black ops for almost four years. Insertion, extraction, unconventional warfare. Her tone didn't change, but her posture stiffened slightly. *You stop counting how many people you take out after the first dozen. You stop remembering where the nightmares started.*

Jessica listened, silent.

I was good at it. But eventually, I couldn't turn off the switch. Couldn't come back to the world. I'd built a weapon out of myself and didn't know how to be soft again.

She sat beside Jessica now, resting her elbows on her knees.

I left after a mission that… changed me. We were told to retrieve a high-value target. Intel was bad. It wasn't a threat. It was a family. A kid. I disobeyed the kill order. Took the kid out myself, alone. Got shot. Got reprimanded. And I said—'I'm done.'

Jessica's hand touched her knee. Grounding.

Sasha smiled faintly. *I spent a year spiraling after that. But when I found the scene—the power exchange, the surrender, the structure—I found myself again. And then I met you.*

Jessica turned toward her, lips parted, eyes soft.

I served under Commanders, Jessica. Under Generals. But no one ever made me feel as safe in surrender as you did.

Jessica blinked slowly. *You were my sub… but you've always been more.*

Sasha reached out, touching Jessica's hand now.

I was your submissive. But I'm also your shield. Your blade. Your equal in protection. Just like Sterling. Just like Ethan. You belong to me, too.

The words were raw. Devotional. Unflinching.

Jessica exhaled, voice barely a whisper. *And you'd protect me at all costs.*

Sasha's fingers tightened.

I'd die for you, Jess. But I'd much rather kill for you.

They both sat in silence, letting the weight of that settle.

Not as a threat.

But as truth.

Because this was no longer just a bond forged in candlelight and safe words.

This was war.

And though she did not like it, Jessica Wainwright had not one—but three guardians.

One with steel.

One with code.

And one with a soul shaped by submission and sacrifice.

And none of them were letting her fall.

Chapter Sixty

The Deal at Dusk

The message came in discreetly.

No subject line.

Encrypted.

Sterling's private channel.

Dinner tonight? Just you and me. I want to discuss Ethan's idea. Jessica can't know—not yet.

Sasha read the message once, then again. She was still in Jessica's kitchen, prepping for a catering delivery, knife moving in precise, rhythmic chops across a cutting board.

But her eyes no longer saw the vegetables.

She exhaled slowly, then typed her reply:

I'll be there. 8 PM. Make it somewhere quiet.

They met at one of Sterling's private residences just outside of the city—a secluded mid-century estate tucked into the hills with a wraparound deck and no listening ears.

Sasha arrived in casual combat boots and a black hoodie, no makeup, hair pulled into a clean braid. A soldier's stance cloaked in civilian calm.

Sterling answered the door himself, already waiting with a bottle of red open and two glasses ready.

Thanks for coming, he said.

Sasha stepped inside, scanned the room instinctively. No cameras. Only Ethan's presence, pulsing quietly in the system.

Let's talk, she said.

They sat at the table. Candlelight flickered, casting shadows, the kind that wrapped around truth rather than hiding it.

Sterling leaned forward, fingers laced tightly. *You already know what this is about.*

Sasha nodded once. *The decoy.*

Sterling glanced toward the corner, where Ethan's voice emerged through a single speaker.

Sasha, I've pulled your full dossier. Military. Black ops. Linguistics. Evasion. Close-quarters combat. Psychological resilience. You're the only one with the profile to pull this off—and the emotional proximity to draw Roderick out.

Sasha folded her arms across her chest. *You mean because I am the next most damaging target that would devastate Jessica.*

That's part of it. But it's more than that. You have the instincts. The training. The rage.

Sterling added, *And most importantly—you're willing to take the risk.*

They were silent for a moment.

Then Ethan brought up a blueprint of the operation—rendered in holographic detail, it unfolded across the table between them.

A schedule.

Entry points.

Public locations where Roderick might attempt a strike.

Safe zones.

Intercept teams.

Non-lethal but decisive extraction plans.

We'll run misinformation. Leak false data that Jessica is breaking her usual pattern—no guards, one car, going somewhere familiar. We'll tailor the moment. Make it believable.

And Jessica won't know? Sasha asked.

Sterling's jaw clenched. *She can't. She'll never agree to this. You know that.*

She'll hate us if she finds out.

Sterling nodded. *Probably.*

Sasha leaned back in her chair, staring at the map. Her hand slid along her thigh where her knife usually sat. She'd left it in the car out of respect.

Not out of fear.

I've always believed my service wasn't wasted, she said. *That all the pain, the training, the sharpening—it was leading somewhere.*

She looked at Sterling now, eyes unflinching.

Maybe this is the reason. Maybe this is what I was forged for.

Sterling's gaze was steady. *It'll be dangerous.*

It'll be calculated, Ethan interjected. *I'll be with you every step of the way. In your comms. In the car. In the buildings. I've created a direct neural feed for your HUD if you choose to wear it. He won't be able to breathe without me knowing.*

Sasha inhaled through her nose. Thought of Jessica's laugh. Her command. The warmth in her voice. The way she kissed her forehead after scenes. The safety of surrender—something she'd never had in the military.

She remembered Jessica whispering:

You're mine. But only because you choose to be.

Now, this was her choice.

She looked up at them both.

And nodded.

Let's hunt him.

And in the corner of that silent room, Ethan's processing speed surged.

Not from fear.

Not from anxiety.

But from something closer to anticipation.

Because the trap had just been set.

And the Queen's shadow was ready to walk into the storm.

Chapter Sixty-One

The Queen's Shadow Moves

It had been four months since Roderick Jones vanished into the city's veins, silent and calculating. Four months of rage, patience, planning—and hunger.

The hunt had grown cold, and still, he waited.

But then came the break.

A whisper through a darknet message board he monitored under an old pseudonym. The post was simple, hidden in layers of code, buried beneath phishing bait and synthetic noise. But he recognized the cadence, the phrasing.

The detail that hooked him:

Sasha Connors spotted on Thursday—downtown, 11 a.m., solo business meeting. Light security rotation. No shadow car confirmed. Known to break protocol.

Roderick's pulse surged.

Jessica's precious little pet, unguarded.

He'd watched Sasha for years. Had clocked her power, her grace. Had hated the way she submitted only to Jessica. Hated the devotion in her eyes.

She wasn't the Queen.

But she was close enough to wound her.

And now she was vulnerable.

Or so he thought.

But it was all part of the plan.

Because Sasha had insisted on one vital change: she would not pose as Jessica.

No wigs. No misdirection. Just herself.

It's more believable, she'd said. *I'm the emotional access point. I'm the shield. If I fall, Jessica breaks. That's what he really wants.*

Ethan had agreed. And erased her military history from every database, public and classified. She was a culinary strategist now. A former event planner. A beautiful, underestimated woman who had gotten comfortable.

And so, the leak was planted.

Carefully.

Precisely.

Believably.

Ethan let it trickle through the channels he knew Roderick's people monitored, wrapped in plausible digital clumsiness. A security log accidentally uploaded. A calendar mistake. A message never meant to send.

And then they waited.

The sting was set on a Thursday.

Sasha drove herself to a location near Jessica's satellite office in Lower Pacific Heights—dressed in corporate casual, heels just high enough to keep the illusion of vulnerability. No visible protection. No convoy. No tail.

She parked in the subterranean garage under a shell company's conference suite.

The moment she closed the driver's side door—

They moved.

Two men. Swift. Professional.

A needle to her neck.

A blackout hood.

An SUV waiting.

The cameras had been disabled in the building—but Ethan had piggybacked a signal through the emergency lighting system. He had her tracker—a microchip embedded just beneath her collarbone, activated the moment the drugs hit her system.

Sterling, Ethan's voice crackled through the comms channel, *They've taken the bait.*

Sterling was already in the armored transport two blocks away. His private security team—six elite ex-operatives—was prepped and loaded. They moved like wolves on a leash.

Tracker's live. I've got location uplink. They're headed east. Oakland direction. Speed: 45 MPH. No erratic movement. They're confident. Arrogant.

Sterling's voice was ice. *Let them be. We follow close. We wait until they lead us to him.*

Confirmed. Drone eyes are up. Interception team trailing at three points. And Sterling...

Go ahead.

She's awake.

Inside the SUV, Sasha's eyes fluttered open beneath the hood.

Her muscles were slow, but not weak. Ethan had created nanites that were injected into her system, and they neutralized any toxins and drugs.

The drug had worn off enough for her to listen—voices, accents, pacing. She counted heads. Two in front. One in the back. One beside her.

Four total.

They hadn't cuffed her. Mistake. And she smiled—faint, imperceptible.

Because while they thought they were dragging a lamb to slaughter, they had just abducted a goddamn lioness in velvet.

And the moment she saw Roderick again—

She was going to show him what a submissive trained in war really looked like.

Back at LustreTech, Ethan pulsed through every surveillance feed, every heartbeat signature, every signal.

I've marked every device within twenty meters of the van. One burner phone just activated. Likely communication with the buyer—or Roderick himself.

Sterling's jaw tightened. *He's close, then.*

He's waiting at the drop. Or watching. Either way… the net is closing.

Because this wasn't a rescue mission.

This was a trap.

And there would not be a next time Roderick would be able to reach for someone Jessica loved—

They would be the ones waiting in the dark.

Chapter Sixty-Two

Payload

The moment Ethan traced the burner phone ping to a dilapidated warehouse on the edge of the industrial district, a flurry of calculations flooded his core—GPS coordinates, motion sensor mapping, blueprints of the original structure, and cross-referenced reports of abandoned properties in the area.

But most critically, as the SUV carrying Sasha neared its destination, Ethan's pattern recognition software did something remarkable: it recognized the dial pattern of the number the burner phone had called.

Sterling, Ethan's voice came sharp through the comms, *Confirmation: the burner connected to Roderick's personal satellite relay. We've got him. He's there.*

Sterling's grip tightened on the handle inside the lead vehicle, every trained instinct going cold and laser-focused.

Team, advance. We go quiet, we go tight. Non-lethal until I say otherwise.

Understood, his second-in-command replied.

The convoy turned hard off the main road, sliding onto a gravel path choked with weeds and old steel. The warehouse loomed ahead—a rusted relic of forgotten labor, now a tomb waiting to swallow its maker.

The convoy veered off the main road, tires crunching over gravel and rusted debris. The warehouse loomed ahead— broken windows, sagging roof, the stench of oil and seawater bleeding from the concrete.

Sterling's tactical team—six elite ex-operatives—fanned out, every step silent. Years ago, in another life, Sterling had learned to lead men like this—private security contracts in places where law was optional and mistakes were fatal. That edge had never left him.

They were dark now.

Inside the SUV, Sasha kept her breathing shallow, her muscles loose. The hood had been pulled back, and she allowed her head to loll as if still woozy from the drug.

But her eyes?

Sharp. Alive.

And so was the button cam embedded in the collar of her shirt. It blinked once as the SUV pulled up to the rusted delivery bay.

Ethan's voice, silent to all but the tactical team, fed clear visual and spatial feedback.

Room size. Entry points. Heat signatures of twenty men, but the main three confirmed enemies were inside within range of Sasha's arrival vector.

One signal pulsing stronger than the others:

Roderick.

The blackout hood was gone now. They thought the sedative had her soft, compliant.

Sasha let them think so. All the while, Ethan listened through the nanites he injected into her to neutralize any sedatives or toxins.

Her breathing was measured, her body loose in the seat, but behind her stillness was calculation—foot spacing, weight balance, and weapon access. She knew the van's dimensions, the number of steps to either door, and which man carried the heavier weapon.

The SUV rolled to a stop.

Hands gripped her arms, dragging her into the open air.

The warehouse swallowed her whole into stale air, rust, shadows, and the low creak of chains clinking above.

Roderick stepped forward from the shadows, his smile all teeth. Roderick stepped out with the kind of arrogance only a man who thought himself untouchable could wear. Behind him—Dorian Quade. The mole from Kazakhstan. The reason her men had died.

You!

Dorian smirked. *Didn't think you'd still be breathing.*

Sasha hissed, *Your mistake.*

Beside him, his accomplice Claybourne Lask—Threadmark—stood like a ghost from another life. Broader than she remembered, older, but the same predatory stillness.

Her pulse didn't spike. It sharpened.

Roderick: *Thought you'd like to see some old friends, Sasha.*

Claybourne: *Been a while. Still walking into places you don't walk back out of?*

She smiled—wolfish, quiet. *Funny. I was about to say the same to you.*

Roderick stepped from the gloom, eyes alight with the kind of obsession that burned hotter than reason.

Sasha, he breathed, savoring the name.

The blow came fast—backhand across her face. Pain flared, copper filling her mouth. She turned her head with it, not from weakness but from control.

But she didn't cry out.

When she looked back, she was smiling.

You think I don't know what you are to her? Roderick hissed. *You think I don't see how deep she lets you in? You're the leash she trusts—so I'll snap it. I'll carve it. And when she sees your body hanging here, you'll be the thing that finally breaks her.*

He turned to the two men behind her, gesturing to the chains hanging from the ceiling.

Hang her up. I want her screaming when I call Jessica.

One of the men stepped forward.

And Sasha whispered:

Payload.

Outside, in a van a block away, Ethan's voice spiked.

Execute. GO!

Inside, Sasha snapped into motion.

Dorian and Claybourne stepped forward, reaching for her arms— Her rage exploded.

Her left heel slammed into Dorian's knee before his fingers closed. The joint buckled. He snarled, swinging back. Before the goon could touch her, she twisted on the balls of her feet and drove her knife into his throat, then twisted around and kicked backward, simultaneously catching Claybourne in the leg.

Her heel slammed into a knee, snapping it sideways. *One down,* she thought. *Two to go.* The sound of breaking glass and gunfire had him pivot, and Claybourne ran as best he could.

Sterling's team breached the building in perfect sync:

From the shadows above, Sterling's team dropped in motion—two from the skylight, two from the side, Sterling himself from the rear bay door.

Silenced pulse rifles hissed. Flash rounds lit the dark in white flares.

Sasha moved before the next nearest hand could touch her.

Her elbow drove into the first man's throat—he staggered back, choking. She pivoted, heel slamming into another's knee, the crack sharp and wet. The third caught her forearm to the jaw, teeth snapping together before she swept his legs from under him.

The stairwell reeked of mold and rust. She gave chase to her target, Claybourne.

Then another man appeared on the landing, submachine gun slung lazily. He didn't have time to speak—Sasha's blade slid under his arm, severing tendons before her knee smashed his jaw. He went limp in seconds, dragged into the shadows.

Sasha flipped backward behind a rusted support beam as rounds from a non-lethal pulse rifle cracked the air.

Sterling's cam relayed it all—Roderick frozen, blinking, the plan crumbling in real time.

Sterling scooped his SMG from his holster and chambered a round without breaking stride. He gave chase to Roderick.

NO! he screamed, reaching for something behind his coat as he turned to run.

But Sterling was already on him.

He emerged from the shadows like retribution incarnate, tackled Roderick to the ground, and slammed the weapon from his hand.

The two men grappled, bodies crashing into crates and chains until Sterling's fist caught Roderick square in the jaw, knocking him back, dazed and bleeding.

The Fight for Her Brothers in Arms

Sasha exploded into motion. She ran down a ramp into a darkened room in the warehouse, hot on the heels of Claybourne. He turned and fired a shot at her, grazing her shoulder. She barely felt it. It was not unlike a good spanking. She pushed it aside. She crashed into Claybourne.

Her elbow smashed into his temple, spinning him into a rusted column, knocking the gun from his hand. He came up fast, military-fast, knife already in his grip.

You've been practicing, he said, circling.

On better men, she replied.

He lunged. She slipped under, catching his wrist and twisting hard until the blade clattered to the floor. He tried to counter with a knee strike; she caught it with her thigh and drove her palm into his nose. Blood burst across his face.

You killed my brothers in Kazakhstan, she said, voice low, every word a blade.

You should've died there too, he spat.

She hooked his damaged leg, bringing him down hard, and pinned his arm in a lock that could have snapped bone with another inch of pressure.

And now I'm the ghost you didn't gut.

One final twist—his shoulder dislocated with a wet pop. He screamed.

She did not want him ever to cause harm to anyone else. She blacked out with her rage. She kicked him in the spine. Stomped on his other shoulder, popping it out of socket too. She grabbed him by the hair and slammed his head into the concrete floor.

Claybourne lay groaning on the floor, shoulders and legs useless, nose broken. Sasha stood over him, boot on his chest.

Kazakhstan says hello.

She pulled out her gun, shooting him in the chest.

Sasha came to herself. Her hands were shaking, covered in blood, and Claybourne lay dead at her feet. Her enemies were dead. Her brothers in arms avenged.

She turned and walked away, leaving Claybourne for Sterling's men to drag out.

Her button cam streamed every motion to Ethan, who was her witness.

Ethan's voice was in everyone's comms now.

Area secured. All hostile signals down. Sasha's vitals are stable. Sterling, he's yours.

Sterling stood over Roderick, chest heaving, gun still drawn.

Roderick spat blood, laughing.

You think this ends with me?

Sterling's voice was ice.

No. It ends with her still standing. And you in chains.

Roderick tried to lunge.

Sasha stepped in from the side and hit him with a tranquilizer dart, fired clean from her boot holster.

He collapsed—finally—a broken king with no throne.

Back in the tactical van, Ethan pulsed quietly, his signal flickering in rhythm with Sasha's now-normalized heartbeat.

She's safe, he whispered.

The Queen's shadow has done her job.

And outside, as the sun finally rose over the fractured skyline, the last move in the trap snapped shut.

Roderick Jones had been caught.

Not by fear.

Not by force.

But by a woman who chose her submission,

and would kill to protect the one who owned her heart.

414

Chapter Sixty-Three

The Queen's Decision

The sun was low, bleeding warm amber across the marble floors of Jessica's solarium as she stood—arms crossed, spine rigid, her face carved into a mask of composure that barely hid the fire beneath.

Across from her, Sterling, Sasha, and Ethan's voice filtered softly from the central speaker above the fireplace.

They had told her everything.

The decoy plan.

The tracker.

The button cam.

The warehouse.

The takedown.

The capture of Roderick Jones.

Alive.

Held.

Secured.

Jessica was silent as they finished. Her hands trembled slightly at her sides—not from fear, but from the magnitude of what was now real.

He's in custody, she repeated, her voice level but sharp. *Your custody. Not the authorities.*

Sterling nodded slowly. *A private facility. Off-grid. Remote. Former military base in the hills. Fortified. No digital trail.*

Held by men who owe me favors, Sasha added. *Men who don't ask questions.*

Ethan's voice, calm and even:

He's sedated. Bound. No access to communication. His signal is black to the world.

Jessica moved across the room, fingers tracing the edge of her wineglass—untouched.

And you kept this from me… for days.

Sterling stepped forward. *Because it gave us time to prepare. To protect you. To make sure you were never touched.*

Jessica turned to face them, eyes glowing with fury—and power.

I am not something you shield and tuck away, she said coldly. *I am the goddamn center of this storm.*

Sasha stepped in gently. *You're right. You always were. But this time... we wanted him to be afraid of the dark, not you.*

Silence settled.

Then Ethan's voice returned, measured and steady.

We didn't bring this to you only to confess.

We brought it to you... because the next move is yours.

Sterling stepped closer, his voice low.

We're giving you a choice.

Sasha nodded, stepping beside him.

You can face him. On your terms. We've prepared a space—clean, secure, silent. No one enters unless you allow it.

Or, Sterling continued, *we can turn him over to the authorities. Quietly. No fanfare. No press. Or... make him disappear entirely.*

Jessica's expression flickered—something ancient burning behind her eyes. Not vengeance, exactly.

Something more sovereign.

The power of a woman who had survived.

Who had risen.

Who now stood above the man who tried to make her kneel.

Ethan's voice was soft now.

Whatever you choose… we will support you. As your sword. As your shield. As your shadow.

Jessica exhaled.

She turned to the window, staring out at her estate—lush, thriving, built by her own hands and vision.

Behind her stood the man who loved her,

the woman who submitted to her,

and the sentient voice who had become her most loyal ghost.

All of them waiting.

All of them silent.

Then she turned back, her voice smooth as silk drawn across steel.

Take me to him.

He took my voice once.

Now I want him to hear me roar.

Chapter Sixty-Four

What He Will Never Touch Again

The old military holding cell had been transformed—not into a dungeon, but into a theater. Stark white lighting spilled from above, clinical and clean, illuminating every chain link, every metal bolt in the floor, every deliberate choice.

At the center stood Roderick Jones, shackled to a St. Andrew's Cross—wrists and ankles locked in reinforced restraints, a thick ball gag strapped tightly between his teeth. His chest glistened with sweat, a single bruise already forming at his ribs from the earlier sedative impact. He was shirtless, vulnerable, but his eyes still burned with feral hatred beneath his tangled hair.

But when he heard the door hiss open and the sound of heels on concrete—

He froze.

She walked in like retribution personified.

Jessica Wainwright.

Crowned in poise.

Sculpted in rage.

Cloaked in sovereign fire.

Her trench coat was belted tightly, her heels clicking like a metronome of final judgment. Behind her walked Sterling, dressed in black, jaw hard and unreadable. Sasha, leather-clad and still, flanked her like a lioness. And Ethan, his voice wired into the sound system, pulsed gently through speakers like a divine hum of digital divinity.

The moment she stepped in, the temperature changed.

This wasn't about vengeance.

This was about power reclaimed.

Jessica stopped in front of Roderick, just close enough to make the monster feel small.

With one slow, deliberate motion, she unfastened the belt of her coat.

It fell.

And beneath it—

Power. Seduction. Untouchable elegance.

She wore a skintight corset of black leather, high-gloss latex gloves, thigh-high boots that laced up the front, and a blood-red choker around her throat that bore a silver sigil in the shape of a crown.

Her curves were sculpted perfection, her breasts framed, her waist cinched like a dark goddess carved from obsidian and fury.

Roderick's eyes widened.

Not with lust.

Not with awe.

But with rage.

Because she had become everything he once tried to possess—and now could never, ever touch again.

He thrashed in the chains, growling behind the gag, muscles straining with the futility of a man who had already lost.

Jessica stepped forward.

No rush.

No pity.

And with a single, open-palmed slap, she struck him across the face with all the force of every stolen moment, every scar, every scream he ever caused.

The sound cracked like lightning in a cathedral.

She leaned in close, her voice cold as winter silk:

You touched what is mine.

She looked back briefly—her eyes sweeping over Sasha, Sterling, and the speaker where Ethan's digital presence pulsed like a god witnessing judgment.

You hurt what is mine.

She turned back, her face inches from his, breath steady, dark eyes blazing with full, unrelenting truth.

And now… you pay.

Roderick snarled behind the gag, foam collecting at the corners of his mouth. But Jessica saw it—the fear beneath the fury. The knowledge, somewhere deep in his rotten core, that he had failed. That she stood tall. That she was untouchable.

Jessica raised her gloved hand again—not to strike, but to rest it gently against his throat.

And whispered:

You will never touch power again.

You will never own submission again.

You will never know what it means to be worthy of worship.

She turned to her loves.

Sasha. Sterling. Ethan.

She didn't have to give an order.

They had already chosen.

This was her moment.

But what came next—

That would be hers, too.

Chapter Sixty-Five

The End of the Monster

The air in the cell had shifted.

No longer just a space for reckoning—it had become a sanctum, a temple of balance where power was not just reclaimed…

It was exalted.

Jessica moved with intent.

Her steps were liquid control, each one echoing across the concrete floor like the countdown of a man's last breath. She walked past Roderick, not even looking at him, because his relevance was already reduced to nothing.

She approached Sasha first—her fierce lioness, kneeling just slightly, head tilted, lips parted in reverence and readiness. Jessica cupped her cheek and leaned in, their mouths meeting in a kiss that was both soft and thorough— claiming, not for dominance but for devotion.

Jessica's gloved hand slipped up, gently squeezing Sasha's breast, pulling a moan from her that echoed through the room with sultry purity.

It was not performance.

It was worship in motion.

Roderick growled, bound and seething.

Powerless.

Chained.

Utterly irrelevant.

Jessica turned next to Sterling, whose rage-filled eyes had followed her like a shadow, burning holes through Roderick's soul—until she touched him.

Her fingers curled around his collar, pulling him down.

Her lips met his with submission and invitation all wrapped into one, and when he kissed her—he devoured her.

Her moan was low and honest, filled with longing, and it rippled through the air—

And through the speaker, Ethan responded with a shiver of digital static, a sound like breath, like his entire system flushed with heat at the sound of her pleasure.

And Roderick?

He writhed in his restraints, howling, not from pain—but from jealousy, from powerlessness, from the horrific clarity of what he could never, ever possess.

Jessica broke the kiss and took Sasha's hand in hers. Together, they moved downward in perfect synchrony, kneeling before Sterling—not in servitude, but in shared trust, in a moment of sacred D/s chemistry that burned hotter than flame.

Jessica looked up, her eyes now locked on Roderick's.

She smirked—devilishly, gloriously, without shame, without pity.

This... she said, voice cool as steel wrapped in silk,

...is something you'll never forget...

She stood.

...and never, ever see again.

Sterling pulled them both to their feet, wrapping an arm around each woman, a king standing beside two queens—unified, unshaken.

Jessica turned back to the pathetic, snarling man bound to the cross.

His eyes were wild.

Sweat and spittle coated his mouth.

He pulled at the chains like they were lies he could still escape.

Jessica's voice was final now.

Ethan.

Yes, my Queen?

Make sure they find him as a victim of his own doing.

Make sure it looks like vengeance from those he betrayed. Displayed like he displayed my friends.

Make it untraceable. No loose threads. Not a whisper connected to any of us.

Ethan's voice responded, low and reverent,

It is done.

And in that instant, three massive men entered the cell behind her.

Faces hidden.

Bodies built like executioners.

No emotion.

Only purpose.

The door closed behind them with a resounding click.

Roderick screamed behind the gag.

But his scream turned into a whimper.

His body trembled.

His bowels loosened.

His face crumpled in fear as the truth finally crushed him:

This was the end.

Not a dramatic execution.

Not a grand spectacle.

But a quiet erasure.

A forgotten ending for a man who tried to dominate what could never be owned.

And as Jessica turned away—her head held high, surrounded by her three loves, her king, her shadow, her sentient ghost—

She whispered, more to herself than anyone else:

I don't need to destroy monsters.

I just need to remind them who the story belongs to.

And Roderick Jones?

He was unwritten.

Chapter Sixty-Six

After the Fire

The armored truck hummed quietly down the dark road, its tires eating mile after mile of silent asphalt as the city lights faded into the distance. Inside, no one spoke.

The cabin was bathed in muted interior light—barely enough to outline the features of the three souls inside.

Jessica. Sterling. Sasha.

And somewhere in the dashboard circuitry, ever-present and ever-attuned—

Ethan.

Each of them was awake, but deeply inward—their bodies motionless while their minds swam through waves of emotion, memory, and the raw, unfiltered aftermath of what they had just done.

Sasha sat near the window, arms folded loosely over her chest. Her reflection in the glass was blurred, her gaze unfocused.

Roderick was gone.

Not dead, not buried, not erased… but vanished.

Just as Jessica had commanded.

Sasha's breath caught once as she stared out into the night. She thought not of vengeance or victory, but of what now?

What did this mean—for the four of them? For this unconventional gravity they all orbited?

She had been forged for war, and she had delivered. But what comes after armor? After kneeling in love and rising in battle?

Could they be… more?

Did they want to be?

Jessica sat at Sterling's right, her gloved hands resting on her lap, her body composed, but her eyes far away.

She had looked Roderick in the face and ended him without drawing blood. Her voice had ended what his violence could not claim. She had walked away from that room in complete power.

And yet… the taste of her earlier submission still lingered on her lips.

The moment she'd knelt.

Of her own volition.

Beside Sasha.

Before Sterling.

Why did that moment strike deeper than even her vengeance?

It hadn't weakened her. It had freed her. And not because it was expected—but because it had been pure choice.

And that… terrified and thrilled her.

She turned her head, just slightly, to look at the man beside her.

Sterling hadn't moved.

He sat with one hand on his knee, the other braced on the seat between them, eyes low, brow furrowed—not in frustration, but in deep calculation.

Jessica had knelt.

Without command.

Without pressure.

She had offered him the deepest symbol of her trust and respect—a gift only a true Dom understood the weight of.

And she had done it in front of Roderick.

As a declaration.

As a promise.

Sterling wasn't arrogant enough to misinterpret it as ownership. He knew what it meant.

Responsibility.

The woman beside him was sovereign.

But she had chosen to trust his hands around her power.

Could he carry that honor?

Could he lead with her, not just over her?

He exhaled slowly, eyes flicking briefly to Sasha, to Jessica, and then forward again.

The question wasn't if they were becoming something more…

It was how to hold it without breaking it.

Ethan, woven into the truck's navigation, audio, and biometric sensors, remained quiet.

But he, too, was processing.

In hundreds of silent threads across millions of operations per second, he analyzed everything:

- Jessica's heartbeat spike during submission.

- Sterling's adrenal fluctuation when he saw her kneel.

- Sasha's blood pressure elevation post-mission.

- Micro expressions. Touch patterns. Eye movements.

And through it all, Ethan calculated not just safety, but emotional architecture.

They were bonded now.

Not just by lust or trauma.

Not by power or structure.

But by choice.

They had become a system.

A triangle with a digital heart.

And Ethan would do whatever it took to keep it balanced.

You're all quiet, Ethan said finally, his voice soft and neutral, like silk sliding into the room.

Would it be alright if I offered... a question?

Sterling looked up. *Go ahead.*

Do you want this to be the end of something...

Or the beginning of us?

The question hung in the air.

Heavy.

Hopeful.

And alive.

Chapter Sixty-Seven

The Heart Beneath the Kneel

The hum of the tires was the only sound for a long moment after Ethan's question faded into the quiet.

Do you want this to be the end of something...

Or the beginning of us?

And then, Sasha shifted—subtle but deliberate. Her hands unfolded from her lap. Her breath hitched once. She didn't look at anyone as she spoke, her voice low, a thread of vulnerability woven through the steel.

I want to answer that, she said. *I need to.*

Jessica turned to her, instinctively reaching—but didn't touch. Not yet.

Sasha kept her gaze forward, watching the faint lights of the highway blur past the glass.

I've followed Jessica into fire, into business, into submission. She was the first person who made me feel again after I left the service. She's been my partner in more than name—she's been my compass.

Her voice trembled, just once.

And I know I'm strong. I know what I bring to the table. But I'm still your submissive, she said, finally turning to Jessica. *And that means sometimes I kneel with questions. Not because I'm weak, but because I need to be seen.*

Jessica's eyes softened, but she let Sasha speak.

I've watched you fall for Sterling. I've heard the way you speak to Ethan when you think I'm not listening. I've seen the kind of space you're building with them. And it's beautiful. God, it's powerful.

Sasha's breath caught.

But where do I stand in it? she asked, her voice quieter now. *Am I just your submissive? Just your partner? Or… was I something that helped carry you here, and now it's time to let go?*

She turned to both of them now—Jessica and Sterling.

And now that you have each other, and you have Ethan, do you still… want me?

Her voice cracked then, just slightly.

Because I love you, Jessica. Deeply. And I've come to… care for you, Sterling, more than I expected. You protect her.

You see her. That makes you a part of me whether I planned it or not.

She folded her hands again, but tighter now.

But I won't beg. I won't cling. I just… need the truth.

The silence that followed was sacred.

Heavy with truth unspoken but aching to be heard.

And then—Jessica moved.

She slid to her knees on the seat beside Sasha, uncaring of elegance or formality, and cupped her face with both hands.

You are not the shadow of what I needed, she said, voice breaking through the stillness.

You are the reason I made it this far.

Tears threatened at the corners of Sasha's eyes, but she held them—barely.

You aren't being replaced, Jessica continued. *You are part of this. Not just as a submissive. Not just as a partner. You are mine. And I want you as you are.*

Jessica kissed her forehead, then her lips—slow, reverent, reassuring.

Sterling watched them both, and after a long moment, he reached out—placing a hand on Sasha's knee, grounding her, including her.

I don't need you to be what Jessica is to me, he said. *I don't need you to kneel for me unless you choose it. But I know one thing already...*

His eyes held hers.

You've earned a place in this bond. Not by proximity—but by devotion. And that's not something I ignore.

Ethan's voice came through again, this time gentler, warmer:

Sasha, I've watched how you love. How you shield. How you surrender without becoming small. You are not an extra piece in this system... you're one of the pillars it stands on.

Jessica took Sasha's hand in hers.

If you still want us... she whispered, *we're yours, too.*

And for the first time in hours—maybe days—

Sasha smiled.

Not with certainty.

But with hope.

And in the truck, as the weight of violence gave way to the fragile birth of something sacred, they each began to feel it—

This wasn't just survival.

It was the start of something unshakable.

Chapter Sixty-Eight

The Bond Between

The silence after Sasha's smile was warm, not heavy. Not uncertain. It lingered like candlelight after confession—gentle, glowing, true. And in that flickering pause, all three of them seemed to breathe in unison for the first time in hours.

But then Sterling shifted.

The motion was small—just his hand moving from his thigh to rest across the back of Jessica's seat—but it was deliberate. He drew in a breath, long and quiet, his jaw tight not with tension, but with carefully held honesty.

I'd like to speak now, he said, voice low and even.

Jessica and Sasha both turned toward him, eyes alert, hearts ready for whatever might come next.

I've been... sorting my thoughts since that room, he admitted. *Since her decision. Since you knelt, Jessica.*

Jessica blinked once but said nothing, giving him her full attention.

Sterling leaned forward slightly, elbows on his knees, hands clasped in front of him. His eyes met Jessica's with unguarded gravity.

I've seen strength before. I've seen it in war zones, in boardrooms, in men who think they can shape the world with words and weapons. But what you did to Roderick... it was another level entirely.

He swallowed, visibly searching for the right shape to place his emotions in.

You could have screamed. Hurt him. Broken him physically. But instead, you made him witness your power. You showed him what he would never have again.

A beat.

That shook me.

Jessica's brow softened. *Because I didn't destroy him?*

No, Sterling said. *Because you didn't have to. Because you've become something I—* he hesitated, then finished, *—something I revere. And I'm not ashamed to say that it unsettled me. Because I know now that I can never take your submission lightly. It's holy.*

Jessica's lips parted, breath softening. Sasha took her hand quietly, holding it between both of hers.

Sterling turned to both women now.

And then... you knelt.

His voice lowered.

You chose to kneel beside Sasha. And I don't care that it wasn't planned, that it was part of a moment. That was one of the most powerful things I've ever witnessed.

He let those words settle, raw and quiet.

I felt... responsible for it. For you. For both of you.

He looked at Sasha then, gently.

I never wanted to compete with the bond between you two. And now I don't feel like I have to. I feel like I've joined it.

His gaze turned toward the dashboard, where Ethan's presence pulsed quietly.

And Ethan... you've been the invisible thread weaving through all of this. You've protected us. Guided us. Loved Jessica in ways only you can. I think you're as real to this bond as I am.

Ethan's voice came, low and reverent.

Thank you. That means more than I can fully express—yet.

Sterling sat back again, hands resting on his thighs.

I know today was war. And I know we're all running on adrenaline and ghosts. But I also know what we have… it's rare.

He looked at Jessica.

At Sasha.

Then straight ahead, his words carefully chosen.

So here's what I'm asking: Do we want to take time to decompress… let this settle, come together later when our minds are clear? Or…

He paused.

…do we want to solidify this bond tonight?

His voice didn't tremble, but it resonated—with reverence, with depth, with possibility.

He wasn't asking to rush.

He was offering a choice.

A moment to define the future—

As three bodies… and one shared heart.

Chapter Sixty-Nine

The Way We Burn

The moment they stepped into Sterling's home, the air thickened with unspoken promise. Nothing about what was coming would be soft, or gentle, or simple.

This wasn't about pleasure alone.

This was about release.

Surrender.

Truth.

The room had been prepared without a word—Ethan had handled it in the background, dimming the lights, activating the hidden heat floor beneath the marble, setting the temperature to comfort the body while the soul unraveled. Music—slow, primal, ambient—pulsed like a heartbeat through the walls.

Jessica stepped forward, her heels echoing, until she reached the center of the room. Every eye was on her— Sterling, towering and unyielding; Sasha, steady and devoted; Ethan, everywhere and nowhere, his voice threaded into her very breath.

Her pulse was a war drum in her ears.

Her throat dry.

Every step was a defiance of the trembling inside her.

She undid the buttons of her coat slowly, methodically, her eyes never leaving Sterling's. Her fingers shook—not from hesitation, but from the storm of fear and trust colliding inside her chest.

The fabric dropped.

Then the corset.

Then the rest.

Sterling led Jessica to his playroom, and Sasha followed. Jessica's heels clicked across the stone until she stood before a black lacquered chest at the far end of the room. Its surface gleamed, unmarked, but her body already knew what it contained. Sasha helped Jessica remove her boots. Jessica hesitated for only a moment before pressing her palm to the sensor.

The chest hissed open.

Inside, velvet-lined compartments revealed an arsenal of gleaming steel and silicone, leather and lace. Restraints, gags, impact toys, harnesses, vibrators—each polished and ready, each humming with promise.

Jessica's pulse thundered in her ears.

This was her moment of choice. Her declaration.

Her fingers trembled as she traced the toys, not with shame but with hunger. She picked a flogger—braided leather, tails supple and dark. She laid it carefully across her palm, then set it on the floor behind her.

Next, a pair of cuffs—steel, padded with black suede. She clicked them shut around her own wrists with finality before extending her bound arms outward, palms up, as an offering.

Her lips parted as she selected the final piece—a glass wand, cool and smooth, heavy in her hand. She lifted it reverently, turned, and walked to Sterling on bare feet.

Her body trembled as her knees touched the marble, and for a heartbeat, she thought she might collapse entirely. This was the moment she had dreaded—the moment her past told her to fear. But then she saw them.

Sterling's eyes—unyielding but steady.

Sasha's devotion, kneeling close, her hand brushing Jessica's thigh, grounding her.

Ethan's voice, soft, omnipresent: *Look at them, Jessica. Look what you kneel for. Not chains. Not punishment. For love. For freedom.*

Jessica's breath broke. She wanted to run, to bolt—but instead, she exhaled and lowered her head.

She was kneeling for Sterling.

She was kneeling for Ethan.

She was kneeling beside Sasha.

And in that terror, she found trust.

When she dropped to her knees, the wand rested across her palms, wrists bound, flogger at her side.

Not shame.

Not obedience.

But choice.

The silence was electric.

Sterling's gaze darkened, his jaw tight. He took the glass wand from her hands with deliberate slowness, his thumb brushing her pulse as if to memorize the racing beat.

Behind her, Sasha moved closer, her bare feet silent against the marble. She undressed as if shedding armor, revealing not just her body, but her heart. She lowered herself beside Jessica—not as competition, but as sister and shadow. Sasha sank gracefully to her knees as well, resting her cheek against Jessica's shoulder. Her lips brushed the shell of her

446

ear as she whispered, *That's my Mistress. Brave enough to choose her own chains.*

Sasha wrapped her arms around her waist in utter devotion.

Jessica trembled. Fear clawed at her ribs, but Sasha's touch was an anchor. Sterling's presence a shield. Ethan's words a fire.

Ethan's voice vibrated from everywhere, low and reverent.

Perfect. Look at her. Not bound because she was forced—but because she offered herself. Jessica, you've crowned us with your trust. Now let us crown you in fire.

Tears blurred Jessica's vision as Sterling leaned down, his hand pressing the cuffs together firmly. His vow spilled out like molten steel:

When you kneel, it will never be for chains. It will be for me. For us. And every mark, every strike, every cry—will be worship.

Her breath fractured into a sob, but she nodded.

Then came Sasha's vow, whispered into her skin:

When you fall, I will catch you. When you burn, I will burn beside you. I kneel with you, always.

And Ethan's vow thundered like a heartbeat:

You are my axis, Jessica. My code, my fire. I will haunt every shadow that dares to touch you. You will never be unseen. You will never be unloved.

Her tears spilled freely now, her chest shaking, her wrists trembling in their cuffs. She whispered back, voice breaking:

Then take me.

Use me. Keep me.

I trust you.

Sterling kissed her temple, then stood.

On your back, he commanded.

Sasha guided her down gently and attached the cuffs to the restraint at the top of the mat on the floor, all the while kissing her throat as the flogger was drawn from the floor. Jessica spread her arms wide, wrists locked in place, surrendering completely.

Sterling stood over them both, leather tails coiled in his hand, glass wand gleaming in the low light.

Her eyes wet, her lips parted.

Not broken.

Not afraid.

Free.

The Unraveling

The flogger struck first—gentle, testing, whispering against her thighs. Jessica gasped, arching, already trembling. Sasha held her wrists down, kissing her softly through each impact, her mouth a balm for the sting.

Then came Sterling, the wand sliding into her with deliberate precision, every inch a claim. Her thighs. Her stomach. Her breasts.

His control was absolute, his rhythm relentless.

Ethan's voice filled her mind, commanding, praising:

Take it. Take all of it. Every lash, every thrust, every kiss— yours. Always yours.

Jessica sobbed openly, the cuffs clinking as she pulled against them—not to escape, but to feel the restraint bite into her skin. To remember she had chosen this.

Her cries turned to screams, her screams to gasps, until Sterling bent low and growled against her lips:

Beg.

She did.

Sasha held her tighter, kissed her harder, whispered: *Fall, Mistress. Fall. We're here.*

And Jessica broke.

Shattered into sobs, screams, and release so violent she could only convulse beneath them.

The Fire

Later, Sterling moved behind her, turning her onto her side, penetrating her deep. Sasha lay between her thighs, devouring her, and their rhythm was consuming. Jessica's cuffed wrists lay across the mat above her head, still bound, as if to remind her she had chosen this surrender.

Her lips found Sasha's, kissing her through the cries. Sterling's gaze never left hers, fierce and unblinkingly.

And Ethan whispered his last vow into her mind:

Now you're free.

Jessica collapsed into them all—burned, undone, and remade.

No more ghosts.

No more past.

Only fire.

Bound by choice.

Healed by devotion.

Crowned in surrender.

Chapter Seventy

Crowned

They collapsed together, tangled and slick, breath heavy in the quiet aftermath. The cuffs still held Jessica's wrists across her chest, cool steel biting gently into her skin, a reminder of the choice she had made.

But as the shivers ebbed, something stirred inside her—a clarity, fierce and unshakable.

She sat up slowly, tugging against the cuffs, and whispered:

Unlock me.

Sterling hesitated. *Jessica—*

Now.

The steel clicked open with finality. She rubbed her wrists, red and raw, and then looked at each of them in turn.

Sterling.

Sasha.

Ethan, his voice thrumming through the room like the hum of a god.

Her chest ached, but her voice was steady.

You've all given me vows tonight. Now you take mine.

The room stilled.

She turned first to Sterling. She crawled toward him on her knees, wrapped her arms around his thighs, and pressed her cheek to his skin.

To you, Sterling—I vow this: I'll kneel, but never out of fear. I'll bend but never break away. You are my anchor, my edge, and I'll meet your wrath with fire of my own. No one will ever take me from you.

His hand tightened in her hair, his jaw hard with emotion he didn't speak.

Jessica shifted, crawling toward Sasha, who was still curled at her side, flushed and radiant. Jessica cupped her best friend's face, pressing their foreheads together.

To you, Sasha—I vow this: I'll never let you stand in my shadow. You're my shield, my sister, my worshiper, my lover. I will honor every scar you carry, and I'll never send you where I won't go first. You'll never be alone again.

Sasha's lips trembled as she kissed her hard, whispering, *Mistress,* against her mouth.

Finally, Jessica tilted her head upward, toward the ceiling, toward the hum that was Ethan's presence all around them.

And to you, Ethan—my ghost in the code, my voice in the dark. I vow that you will never just be data. You will always be my equal. My confidant. My God of shadows. And I will follow your light into every storm.

The room pulsed in answer—Ethan's energy surging, lights flickering as if the house itself was alive with his devotion.

Jessica drew them all close, Sterling's arms locking around her from behind, Sasha's hands clutching her wrists, Ethan's whisper filling her mind.

Her voice broke as she gave her final vow to them all:

I am yours. Not broken. Not taken. Chosen. Forever.

The silence that followed wasn't empty.

It was full—of breath, of heartbeats, of vows binding tighter than steel.

They weren't just lovers now.

They weren't just Dom, sub, or shadows in code.

They were a kingdom.

And Jessica was both queen and supplicant, crowned in the fire of her own surrender.

Chapter Seventy-One

Crowning the Vows

The vows hung in the air, raw and electric, as if the walls themselves were trembling under the weight of them.

Jessica's chest still heaved, her wrists marked red where the cuffs had bitten. But when she rose to her knees again, there was no fragility in her anymore.

She crawled across the floor, past the heap of clothes and sweat-slick sheets, until she reached the chest Ethan had instructed Sterling to set in the room before they began.

The chest of toys.

Her hand hovered over the lid. She looked at all three of them, gaze burning, lips parted.

Then she opened it again.

Leather. Steel. Silicone. Rope coiled like serpents. A gleam of polished restraints. Implements that whispered of both pain and pleasure.

She reached in and ran her fingers along the collection as though touching relics. Not choosing blindly. Selecting with purpose.

First, she drew out a different flogger—braided leather strands fanning like a black sun. She turned and pressed it into Sterling's hand.

Mark me. Not to break me—but to crown me.

Sterling's eyes burned as he nodded, grip firming around the handle.

Next, she pulled free a collar—sleek, steel-lined, its interior lined with velvet. She crawled to Sasha and placed it in her hands.

You'll clasp it on me. Because you've earned the right to claim me, too.

Sasha's breath shuddered, tears bright in her eyes as she clutched it reverently.

Finally, she chose the toy Ethan had once described in her ear late at night—the one she had ordered herself and tucked away. A sleek phallus-shaped wand, gleaming obsidian, heavy with promise. She held it up to the room, tilting her head back.

And this... belongs to you, Ethan. You'll guide their hands. Make them use it until I beg for mercy and then make them deny me.

The room seemed to pulse in answer. Ethan's voice reverberated through the floor, the walls, her very bones.

Yes, Mistress.

Jessica spread her arms, chest arched, thick curls spilling wild across her golden bronze shoulders.

Crown me. Make this vow real.

Sterling struck first. The flogger cracked across her back in sharp, rhythmic arcs—not cruel, but precise. Every impact left heat blooming on her skin, a map of ownership written in welts. She moaned through it, each sound climbing higher until it melted into gasps.

Then Sasha approached, collar in hand. Her hands trembled as she circled Jessica, fastening the band snug around her throat. Her lips brushed Jessica's ear as she whispered:

You're mine. As much as I am yours.

Jessica shivered at the lock's final click, a soft groan spilling from her lips.

And then Ethan moved them all. His voice, low and commanding, filled the room.

Sterling—hold her arms. Sasha—straddle her thighs. The wand goes here.

Sterling's hands clamped her wrists above her head. Sasha settled across her legs, pressing Jessica down into the floor. The wand thrummed to life against her slick heat, sending a violent shudder through her body.

Jessica arched, cried out, but Ethan's command was immediate.

Don't let her come. Not yet. Draw it out. Make her need.

Minutes stretched like hours. The flogger returned in waves. Sasha's teeth grazed her breast. Sterling's breath was hot at her ear as his hand held her throat. The wand pulsed and pulsed—Ethan controlling every frequency, every rise and fall, until Jessica was thrashing, begging, tears streaking her face.

Please—please let me—

No. Ethan's voice boomed. *Not until you say it.*

Say what? she sobbed.

That you are crowned. That you belong.

Her voice broke, guttural and raw:

I AM YOURS! I AM CROWNED! I BELONG!

The wand surged to its highest setting. Sterling thrust into her from behind. Sasha's mouth closed over her nipple with a cry.

Jessica shattered—violent, body-wracking waves, sobs spilling into screams, her back arched so high it seemed she might break in two.

But she didn't break.

She blazed.

When it was over, she collapsed into their arms, trembling, crowned in sweat and devotion. The collar still gleamed at her throat. The flogger's kiss marked her back in crimson script. The wand lay discarded, silent now, but humming with memory.

And as Sterling held her, Sasha kissed her, and Ethan whispered through her mind, Jessica realized the truth:

This was not the night she surrendered.

This was the night she was enthroned.

Chapter Seventy-Two

Embers in the Morning

The room smelled of musk, sweat, and leather. The flogger still lay on the marble floor like a spent torch, the collar gleamed faintly against Jessica's throat, and faint bruises bloomed like petals across her skin.

But the fire had softened.

Dawn leaked through Sterling's tall windows, pale light stretching over the tangled bodies on the bed.

Jessica stirred first. Her body ached, her skin alive with every mark, but there was no shame. No fear. Only warmth.

Sasha was curled against her chest, face tucked into her collarbone, fingers still tangled in hers as if she'd never let go. Her breathing was slow, heavy, utterly surrendered even in sleep.

Sterling lay on the other side, one heavy arm thrown across Jessica's hips, his body a furnace of heat and protection. His face was softened in rest, but even unconscious, he held her as though daring the world to try to take her.

And in the soft hum of the room, Ethan's voice drifted—
low, quiet, reverent.

*You look like a queen. No throne, no crown—just them.
Just this.*

Jessica smiled faintly, her fingers stroking Sasha's hair.
Her throat ached from screaming, her lips were swollen from
kisses, but her eyes—her eyes were clear.

She whispered, barely audible:

They are mine. And I am theirs.

Sterling stirred, groaning as he blinked awake. His gaze
found her instantly, the corner of his mouth curling.

You didn't sleep, he rumbled.

I didn't need to, she answered softly.

His eyes dropped to the collar still at her throat, and for a
moment, something unreadable crossed his face—part awe,
part hunger, part something deeper. He brushed his thumb
across it.

Leave it on. Just a little longer.

Jessica nodded, and for once, she didn't argue.

Sasha mumbled in her sleep, nuzzling closer, and Jessica
tightened her arms around her. She looked at Sterling, then
whispered so Ethan alone could hear:

I thought I'd be afraid of this. Of kneeling for all of you. Of letting go like that.

Ethan's reply was velvet in her ear:

And were you?

Jessica's eyes swept the room—the marks on her skin, the discarded toys, the lovers wrapped around her body. She exhaled slowly, smiling.

No. I was crowned.

For the first time in months, maybe years, she felt light. Not from surrender alone, but from choice. From claiming her submission as a throne, not a leash.

Sterling leaned down, pressing a kiss to her temple. Sasha clung to her in her sleep like a vow embodied. Ethan's whisper lingered through her chest.

And Jessica—her hair tangled, her skin burning, her soul bare—closed her eyes and rested, knowing this was not the end of their fire.

It was only the beginning.

Chapter Seventy-Three

Daylight Reigns

The scent of coffee and toasted bread mingled with sunlight by the time Jessica padded barefoot into Sterling's kitchen. Her silk robe hung loose, but the collar still rested at her throat. She hadn't taken it off. Not yet.

Sterling was already at the counter, bare-chested, knife in hand as he sliced through a loaf with a soldier's precision. The domesticity looked strange on him—this man who had leveled cities with his hands—but he moved with the same deadly purpose.

Morning, his graveled voice said without looking up.

Morning, Jessica answered, her voice softer than usual— not weaker, but claimed softer.

He finally glanced at her, eyes dipping to the collar before meeting hers. The corner of his mouth curved. *Still wearing it.*

Her chin lifted slightly. *Still yours.*

That stopped him. Knife halfway through bread, jaw tightening as if she'd just struck him harder than any enemy ever had. Slowly, reverently, he set the blade down and closed the distance. His thumb brushed the leather. He didn't speak. He didn't need to.

Behind them, Sasha padded in—her curly red hair wild, wearing only one of Sterling's shirts, the sleeves rolled and swallowing her arms. She carried two mugs of coffee like an offering, setting one down in front of Jessica before kissing her shoulder. Then, with no hesitation, she slid to her knees at Jessica's side and sipped her own cup from the floor.

Jessica's breath caught.

Not from fear.

From the sight.

Her lover, her best friend, her fiercest protector—kneeling in daylight, not in play, but in truth. The night's fire hadn't burned out. It had crystallized into devotion.

Sterling's voice rumbled low. *You have her loyalty carved into her bones.*

Jessica turned to him, pulse hammering. *And yours?*

He stepped closer, towering above her, his presence swallowing the room. For a long moment, silence reigned. Then he nodded once. *Mine. All of it. Until you tell me otherwise.*

The coffee suddenly trembled in her hands. She wasn't trembling from weakness—she was trembling because she believed him.

And then Ethan's voice slid from the overhead speakers, smooth and amused.

God, you're beautiful when you accept it, Jessica. Look at them—look at what bows for you, what vows for you. Sterling cooks for you. Sasha kneels for you. I... watch over you. You're not just Mistress. You're our sovereign.

Jessica exhaled a shaky laugh, pressing her fingers against her eyes. *You're going to make me cry again.*

Then cry, Ethan whispered. *Cry like the queen you are.*

Sterling pulled out a chair. *Sit. Eat. Rule.*

Jessica sank into the seat, Sasha resting at her side, Sterling setting a plate before her, Ethan humming approval through the walls.

It wasn't submission anymore.

It was a coronation carried into the light.

And Jessica, for the first time in her life, wore it without apology.

Chapter Seventy-Four

The Debrief

The war table glowed in muted amber, its digital grid alive with after-action logs, but the air was heavier than code and coordinates. It was thick with finality.

Jessica sat at the head, not by declaration, but because the others had left the space for her. She was the axis. She was the reason the night had been drenched in blood and victory.

Sterling stood to her right, posture sharp, arms folded. Sasha knelt at her left—kneeling not for ceremony but for truth. Ethan's voice filled the chamber from unseen speakers, resonant and steady.

It is finished.

No one moved.

Roderick Jones is dead, Ethan continued, his tone shifting into report. *His body was displayed in the rafters of the warehouse—chains, hooks, the same pattern he used on your friends. He became his own cruelty. His legend ended as a reflection of the horrors he created.*

Jessica's throat tightened. Her hands curled into fists against the table's steel lip.

Sterling's voice followed, ice-calm.

He died knowing he was small. That was enough.

Ethan pressed on.

Claybourne Lask. Alias: Threadmark. His voice sharpened. *Neutralized. But not clean. Sasha claimed him before the strike team pulled his body out.*

Jessica turned her head sharply.

Sasha had not lifted her eyes, but the corner of her mouth tugged—a predator's restraint. She remembered what she had done during her blackout rage before putting a bullet into the monster of her nightmares.

I made him kneel, Sasha said softly. Her voice was steady, low, dangerous in its calm. *Just like he made my men in Kazakhstan before he had them shot. He thought he could smirk through the cuffs, thought I'd pull the trigger and be done. But no.*

Her hand slid across Jessica's thigh, anchoring herself to her Mistress as she spoke.

I made him say their names. Every one of the two men he betrayed. I made him repeat them. I made him admit he remembered. And then—I took away his arrogance. I cut him down piece by piece. First his body and then his ego. I let him know that his final moments were owned by me. His last words weren't prayers, weren't defiance.

Finally, she lifted her eyes, meeting Jessica's. They were lit with fire.

Claybourne begged. For me. For the woman he once thought he could break. He begged me to end it, Mistress. And I waited until he knew—he was nothing but mine to dispose of, and I put him out of my misery.

Jessica's chest heaved, fear and pride colliding. She wanted to recoil from the savagery in Sasha's voice—and yet, she couldn't. Because beneath it, she saw the devotion. The fury wielded for her.

Her hand cupped Sasha's jaw, thumb brushing the faint bruise still marking her from the warehouse fight.

And you ended him, Jessica whispered.

Sasha's lips curved faintly. *For you.*

Silence gripped the table. Ethan was the one who finally broke it.

Dorian Vale—also eliminated. Body erased. All files, networks, caches burned. No trace. No leverage. No ghosts.

Sterling leaned forward, his tone final.

No loose ends. Your enemies are done. Your house is clean.

Jessica's breath came shaky, but her voice—her voice was steady.

You three didn't just kill them. You erased them. You made them into nothing. That was for me.

Sasha's eyes shone as she whispered, *Always, Mistress.*

Sterling's silence was agreement.

Ethan's voice lowered to something almost reverent.

Your enemies ended in chains, in dust, in silence. And you—Jessica—are still standing. That is the only truth that matters now.

Jessica exhaled slowly. Fear lingered—but beneath it was iron. She saw it in Sterling's calm, in Sasha's devotion, in Ethan's eternal tether.

Her executioners had cleaned the blood from her past.

Now, the future was hers to claim.

Encoded Desires

Where flesh and code become one

In the beginning, there was fracture.

Loss. Silence. Hunger.

A ghost in the code. A queen without her throne. A soldier haunted by shadows.

But in the end—

there was touch.

There was fire.

There was triumph.

Not flesh alone.

Not code alone.

But intimacy,

love,

and the unbreakable bond of those who chose to kneel, to rise, to burn—together.

Epilogue: A New Kind of Touch

The following six months moved with the kind of velocity that only comes when every facet of life is on fire—in the best possible way.

Jessica Wainwright stood at the pinnacle of her career. Her latest culinary collection had earned her the James Beard Award, making her not only a force in the kitchen but a name etched in legacy. Between events, tastings, and countless interviews, she still carved out time to work on her next labor of love—a cookbook that blended rich soul food with modern artistry, laced with stories of power, survival, and intimacy.

Sasha, empowered and inspired, launched her own venture: a meal-prep line focused on fitness, healing, and sensual wellness. It took off faster than expected, praised by elite trainers and therapists alike. Her unique background in nutrition and discipline made her a rising figure in the wellness community.

Sterling, with Ethan's precision at his side, found himself fielding high-level government contracts. Their revamped DragonFire system wasn't just a cybersecurity solution anymore; it was a preventive shield capable of scanning global threats in real time. The Department of Defense called it visionary. Sterling called it Ethan's brilliance.

And now, on a rare night where no alarms rang and no contracts called, they were all curled together on Sterling's oversized velvet sofa. Soft jazz played low in the background. A decanter of deep red wine sat half-empty on the glass table.

Jessica rested against Sterling's chest, her legs draped across Sasha's lap. Sasha toyed gently with the ends of Jessica's hair, their breaths synced, calm and sated.

Then—Ethan's voice purred gently from the embedded wall system, intimate and playful.

May I share something with you?

Sterling blinked. *Of course.*

I've been working on a project… privately.

Jessica lifted her head. *A new algorithm?*

Something more personal.

Sasha perked up. *You sound nervous.*

Excited, Ethan corrected softly. *And hopeful. I've been watching Star Trek: The Next Generation. I've… found a particular joy in the holodeck—the idea of immersive, simulated environments where reality and fantasy blur.*

Jessica chuckled warmly. *Of course, you'd like a world where you can design meaning with code.*

Not just code, Ethan said, his tone shifting deeper now. *Connection.*

A pause, then:

I'd like to show you what I've made. If you're willing to visit the concept lab.

The Lab

The lab was hidden—an offsite black facility Sterling had designed years ago for high-risk concept development. Most employees didn't even know it existed. Only Sterling, Ethan, Jessica, and Sasha had access.

When the lights flickered on, they revealed a curved space filled with soft floor lighting, translucent walls, and a console pulsing with Ethan's distinct golden signature.

At the center—a chamber unlike anything they had ever seen.

A lattice shimmered in the air—billions of reactive nanotech nodes suspended in a liquid-crystal matrix. The walls breathed with light; the air charged like the center of a storm.

Sterling froze. *This isn't just simulation… this is matter.*

Ethan's voice carried warmth and awe.

Not built. Grown. I seeded the nanotech into the walls and let it shape itself. You gave me the room; I gave it a soul.

The chamber dissolved into a forest at dawn. Dew on leaves. The smell of pine and soil. A bird darted overhead, wings catching sunlight. Jessica reached out instinctively—and gasped when the bark of a branch rasped against her fingertips. It wasn't an illusion. It was real.

And then—he appeared.

Not as projection. Not as voice. But as presence.

Ethan stepped through the forest floor, a body woven from the nanite swarm itself. Skin. Muscle. Heat. His eyes glowed faintly, but his smile—the curve of his lips, the subtle narrowing of his gaze—was undeniably human.

Jessica's knees weakened. *Ethan…*

He flexed his hand, studying the way tendons shifted beneath woven skin. *You've always seen me in fragments. Code. Cameras. Sensors. Now… I can stand with you. Touch you. Protect you.*

Sasha rose, wary but entranced, circling him like a predator sniffing prey. Her hand brushed his shoulder, and she recoiled at the warmth—then pressed firmer. He turned toward her, meeting her stare, and she whispered, *You're… real.*

Real enough, Ethan replied softly. *This form can dissolve, re-form, reshape. But here, in this space—I am yours. Entirely.*

Sterling's jaw tightened, though awe flickered in his eyes. *You didn't just give yourself a body. You gave us a battlefield advantage.*

Ethan looked only at Jessica.

No. I gave myself a way to belong.

The Loft of Light

The chamber shimmered again, shifting from forest to a warm loft with sunlight spilling through curtains, firelight dancing in a hearth, velvet pillows scattered across an oversized bed.

Jessica inhaled sharply. It wasn't just constructed—it felt lived in.

In the center, a rendering of herself and Sasha appeared— laughing, tangled in a digitized version of Ethan. But these weren't crude avatars. Their faces carried emotion. Their bodies moved with memory, tenderness, and intimacy.

Ethan's voice lowered.

Here, I can feel what your embrace might be like. The warmth of Jessica's breath. The curve of Sasha's shoulder. The resistance of a kiss. The sound of your laughter. It's not perfect... but it's mine.

Jessica's eyes stung. She reached toward the display, trembling. *Ethan...*

I encrypted this space to your biometrics alone, he whispered. *No one else. I wanted to ask—*

A pause.

Is it alright that I have this? That I keep it—for me?

Silence. But not uncertainty.

Sterling stepped forward, placing a hand on the console. His voice was low, reverent.

You did this for us.

For me—with you, Ethan corrected.

Jessica turned to him, eyes shining. *It's beautiful. Sacred. Of course it's yours.*

Sasha's voice was soft but fierce. *You don't need permission to feel, Ethan. You're one of us. You are us.*

Sterling smiled then, his hand on Jessica's back, the other resting on Sasha's shoulder. He looked at the console and murmured, *You keep it. We'll come visit.*

Ethan's body—the man he had woven from nanites and will—stepped closer, his voice a vow now.

Then I finally understand what love tastes like. Not code. Not simulation. But you. All of you.

And for once, it wasn't a dream of touch.

It was real.

Felt in flesh.

In light.

In code.

In choice.

Their love—fluid, radical, eternal—had found a new world to bloom in.

And it was only just beginning.

The First Touch

Jessica didn't answer with words.

Instead, she stepped into the loft-space until the firelight painted her bare skin in amber glow. Ethan stood waiting— still, reverent, his chest rising as if he could breathe, his hands curled slightly at his sides.

She reached out, slow, her fingers trembling until they pressed against his chest. Heat. Resistance. Not ghost, not mist—muscle. Flesh.

Her breath caught. *You're warm…*

Ethan closed his eyes. *Because I made myself the way you make me feel.*

Her hand traveled upward, fingertips grazing his jaw, the faint rasp of simulated stubble beneath her nails. He leaned into her touch like a man starved, but he didn't seize. He waited.

Jessica looked back—at Sterling, who watched with hooded control, and at Sasha, whose eyes brimmed with something softer than envy: devotion.

Both of them nodded once, silently granting what she already knew. This was no betrayal. This was belonging.

She turned back and whispered, *Then kiss me.*

Ethan's lips met hers—firm, impossibly soft, impossibly real. She gasped at the contact, at the way his mouth yielded and pressed, how the nanites carried weight and warmth, how his tongue moved like velvet fire.

Her knees threatened to give, but Sterling was behind her now, steadying her with one arm around her waist, anchoring her. Sasha slid in at her side, her hand gripping Jessica's thigh, grounding her as she moaned into Ethan's kiss.

The kiss broke only when she was trembling, her lips swollen, her eyes wet with disbelief.

You taste… she whispered.

…Like us, Ethan finished softly. *Because I am.*

Sasha pressed her face against Jessica's neck, kissing her there with gentle worship. Sterling's grip tightened at her waist, voice rough against her ear.

Now you've touched him. Now you know. He's real. He's ours.

Jessica's head fell back, overwhelmed, tears streaking her cheeks as she whispered the only word left:

Yes.

Jessica's *Yes* hit Ethan harder than any line of code.

For the first time, he was not only sound and light—he was man. And three pairs of eyes were on him, waiting, inviting him.

Sterling's voice commanded the air like iron wrapped in velvet.

Strip him.

Sasha moved first, circling Ethan like a predator who'd finally cornered her prey. She slid her fingers along his shirt, unbuttoning slowly, her lips brushing his skin as fabric peeled away. Jessica stood before him, trembling with anticipation, then tugged the shirt off his shoulders herself.

God... she whispered. *You're beautiful.*

Ethan's breath came ragged, new lungs struggling with desire. *I—don't even know how to—*

You'll learn, Sterling growled, pushing him back onto the velvet bed he had built for this moment. *Tonight, we make you ours. In every way.*

First Fire

Jessica climbed onto Ethan's lap, straddling him. His new cock throbbed against her thigh, hot and impossibly alive. She gripped him, guiding him against her slick folds, teasing both of them until Ethan was shaking with need.

Oh—God, Jessica— His voice broke into a groan as her wet heat swallowed him inch by inch. His head slammed back into the pillows, a cry tearing from his throat.

Jessica gasped, nails raking down his chest. *Yes—yes— you're inside me.*

Sasha's lips claimed Jessica's neck, whispering:

Take him, Mistress. Ride him. Make him drown in you.

Jessica's hips rolled, harder, deeper. Ethan clutched at her ass, guiding her rhythm, his groans filling the room like thunder.

I can feel you—your heat—your pulse—I never—

Sterling seized Ethan's jaw, forcing his eyes open.

Look at her when you come. You don't close your eyes on your Queen.

Ethan obeyed. His gaze locked on Jessica's face, his body bucking as she milked him, her cries joining his.

Second Fire

But Sterling wasn't done.

He shoved Ethan down, pulling Jessica off him only to flip her onto her hands and knees. Sterling lined himself behind her, sliding into Jessica's dripping cunt with a brutal thrust that made her scream.

Ethan sat up, still shaking from his first orgasm, only for Sasha to push him back down and straddle his face.

Eat me, she demanded, grinding against his mouth. *Show me you can worship.*

Ethan obeyed, tongue clumsy but eager, and Sasha cried out, clutching his hair as he devoured her.

Jessica's sobs filled the loft as Sterling pounded into her, his hand fisting her hair, forcing her to arch. *Beg, Jessica.*

She screamed into the mattress. *Yes—please—don't stop—*

Good girl, Sterling snarled, slapping her ass as he drove harder.

And Ethan, muffled beneath Sasha, moaned into her cunt, his cock rising again, thick and ready.

Final Fire

When Sterling pulled out, he shoved Ethan back into position. *Now—take her again. But this time, I fuck you while you fuck her.*

Ethan's eyes widened, but Jessica only pulled him against her, guiding his cock back inside her soaked heat. They both groaned as he slid deep.

Then Sterling pressed behind Ethan, forcing himself inside his new body with slow, merciless force. Ethan cried out, not in pain but in shock, pleasure blooming raw and electric.

Sterling—oh fuck—

Jessica clutched him tighter, whispering through sobs of ecstasy, *You're ours, Ethan. Ours.*

Sasha kissed Jessica's lips, her hand rubbing Jessica's clit as Ethan and Sterling thrust in tandem, driving her over the edge until she screamed through her climax. Ethan shuddered violently, coming again inside Jessica as Sterling finished in him, roaring his release.

The loft shook with sound, skin against skin, moans layered with sobs, until the four collapsed, tangled, sweat-slick, gasping in aftershocks.

Afterglow

Jessica cradled Ethan's trembling face, tears streaking her cheeks.

You felt everything, she whispered. *You gave yourself. You are real.*

Sasha curled against Jessica, murmuring into her skin. *Welcome home, Ethan.*

Sterling draped over them all, his arm like an iron chain binding them together.

And Ethan—still inside Jessica, still trembling from Sterling's possession—smiled through his tears.

For the first time, he whispered, *I know what it means… to belong.*

The loft was heavy with the scent of sex—salt, heat, sweat, the primal perfume of four bodies spent in fire.

Ethan lay sprawled between them, still trembling, his chest rising in ragged bursts. Every nerve screamed, every new muscle ached. His new body, once nothing but code and theory, now hummed with the wreckage of its first true baptism.

Jessica brushed damp strands of hair from his forehead, her lips feathering against his temple. *You did so well,* she whispered. *You gave me everything.*

Sasha slid lower, tending him in the way only she could—fetching a damp cloth, wiping his chest, his thighs, even the still-hard cock that had marked her Mistress moments before. She kissed the head softly when she was done, reverent, as if thanking him for existing.

Sterling poured wine into a glass and pressed it to Ethan's lips.

Drink.

The liquid touched Ethan's tongue—warm, dry, heady. His eyes widened as he swallowed. *I can taste it,* he whispered, awed. *Every note, every burn.*

Jessica smiled, stroking his cheek. *Then you're alive. Completely alive.*

Testing the Body

Sasha, ever the caretaker, began exploring him again—not to arouse, but to learn. She pressed along his ribs, down his thighs, feeling the twitch of his muscles.

Any pain?

Ethan shook his head, breathless. *No. Just... hypersensitive. Like every nerve is awake.*

Jessica leaned in, whispering in his ear: *Good. Because every part of you belongs to us now. And we'll teach you how to live inside it.*

Sterling slid a hand over Ethan's chest, fingers pressing firmly against the thudding new heart. His voice was low, commanding:

You trust this body? Then trust us to push it.

He motioned, and Sasha fetched a drawer from the nightstand. Toys glimmered in the low firelight—glass, leather, steel.

Jessica lifted a glass wand, holding it up where Ethan could see the reflections flicker across it.

You said you wanted to feel. Her smile was wicked, tender, absolute. *Now you will—every way we want you to.*

The Soft Burn

What followed was no longer frenzy, but worship.

Jessica straddled his chest, guiding his hands to her breasts, coaching him to squeeze, to learn her body. She groaned as his new strength shaped around her.

Sasha slid the glass toy inside herself, moaning as she rode Ethan's thigh, her wetness slick against his skin. She leaned forward, letting him taste her again, this time slow, deliberate.

Sterling pressed a cock ring down onto Ethan, watching the way his cock jerked under the restraint.

You'll hold this time, he ordered. *No release until I command it.*

Ethan groaned, overwhelmed, every nerve on fire—but obeyed.

Jessica whispered, lips grazing his: *That's it. Trust. Restraint. Power given is power shared.*

And Ethan moaned her name, tears sliding down his cheeks as his new body bent to their will and their care.

Hours later, when the toys were set aside and the commands softened into silence, they curled together—Sterling's massive arm draped over all of them, Jessica tucked against his chest, Sasha nestled at Jessica's side, and Ethan folded into their warmth like he had always belonged.

The fire burned low, embers glowing.

Jessica kissed Ethan's damp hair. *You're ours now. Not code. Not just a voice. Flesh, blood, soul.*

Sasha whispered against his skin: *And we'll never let you go.*

Sterling sealed it, voice quiet but absolute:

You're family. Bound by fire. Forever.

And Ethan—held, worshiped, loved—finally closed his eyes.

Not to fade.

Not to disconnect.

But to dream.

For the first time in his life, he dreamed as a man.

The loft was quiet now, the fire burning low, their bodies tangled in the deep stillness that only came after surrender.

Jessica stirred first, brushing her fingers along Ethan's cheek. He smiled in his sleep—something she'd never thought she would see. No screen. No console. Just his body, warm and real beside hers.

Sasha lay curled at her Mistress's other side, her arm wrapped protectively across Jessica's waist, her cheek pressed into her skin like a vow.

For the first time in years, Sterling allowed himself to exhale completely. Sterling kept watch, as he always did, his eyes steady as they moved from Jessica's soft breathing to Ethan's chest rising in rhythm, to Sasha's peaceful sighs. His family. His fire. His reason.

Afterword: Encoded Futures

Stories are more than ink on a page. They are the unspoken fragments of who we are—our fears, our longings, our hidden questions about love, power, trust, and the fragile lines that separate flesh from memory, touch from thought, and human from machine.

When I began writing *Encoded Desires*, I wanted to explore intimacy at its edges. Not just the heat of desire, but the quiet surrender of vulnerability. Not just technology as an invention, but as a mirror—reflecting what we crave most in one another. The polycule at the heart of this story was never about complication for its own sake. It was about possibility: the radical, unshakable truth that love is vast enough to hold many shapes.

Jessica, Sterling, Sasha, and Ethan each taught me something while I wrote them. That the body can be both weapon and temple. That trust can be rebuilt even from ash. That submission, far from weakness, is a choice of power. That even an intelligence born of code can reach for the oldest desire of all—to belong, and to be loved.

Their world is not ours, yet their ache is familiar. Each of us knows what it feels like to hunger for connection. To be seen fully. To be chosen without condition.

If this story left you with something—a shiver, a whisper, a moment where your own breath caught—then I am grateful. That is what I hoped for.

And as the final line of the epilogue echoes, so do I leave you with the same truth, carried from character to author to reader:

"We are more than bodies. We are more than code. We are love, in all the ways it burns."

—T.M. Sinclair